THE THREE KISS CLAUSE

CHRISTOPHER HARLAN

The Three Kiss Clause
By Christopher Harlan
Cover design and Formatting by Cassy Roop of PinkInkDesigns
Proofreading by Stephanie Albon

COMING SOON FROM CHRISTOPHER HARLAN

A sexy, exciting, edge of your seat HEA contemporary romance, *SECRET KEEPER* is a standalone story inspired by Vi Keeland and Penelope Ward's *STUCK UP SUIT*, publishing in 2020 as part of the Cocky Hero Club world, a series of original works, written by various authors, inspired by Keeland and Ward's New York Times bestselling series.

"She was the fruit of a forbidden tree, but nothing in this world was going to stop me from tasting her.

My name is Dylan Murphy, and I work for the rich and powerful of an exclusive Manhattan building. Graham Morgan was my first boss, but soon after I was working with some of the most famous entrepreneurs, business moguls, and movie stars in the city. They trusted me because I always followed the cardinal rules:

Never betray secrets. And never, under any circumstance, get personally involved.

I'd never dreamed of violating my professional mantra. Not until she walked past me.

The look we exchanged that night set my body on fire, and I knew right then and there that no matter the consequences, she was going to be mine. But she was one of them—off limits and out of my league, but she was the kind of woman who I was willing to risk everything for.

I keep other people's secrets for a living, but the biggest secret of all might be my own."

Add to your Goodreads here—> https://www.goodreads.com/book/show/48258882-secret-keeper
Join Vi & Penelope's Cocky Hero Reader Group here—>
https://m.facebook.com/groups/874368842925701?ref=share

Make sure you sign up for my *NEWSLETTER* so that we can stay in touch, you can have access to all my giveaways, new releases, and cover reveals. Don't worry!
You'll never be spammed, shared, or sold.

FuckBoy

—Someone who is only looking for a piece of ass to use then throw away... He will always come crawling back because he is a horny prick and can not withstand the dispossession of one of his baes, because he has more than one that's for sure.

FuckBoy Syndrome

—A chronic disease, in which a chemical imbalance located between the testicles and brain cause the affected male to act and think in a distorted and perverted way. No one knows the exact cause of Fuckboy Syndrome, but it is said to be both genetic and conditioned. If this disease is left to manifest, it will consume the fuckboys life and actions.

—*Urban Dictionary*

THE THREE KISS CLAUSE

PART ONE
THE CONTRACT

PROLOGUE
EPISODE #87

WELCOME TO EPISODE EIGHTY-SEVEN of your favorite podcast, *Women on D*cks*, where me and my favorite female guests talk about all things guy related. As always, this is your girl, Tori Klein, and even though I don't have any guests today, I do have two super exciting announcements for my loyal army of *TorMenTors*.

First, I'm beyond amazed to say that we just passed one million subscribers on iTunes!

I can't even begin to express how lucky I am to have the greatest fans in all of Internet Land! Seriously, you all rock, and none of this would be possible without your support. So, in honor of our one millionth download, I'm giving away a bunch of cool *Women On D*cks* merch, as well as some of my brand-new *Tormentor Army* shirts, signed by yours truly. All you have to do is leave some love in the comments and I'll choose ten—that's right, ten lucky winners. All names will be announced on Wednesday's vlog!

You're probably wondering what my second piece of amazing news could be, right?

I can't keep you guys waiting any longer.

I've been teasing about it for a while now, and its finally time for my big reveal.

So, about a year ago, one of our own loyal supporters reached out to me about a project she wanted to work with me on. After some careful consideration, followed by a crazy amount of hard work, I'm happy to announce that soon you'll be able to grab a copy of my very first book!

That's right, TorMenTors, soon your girl is going to add published author to her growing list of titles. My debut book, which I named after my most downloaded episode of this podcast—*Fuckboys*—will soon be available at a store near you. I don't have any details or dates for you yet, but stay tuned.

That's all for now, guys. Gotta run. Remember to leave that comment for a chance to win all that amazing merch, and stay tuned for updates!

And, as always, support your girl by hitting that subscribe button and leaving a review!

CHAPTER 1

Tori

I STARTED MY PODCAST WHEN I came to the realization that all women eventually come to—that men are slaves to the masters that are their dicks. It's a simple truth, and the sooner you realize it, the better off you'll be

If you follow me on social media you already know how I feel about this topic, it's pretty much the focus of all of my content. And if you do follow me, I know you've seen (and hopefully used) that very hashtag I created—*#slavestotheirdicks*. But just in case you're not one of my loyal *Tormentor Army*, hit me up on Insta, *@Tor_MEN_Ted*, and make sure you subscribe and hit that notification bell on my YouTube channel—I vlog twice a week.

If you don't know me from either of those platforms (well, get on that!), then I should probably introduce myself properly.

I'm Tori Klein. Feminist influencer. Vlogger. Podcaster. Regular woman trying to get through the day. Oh, and I forgot to mention that soon I'll be a published author as well—but I'll get to that part in a second.

The first time someone called me Instafamous I almost hurled. I'm not in this for any kind of fame or recognition, but it kind of comes with the territory. Eventually I caved and just accepted that I'm kinda sorta famous, but only for the small percentage of the population that know my vlogging and podcasting.

Let's just say I get recognized more at Starbucks than anywhere else. But whether the old lady at the grocery store recognizes me or not, I still make a living off my social media accounts and the sponsors of my podcast. But I'm never satisfied, no matter how many new followers I get. I always want to reach more women. I always want to spread the gospel of #MenArePigs. And that's why I'll soon be adding published author to my growing list of job titles.

I decided to write a book so I could send my message to even more people than I could reach on Insta, or YouTube, or even on my podcast. A book is another platform, another chance to grow my rabid following of *TorMenTors* and spread the gospel of #slavestotheirdicks.

But there's a catch, of course—there's always a catch.

The thing is, I'm not *technically* published just yet, but it's practically a wrap. A fan slid into my DM's about a year ago and told me that she worked for one of the top publishing companies in Manhattan, and that my content is something they're missing in their catalog. So, long story short, I have what she called a 'pitch meeting' there tomorrow. From what she tells me, that whole meeting thing is basically just a formality.

If all goes well—and how could it not when they read my insights into the male sex—you'll be able to order your very own copy of *Fuckboys* on Amazon. And if you're super lucky, maybe you'll even get to meet me at your local Barnes & Noble when I'm signing copies on my sold-out book tour—I can't wait to meet you, by the way, and I thank you in advance for supporting my career! #*Tormentors!*

But before taking our epic selfies in front of my signing table (please use the hashtags #torikleinisawesome #shessoapproachable #myfavoriteauthor #fuckboys, and always remember to tag me).

Before you check out my pages or (eventually) read my book, we do need to clarify a few things, because there's some misinformation floating out there about me and my beliefs, mostly from the trolls in the comments section.

1.) **What I'm not:** the radical feminist, man-hating bitch I've been accused of being more times than I can count.

2.) **What I am:** a strong, fierce, ambitious woman who isn't afraid to speak her truth for the world to hear, and to inspire other women to do the same.

And what's the number one question I get from women who are looking to start their own vlog or podcast? Easy. *How do you find time in the day to do it all, Tori?*

I'll tell you a secret, I don't do it all. No one can manage a social media empire like I have without some serious help, and in that case the help is my other half. No, not *that* kind of other half, I'm as single as they come. I mean my bestie, Shoshana. She's been a fixture in my life since college, and she helps me edit, come up with concepts, find guests, and even manage my pages when I'm too busy. I honestly don't know what I'd do without her.

How would I describe our friendship? Let's just say that we're... well, we're a little different—opposites in almost every way that two women can be, but if Paula Abdul taught us nothing else, it's that opposites attract.

When I'm not in front of my camera or behind a microphone, I'm intense, reserved, and usually distrustful until I get to know someone. Shoshana is Ms. Loves The World—trusting, outgoing, happy-go-lucky, and the coolest strange person you'll ever meet. She's also weird as hell, in the best possible way.

When it comes to guys, we also exist on opposite sides of the universe. I see men for the stray alley cats that they are, but my other half believes in their goodness, no matter how many times she's been screwed over by them—and trust me, it's no small amount of times.

We talk about this subject all the time, and not just for the vlogs. We just love to debate each other when it comes to anything guy related. Besides all the other time we spend around each other (sometimes I feel like she's my work wife), we also have weekly sit down lunches at different restaurants around the city to discuss upcoming episodes and themes we want to explore. A few days ago we got into it about the differences in our perspectives when it comes to the opposite sex.

"I know that it's kind of your thing—you know, hashtags and all, but you really can't call all men pigs, Tor, it just isn't accurate." She was referring to a vlog I was editing at the time—guess what I was going to title it?

"I'll never understand how you can disagree with me after all the bad experiences that you and all the women who follow me have had. You know I'm right, that's why I have such a following. I speak the truth."

"I know no such thing, thank you very much. And I can

disagree comfortably because, unlike my hater of a best friend, I'm not a bitter old lady with a dried-up vagina full of dead spiders."

That's what I'm talking about—Shoshana can say some crazy shit that's somehow still pretty spot on. "Wow," I said, "just... wow."

"Well, in my head I was imagining your vag as either a desert or a frozen Siberian tundra—I just couldn't decide which metaphor was more appropriate—so I went with spiders and cobwebs."

"You realize that you just made my nether region into a B-horror movie troupe."

"Of course I realize. If there's one thing you know about me, Tor, it's that I always realize, even if I pretend not to. But the metaphor makes sense. Your vag should be a bustling spring full of chirping birds and waterfalls. You're young, hot, and more than a little bit famous—you should be putting yourself out there for all the eligible men who aren't the kind of guys you vlog about."

Here's a classic example of where where me and Shoshana disagree on our basic outlook on Guyland—she thinks most guys are good, with the occasional bad apple mixed in, while I think almost all of them are bad apples—the mushy, bruised kind that has a worm inside when you bite into it.

"I appreciate that you put all this mental energy into the state of my vagina, Shosh. I really do, but you don't have to worry about me. I don't need some guy in my life to turn a desert into a spring."

"In your opinion," she joked.

"My vag, my opinion," I joked back. "And there are better things to think about than my sex life."

"That's a contradiction in terms. How can I think of something that doesn't exist?"

"Ouch." She wasn't wrong, though. Shoshana has a sense of

humor that can make you laugh hysterically while simultaneously making you question every aspect of your existence. When she joked, sometimes you smiled because your diaphragm demanded contraction and your lungs just pushed out loud giggling sounds. But other times, like when she pointed out my non-existent dating life, you smiled because her accuracy frightened you. "Gotta say, that one stung a little."

"I wasn't trying to sting," she said. "I just worry about you. I want you to get out there. I think about it all the time."

What I never told Shosh—the truth that I worked my ass off to hide, was that I thought about it all the time too. *It*, in this case, being my relationships with guys. Or, as she put it, my *non-existent* relationships with guys. It's almost like there are two of me—the feminist social media mogul who made her name spreading the word that all guys were all sex crazed pricks, and then the inner me—the one who still held onto a belief that maybe, just maybe, there was at least one good one out there—the perfect apple at the bottom of the barrel.

Usually the first version of myself won out, but that didn't mean the other one wasn't in there, somewhere deep inside, waiting for the prince to step out from behind all the frogs.

"Thanks, Shosh, but you don't have to worry about me or my... area."

"Did you just call it your area?" She started laughing hysterically.

"I might have. Just maybe."

"Fine, we'll move on, but it's a hard thing to not think about. That hot guy over there is probably thinking about it right now."

"There's a thought—some random guy thinking of me like that."

"You're missing out, he's a cutie and a half." At that point she stopped looking at me entirely and just ogled the random dude, who apparently sat just over my should. "Hey," she said. "I have an idea—what do you say I wave him over? Maybe he has spider-poison in his pants."

"What? Listen to what you just said."

"You know, I heard it as it was coming out, and just so you know, it sounded super clever in my head. Cause, you know, the vagina spiders?"

"I got it. They can't all be home runs, you know?"

"Sadly, I do. But, still." She went to put her hand up and I grabbed it without even thinking about it. "Don't you dare wave at some strange guy."

"Well, he wouldn't exactly be strange if I waved him over and he introduced himself, would he? God, Tor, you're the dumbest smart girl I know."

"I don't need some weirdo to chase away anything in my pants, thank you very much."

"Your man-hating is going to leave you a bitter old lady one day. And as your best friend, I just can't have that. You're too awesome to end up that way."

There was the line. The one I'd read a million times in a million comments on my videos. If it wasn't there, it was some troll in the reviews of my podcast episodes. 'Tori hates men.' I heard it so often that it was like the same jab coming at my face again and again—I learned how to defend it instinctually without even thinking about it. "I don't hate men. How many times do I have to tell you that?"

"I'm not sure—how about as many times as it takes to sound convincing. So, like, maybe a bazillion more or so. I'm not sure."

"Look, you can't be like those Insta trolls I had to block. I do not hate men, I just... have some strong opinions on them. And those opinions are based on some real experiences. You know what I'm talking about."

"Of course I know what you're talking about. I was there, remember?"

She was *there*. There for the most painful experience of my life—the one that almost broke me. "Of course I remember," I told her. "How could I forget? But I wasn't talking about him, just experiences with men, in general. Look, I'll be the first to admit that I don't have a lot of experience to with guys, but that doesn't mean I can't speak with authority."

"Actually, Tor, that's exactly what that means."

" I mean, come on, Lord knows you have enough experience for the both of us. After some of the guys you've been with, you of all people should get how treacherous guys can be."

She raised an eyebrow and put her drink down. "Wait, hold on, before we even get into your lack of experience, I'm pretty sure you just called me a slut. Am I off on that?"

I can't help the smile that crossed my face. "I heard it as I was saying it. I didn't think you'd catch it."

"So I'm an oblivious slut, huh? Look, I may not have gotten a 1575 on my SAT's and been accepted to four Ivy League schools like some people, but I'm hardly an idiot."

I laughed so hard I almost spit out the drink I'd just stupidly taken a sip of. "You're the furthest thing from an idiot. And it should have been five, by the way."

"Huh? Five what?"

"Ivy's. I should have been accepted to five. But, you know, Stanford and all that."

"I have no actual idea what you just said, but I think I just caught a whiff of something snobby. It smells a little funky."

"I think that might be your lunch you're smelling."

Shosh was the queen of ordering too much food and eating almost none of it. "Oh yeah, look at that. That makes way more sense than what I said. But, still, with the snobbery."

"It's not me being a snob, it's true. That school has like a six percent acceptance rate."

"Let's get back on track here, I'm bored with all the school talk."

"Oh, don't do that," I told her.

"What?"

"Play the dumb role. Not only does it offend every feminist sensibility I have, it's also blatantly not true. We both know you're way smarter than I am."

"I know no such thing. You're the smart and pretty one. I'm just the one who can whip up witty Instagram stories and inventive hashtags."

Don't let Shoshana fool you. Her false modesty is just that. She's also beautiful, crazy smart, and if she put any thought into starting her own social media pages, I'd be in some trouble. She always tells me that she loves being the behind-the-scenes girl much more than she likes being on camera. I interviewed her on one of my early vlogs and it was one of the most awkward and funny things ever. It's still one of my most watched videos.

"You're a lot more than just social media savvy, and you know it."

"Agree to disagree," she told me. "But let's get back to you. Talking about me is boring. I already know all about me."

"Let's stay on you for one more minute. You think I'm crazy

for my views on guys, but just look at your last four—that's *four*—boyfriends."

"What about them?"

"I think you'd agree that they were shitheads, one and all, and each one was worse than the last, if I'm keeping my douche bags in order."

"You're not totally wrong. Oh, did I ever tell you that I kept all their numbers? I have them all in my phone as 'Ex-Dicks #'s 1-4.'"

"Really? Even Dillon?"

"Even good-old Dillon."

Dillon was the absolute worst of the four—the last one in a long line of assholes Shoshana decided to give a chance to be with her. I didn't like him from the second I met him. I never told Shosh, but when she first introduced me to Dillon he grabbed my ass when he hugged me hello. I knew he was a prick, but anytime I open my mouth about her choice in men she just writes it off as my 'man-hating.' Yet another example of what I always say about guys—their dicks have a gps to all the vaginas in the room. #slavestotheirdicks.

"Why keep their numbers? And don't tell me you'd ever call or text that creep again or I'm gonna flip out."

"No, never," she said. "But I like to keep their numbers mementos."

"Mementos?" I asked.

"Yeah. Like a little piece of my past mistakes to remind me of where I've been. But I won't deny that I've had some bad luck with the XYs recently."

"Four bad guys in a row isn't bad luck, Shoshana. It's evidence of why women need this book I wrote. I didn't even realize how many women had such bad experiences until I started to write down all my past podcast guests' stories. It's crazy."

"And you think that means that all men are like that?"

"No, it doesn't mean that at all, but it definitely means that there's *something* to the points I make in my book. I'm not totally crazy."

"No one's totally crazy, Tor. I mean, maybe like, Charles Manson or something, he was pretty batshit. But when it comes to someone like you, I'd say you're only like... maybe sixty-five percent crazy. That's not bad at all. The national average is probably higher."

"It's not my fault that all my female guests want to talk about is how the men in their lives—brothers, friends, boyfriends, husbands, fathers and yes, wait for it, even *grandfathers*—are running around twenty-four seven trying to stick their little dicks into everything."

"Don't say that, Tori. That's not fair. Some of them may have pretty substantial dicks."

"I'm sure they do. I wouldn't know."

"Wait, how big was... He-Who-Shall-Remain-Nameless' dick? I never asked you. I know you didn't measure it or anything. Unless you did, which would be some kinky shit for you—but forget that, just give me an approximation? Was it like a pencil—long and thin? Or was it more cucumber-ish?"

"Shosh, stop it..."

"Wait, don't tell me he was packing a full eggplant down there?"

"Shoshana!"

"Sorry. Sorry. I got carried away with thoughts of..."

"I don't want to talk about *him*—ever, really, but especially not right now."

The *him* was my ex boyfriend from college—really the only boyfriend I've ever had. I'm not going to mention his name because I might speak his evil into existence. If I stood in front of a mirror and invoked his stupid name three times I'm sure he'd appear behind me with a full hard on, ready to stick it into the first willing woman he found.

That whole experience changed my opinions on guys. It was a few years ago, and I've basically been as celibate as a Tibetan monk ever since. That's by choice, mind you. If there's a universal truth that every one of us XX's knows, it's that no matter who you are, what you look like, or where you live, there's never a shortage of men willing to fuck you if you offer them the chance.

After college, relationships and men were like that drink you order on your twenty-first birthday, have way too much of, and then can never smell again without vomiting on the floor.

Instead, I chose to podcast, vlog, and now write about other women's experiences with their own fuckboys (the title of my upcoming book, btw)—how they were hurt, what was expected of them, how they were treated.

"I get it," Shoshana said. "I know he hurt you bad, but still, you can't blame all men..."

"Shoshana, seriously, I really don't want to talk about him."

"I know, just let me finish. I'm pulling the bestie card. That's a thing. I know that whole thing back in school didn't go the way you thought it would, but welcome to the club."

"You're making my points for me."

"No, I'm not. You're missing my point. I'm not even talking about him. I'm talking about you and all of us. There are some things that bind us together as women—the two that pop into my mind are getting our periods and having shitty ex boyfriend horror stories to share with friends—it's a female universal. Doesn't mean we all have to become bitter at the ripe old age of twenty-eight!"

"I'm not bitter, and like I've said a million times already, I don't hate men. I just see them for what they are. There's a difference."

"And what are they?"

"Penises attached to arms, legs, and the occasional semi-functioning brain. They're walking hard ons, Shoshana, and basically all of their behaviors are focused on one activity and one activity only—screwing as many women as they can before the sun sets, at which time they rest up, so that they can get their fuck energy back for the next day's hunt. They're like sexual nomads, wandering the vast plains of America looking for willing vaginas."

"Wow," she said.

"Wow, what?"

"My best friend is profoundly messed up."

"I'm not messed up because I speak the truth."

"Before I respond, kudos to the expression 'fuck energy' right off the top of your head—that was a special moment right there. Now, even you have to admit that there XYs out there in Guyland who aren't what you're describing." She was right, of course, and I know not ALL men are piggish fuckboys, but I couldn't shake the feeling that most of them were—at least the ones I heard about every day.

"Not all of them, no."

"Don't get me wrong, I still want you to get that book deal—partially because I love you—like ninety-five percent that, but also because I really want to appear in the acknowledgments of a book sometime in my life. So yeah, good luck."

"Awww," I said really sarcastically. "You're so sweet."

"I have my moments. Just consider my point of view. I'm a woman too, you know? I have a vagina just like you, only mine is alive and well."

"No spiders in yours?"

"My exes exterminated them for me. Now it's like an oasis in there." She sat up really straight at that point, like a lightbulb had just gone off in her crazy little head. "Wait, maybe that's it! I never thought of it before."

"Thought of what?" I asked.

"The reason why you have such an obsession with men's sex lives."

"Edify me. I'd love to hear this."

"First, answer me something, for my own research purposes. What did you do with the vibrator I got you for your birthday last year?"

"Jesus, Shoshana, lower your voice."

We were getting lunch at the time of this discussion—some vegan place that she found right after her conversion to all things non-living. She was flaky like that. I gave her veganism about as long as I gave her whenever she texted me to say that she'd met 'the perfect guy'—usually at a Walmart, or some other location where no woman has ever met the right guy—about two to four weeks, max.

Knowing how fickle she was, I assumed our next lunch date debate would probably be at a steakhouse, which was just fine with me.

"What, now you're embarrassed?" she asked, taking a bite of

her sweet potato... something or other. "You didn't care if anyone heard you declaring the inherent evil of the entire male species, but I mention touching yourself and you get all..."

"Shhh."

"Oh, wow," Shoshana said. It was judgmental. It was something I'd do. I did not appreciate it. I can't take my own medicine. I can't take just as good as I give. "I just figured you out. Like, a lightbulb just went off. Can you see it?"

I look over her head and we both laugh. "Nope. Strangely, I can't."

"Don't worry, it's there, whether you see it or not. It's glowing just as bright, regardless. It's like that thing, when a tree falls in the forest."

"And what is said lightbulb illuminating for you?"

"Something I should have realized years ago," she said. "It's so simple that I never saw it. You're afraid of sex."

"What? You're nuts."

"Interesting that you bring up nuts, firstly. And secondly, I think I'm onto something here. Let's examine the evidence, shall we?"

"Oh, there's evidence now?"

"Hear me out. You're obsessed with men having sex. Or, at least with them *trying* to have sex all the time, like it's some global conspiracy to keep women down instead of a natural biological thing. You see men wanting sex as threatening, and you're uncomfortable talking about masturbation or orgasms."

I hate that Shoshana has an undergrad degree in Psychology. You know what they say about having a little knowledge about something—well, that's her when it comes to anything psychological. She remembers a few lectures from college and tries to use them to 'diagnose' me with whatever she thinks is wrong.

"I don't like talking about getting myself off in public with a... how would you even classify that thing?"

"As a big fake black cock," she blurted out. I almost turned right red. "Oh, wait, that's not totally accurate. You have a big fake black cock that vibrates at five different speeds."

I lowered my voice to practically a whisper. "Right. Thanks for the reminder. But not wanting this whole restaurant to hear about my multi vibration black cock doesn't make me a prude. It just makes me someone with standards."

"I have standards, too—I got you the largest size they had! The guy had to go into the back to get it, Ms. Unappreciative. But I figured, go big or go home. And also, don't get all high and mighty on me, Tori, we're just two girls talking. It's not like I whipped out the little bean tickler right here at the table."

I started giggling. "Excuse me? The bean tickler?"

"Yeah," she said. "You know? The joystick. The pussy pleaser."

"Oh my God, how are we even friends?"

"Wait, I wasn't done. The hole pole, Happy Feelmore, BOB."

"Excuse me, BOB?"

"Yeah, Battery-Operated-Boyfrind. BOB. We all know BOB—some of us know him a little better than others. BOB's not a bad guy—he's there to help bring us to a higher plane of existence. We love BOB. We need him in our lives."

I started cracking up then, and so did Shoshana. "Look, I'm not scared of sex, alright. Nor am I an old lady with a cobweb vagina."

"Actually, I said that you had spiders and cobwebs *in* your vagina, but whatever."

"Well, I'm not that... I'm just... guarded when it comes to that kind of stuff. He-Who-Shall-Not-Be-Mentioned took care of that for me. Now I spend so much time giving men shit for their sex lives that I don't really have much of a chance to have my own. I mean, what guy would even try to approach me? I scare them away, and I have really high standards. It would take a lot for me to even feel something like that towards a man."

"Look, all I'm saying is that it's possible to separate the two," she told me. "You can still be a woman without feeling guilty about it. It's okay to like men, to want them, to have those feelings towards them. It is okay to enjoy a sexual relationship with a man. That doesn't invalidate your book or your social media presence. What invalidates it, is that you don't ever actually put yourself out there and try—you're commentating from the bench. You need to get in the game."

When Shoshana speaks like she did at lunch yesterday, I always want to believe what she's saying to me, but I can never seem to get there. It's like I have this shield around me when it comes to guys. I know where that shield comes from, but I can't get rid of it. On top of that, every time I talk to another woman about her experiences, all of my feelings on men come right back to the forefront of my mind.

I look down at the worn advanced copy of my book and take an especially deep breath. It's filled with colored post its and so many highlights that it looks like a coloring book. I'm not the nervous type, but I hope tomorrow goes well!

I know this is my first rodeo, and I'm way more of a podcaster than I am an author, but I really think this book is going to set the publishing world on fire!

CHAPTER 2

Cormac

The Following Afternoon

THANK GOD THIS WOMAN IS HOT, because this book of hers
is total crap!

That's probably not the most appropriate thing for a partner
in a huge publishing company to think while an author is pitching
a book they've poured their heart and soul into, but I've seriously
never read such crap in my entire life, and I read books for a living!
I look back down at the text just in case I'm being unfair.

Nope. No, I'm not. What do all these buzz words even mean?
There's just one after the other.

Toxic masculinity?

Manspreading?

Mansplaining?

The Patriarchy?

Who made up all of these stupid terms? I look over and see one of my two partners, Elissa, smiling and nodding so hard that her neck must be getting sore. My other partner, Cynthia, approved of this drivel *in absentia*. She took some of that fuck-you money she has from being the founder of such a successful company and is currently touring Europe with her husband. She's such a work horse that she's reading samples somewhere in Amsterdam or Prague, or wherever.

As for me? I have to sit in this uncomfortable chair, reading even more uncomfortable words as my other partner seems to have taken a few shots of Kool-Aid before this meeting even began. I'm in The *Twilight Zone* right now.

"Excuse me? I interrupt.

"Yes."

"I hate to be the ignorant one here, and I can't believe that I'm about to say this to a woman I just met, but your title?"

"Fuckboys?" She asks like it's nothing. "What about it?"

"What is that?"

"A fuckboy?"

"Yeah. It's the title of this book but I don't even know what that is. Can you explain for us unindoctrinated?"

"Sure. I guess the simplest way to describe a fuckboy...sorry, does it bother you that I keep saying that word again and again?"

"It's the title of your book. If it bothers people then it's a problem, isn't it?"

"Yeah. I mean, I guess, but...anyhow, it means a guy who sleeps around, but only wants to hookup with girls and will tell them anything they want to hear, and who doesn't want anything close to a relationship. There are other definitions, but I'm easing you into it."

"Other definitions?"

"Yeah. A lot, actually. Have you ever looked on Urban Dictionary?"

I shake my head. "Nope. Can't say that I have."

"You should. There are some hilarious definitions on there. Way better than I just described."

"You care to share one?" I ask. I don't really care what a fuckboy is, but the conversation I'm having is way more interesting than this feminist drivel she's trying to pitch me. I'm just trying to keep myself awake and sane at this point.

She pulls out her phone. "My favorite is from the guy who said, and I quote, 'a "fuckboy" is the lowest possible form of the vile, degenerate waste pouring from the proverbial asshole of society.' There's more, but I think it gets a little vulgar."

"We sure wouldn't want to let that happen, would we?"

She can finally sense my sarcasm, and she makes that sexy face of hers into a scowl that excites me and turns me on at the same time. She really is gorgeous.

Tori Klein.

I read up on her a little after Elissa set up this meeting.

She describes herself as a, and I quote, *liberal third wave feminist* (I didn't know they came in waves, but whatever), and apparently, she's some kind of hot shot social media person. But as far as I'm concerned, the only thing this girl has going for her is her face and body, because Lord knows her book is some man-hating craziness. But back to that face and body for a minute—both are ridiculous! I can't stop staring at her neck. She's wearing this necklace that hangs just to where I can't see the things I want to.

Her hair hangs to her shoulders, and she has these legs that make my dick twitch right here in my seat. I can't keep my eyes off her, no matter what I think of this crap she thinks I'm crazy enough to actually publish. She's not just the hottest woman to ever pitch a book in this office, she's one of the most gorgeous women I've ever seen. It's getting harder and harder... to concentrate, that is.

I snap myself back into reality, and out of the fantasy I was just having about bending her over this conference table. I see Elissa still has that shit-eating grin on her face. I have partners—two of them, both women—and they both loved the sample chapters that Tori provided to us. But they know as well as I do that our company has a policy of 'unanimous or no' – meaning that we all have to agree that we're going to accept a book for publication or the book gets rejected. Every one of us has veto power, and based on the silly, happy grin on Elissa's face, I think I'm going to be the only sane person who actually uses theirs.

She keeps talking for a few more minutes, going through all of the horrible things men are—let me see if I remember her words accurately: *sex-crazed maniacs, fuckboys, slaves to their dicks*, which she gave a verbal 'hashtag'—a pet peeve of mine in case you were wondering—until finally I can't take any more "Okay, okay, I've heard enough."

"Cormac?" My partner is looking over at me with more than a little judgement in her eyes.

"I'm sorry, Elissa, but I really can't listen to any more of this drivel."

The only reason I'm still sitting at this table is because of how sexy this woman is. She's bat-shit crazy if she thinks this book is getting published by us, but with a body like that I'm almost ready to forgive her. Almost.

"What's the matter?" She asks. She's looking right into my

eyes. Thank God I'm sitting down when she does. For a second, I forget her question, but when I pause way too long Elissa jabs me in the side.

"Cormac," Elissa says, interrupting what I'm about to say. "Why don't we just let her finish what she was saying?"

"Because I don't want to waste her time. Or ours. I don't need to hear anymore of this."

I'm not trying to be a total dick, but that's how it's coming across. I can see Tori's face change as soon as she sees where this is heading. First, it's a look of concern, but then pretty quickly I see a tinge of anger replace it.

"Look, Mr..."

"Cormac is fine," I tell her. "Or should I call myself... hold on, let me find it." I page back through her last chapter until I find what I'm looking for. "Ah, here it is. Maybe I should call myself a '...cis man patriarch.' But I guess that's a little wordy to say, huh? Doesn't really roll off the tongue, does it?"

Tongue. I wonder what hers would feel like in my mouth. Fuck, Cormac, focus!

My partner jumps in to do what she always thinks she needs to do—apologize for me and make excuses for my behavior. She thinks I'm rude. I think I'm honest. "Tori, I'm so sorry, he's just a very blunt person."

"Now Elissa, don't go mansplaining away my behavior." Not sure why I'm using the sharpest tone I can find, but every word coming out of my mouth is fire. Don't get me wrong, she seems like a nice enough person, and she could stop traffic with her face, but every time I think about all the man-hating bullshit she's peddling my way I get angrier and more defensive. And the more sarcastic I get, the more aggravated I see her becoming. "Wait, did

I use that right? There are so many derogatory terms beginning with the prefix 'man', it's hard to keep them all straight. You'd think these radical feminists would be more creative with their made-up terminology."

"Cormac!" Elissa yells again. Even though she's younger than me, she's starting to sound like my mom.

"What is it?"

"I've got this one, Elissa." I turn back from my partner to the sound of Tori's voice. "Listen, Cormac, I'm not sure what your problem with me or my work is, but..."

"Really?" I interrupt. "You don't see how a male publisher might have a problem with some of the ideas that you're trying to put out regarding all men. Or, as you call us, *the patriarchy?*"

"I wasn't talking about you." She says. "You're getting a little defensive considering it's a book. If you disagree with the content of the book you could at least handle it with a little more professionalism."

What the hell did she just say? On top of insulting my entire gender, she also just called me unprofessional. It takes a lot of balls to insult a guy who holds the fate of your publishing future in his hands. I don't know if I should be offended, or proud of her for defending her work so hard. Nah, I'm going with offended.

"Excuse me?" I ask. "Are you saying that I'm being unprofessional?"

"You cut me off in the middle of my pitch and you've been pretty sarcastic with everything else you've said to me. I'd think, for a company this large, you'd at least let an author finish before politely rejecting her—*politely* being the key word."

"Well I'm sorry for my sarcasm, Ms. Klein, but..."

"Tori." She says, cutting me off. "If we're on a first name basis then it should go both ways, right?"

"Fine." I say. "Tori, then."

"It's short for Victoria, but no one really calls me that."

I start to feel bad about this whole thing, but I really can't have a book like hers published with my company's name on the back cover. I don't think she's a bad person, but she's got some really bad ideas about men. "I see." I soften my tone a little. If we keep going like this I'm going to confirm all of the bad things she clearly thinks of me. "Look, Tori, I didn't mean to cut you off, and if you want you can certainly finish anything that you wanted to say to us, but I also don't want to waste anyone's time here—yours or ours—and the truth is, that unless your last words are about how this whole book is some long piece of satire, I can't vote yes to have it published here. I find a lot of what you wrote insulting and way too general."

"Insulting?" she asks.

"Yes, insulting. Half of the population is male, Tori, as I'm sure you know this already, and it's about the same percentage of people who buy books that we publish under our banner. I can't publish something that's going to alienate fifty percent of the people who keep our doors open. My opinion aside, that's just bad business."

"So that's how it is here, huh?"

"Meaning what, exactly?"

"Meaning I didn't know you made your publishing decisions based on money. I thought maybe the artistic integrity of the book would be something you'd take into consideration."

Artistic integrity? Is she serious? "Of course it matters what the book is about. And for the record, it's not about me liking or not liking it, it's about what kind of fit it's going to be for our company and our audience. This is a business, Tori, not an art gallery."

"Cormac," Elissa says, jumping in before the conversation gets too heavy. "Can I talk to you for a second, privately?"

I feel another scolding coming on, but I'll always hear Elissa out. "Of course. Excuse us."

I prepare myself for the lecture that I know is coming. The background to this whole meeting is that it was Elissa who reached out to Tori in the first place—which I think is completely inappropriate. The truth is, our company has been losing popular authors to up and coming rival companies for a while now, and Elissa is the most ambitious of the three partners. She'd do anything to keep Tori around.

"Listen," she says. "I get where you're coming from, that's why I tried to warn you as to what her book was about."

"Warn me? Elissa you said she was—wait, I think I remember your exact line—you said she was 'a progressive social media personality that vlogs and has a podcast about women's relationship experiences.' You didn't say she was a full-fledged radical feminist who hates men! You might have warned me about that part."

"Okay, fine. Maybe I was a little conservative with how I described her, but Cormac, you're not a social media person, you have no idea how popular the woman sitting there watching us talk really is. She has a rabid following."

"Including you."

That last part was a dig. I'm not a conservative guy—at all—but when it comes to things like this, I find Elissa's behavior a little south of appropriate. Apparently, Elissa reached out to Tori on social media and tried to court her business. Usually it works the other way around—authors pitch us, we don't pitch them. We're not a bunch of literary ambulance chasers, but I think Elissa is starting to panic about our bottom line.

"Yes, including me. Regardless of what you think—and it's clear what you think—her messages to women have a lot of value. Especially in the #metoo era. Her platforms are all about female empowerment and self-actualization. I don't see how that's a bad thing."

Self-actualization? My partner sounds like a bad self-help book you pick up on the discount rack at a bookstore. "I'm fine with empowerment, just not at the expense of trashing an entire gender. Do you really buy into all this man hating stuff?"

"She's not like that, I promise you. I know you won't believe me, but it's more complicated than you think."

"I'm sure it is."

"Look, I don't have time to convince you of her message, but what I can do is tell you that you need to stop thinking purely like an editor and more like a businessman. You had it backwards in there."

Here it is. The money pitch.

"Meaning I should just blindly say yes because she has a lot of followers and subscribers and can bring us money we so desperately need? That kind of businessman?"

"For every man she might alienate with the content, she'll bring in five women. It's still a net gain for us, which means more sales. This could be a New York Times bestseller, no matter what you think. And we can't afford to lose another popular author."

And that was her dig right back at me. She still blames me

for our most popular and bestselling author leaving the company, even though that decision had nothing to do with me.

"I'm sorry." I say, trying to compromise. "I'll let her finish, alright, but I can't sign off on this just because you're scared we're going to go out of business. No one author has the power to make or break a whole company. It doesn't work like that."

I can tell that she doesn't like what I'm saying, but I can't make everyone happy. I have to do what I think is best, and no matter how many new readers she brings to the table, I can't give this book the green light.

But there is something I want to know—something that's been bothering me this entire pitch—and not just the content of the book. I have a question for my favorite feminist. "Sorry about that, Tori."

"No problem. Should I go on?"

"Actually, if you'll indulge me, I have one last question for you about this whole book."

"Sure. Fire away."

"Something you wrote in the introduction struck me as odd. I've been meaning to ask you about it since this meeting started."

"Which part?" she asks.

I flip back to the beginning of the book. "Here it is. Your book is mainly transcriptions of interviews you did with women on your podcast and in your vlog, right?"

"Mostly," she says. "Like, maybe 75% that and the other 25% are my own thoughts and conclusions. You know, the parts you hate."

"Right, that. In your first paragraph, you talk about how even though you're writing a book all about men, that you've never really been in a serious, long term relationship with one yourself. Is that true?"

She takes a big deep breath, which gets me even more curious. "Technically, I've only been in one real relationship—in college. It didn't end well."

"I see. And is that how you came to all your conclusions on men? Based on one bad experience?"

"No, Cormac," she says with an edge to her voice. "It's not. You really think I'd have one bad experience and then write a whole book? It's not as simple as all that. Like you said, most of the book is *other* women's experiences. But the whole social media thing started with my own."

I think about what she just said, and I'm torn between wanting to ask my next question and not coming across as too much of an asshole. The curious part of me wins out. "So, can I ask you something else, then?"

She takes a deep breath, so loud that I can hear it from across the table. Clearly, she's had enough of me, but I can't help myself. "Go ahead."

"How can you claim to be some kind of expert on men when you've never been in a real relationship, save for one relationship in college? Doesn't that seem a little contradictory to you?"

"Contradictory?"

"Yeah. Meaning, you're repeating other women's experiences, but past your one experience in college, you don't have any of your own."

"Cormac, I think you're out of line here," Elissa interjects.

"It's okay, Elissa," Tori says. "I don't think I need to be in a bunch of relationships to draw some basic conclusions about them."

Wrong answer. I was hoping for some self-reflection. Some acknowledgement that maybe she's not quite the expert she thinks she is. Instead, she just dug her heals in and killed any chance of me saying yes to this drivel. "Alright, then." I stand up. "With all due respect, I have to say no to this. I don't think you have a leg to stand on with it, and I don't think it's even marketable, save for maybe to your followers. You have some interesting stories in there, but all the other things—your conclusions—I just can't get there, Tori. I'm sorry."

I get up to head back to my office.

Before I'm completely out of the room I steal one more look at her.

She really is so beautiful, even though she looks like she's ready to kill me.

It's a damn shame she hates men so much.

CHAPTER 3

Tori

WHAT AN ARROGANT ASSHOLE!

If I'd known my first book pitch was going to be like my actual first time—messy, uncomfortable, faster than I imagined, and ultimately disappointing—I would have mentally prepared myself. But I believed Elissa when she said that this was just a formality. She said that she loved the samples I gave her, and so did their other parter, Cynthia. She never mentioned that the third partner I'd be facing was their hanging judge.

"What the hell?" I don't mean to sound bitchy—Elissa did me a favor by reaching out to me in the first place, but I definitely feel like I got sideswiped.

"I'm sorry, Tori. I had no idea anything like that was going to happen.."

God, that Cormac was a total jerk to me! I mean, who does

he think he is? Like it matters that he has crystal blue eyes you get completely lost in when he talks, or that he's over six feet tall and built like a gym rat. That doesn't give him free range to be a douche. I feel so silly that I walked into this.

If I didn't have so much respect for Elissa, I would have followed him out of the room and told him what I really thought of him. But I appreciate the opportunity she gave me, even if the whole thing went south. She comes around to the other side of the table and sits down next to me. She's only a little bit older than me, but she's treating me like she's my mom.

"I feel terrible Tori. I know I made it sound like this was going to be... easier than it was."

Easier. That's an understatement. She made it sound like I already had a book deal and all I had to do was sign the paperwork. "You didn't know he'd react like that? He's your partner."

"He is that," she says. "He's also a friend, and I have to be honest, I've never seen him treat an author that way. Something in your book must have really rubbed him the wrong way. Trust me, the last thing I'd ever do is purposely walk you into something like that. I really had no idea. I'm so sorry."

"Thanks, Elissa, but you really don't need to apologize to me, it's not your fault. If he hated it, he hated it, there's nothing I can do to change his mind, I guess."

"Actually, that might not be completely true."

I make a puzzled face. "Huh?"

"I didn't tell you this before because I didn't think I'd need to, but I think now is a good time to go over some policies that our company has. All of us—myself, Cormac, and Cynthia are all equal partners when it comes to publishing deals. Meaning that we're either unanimous in accepting a book, or unanimous in rejecting it." *Great. Fuck. My. Life.* "So, as much as I love you, I can't override that policy to push your book through."

"No, of course not, and I'd never ask you to. So I guess I'll shop the book around somewhere else. Maybe you could point me in the right direction and..."

"Hold on. I said that I couldn't change the policy for you. I didn't say that your chances of getting published under our banner are hopeless."

Holy crap. Is she serious? Wait, I don't want to get my hopes up only to get burned again. I have to be cautious. "Okay, I'm listening. I've got to be honest though, it sounded pretty hopeless a minute ago."

"Cormac's a brilliant copy editor and has a great eye for what's marketable and what isn't. While I think he's completely off base about your work, I'm not going to write his opinion off completely. I sent a copy of the book to Cynthia while she's in Europe. She feels the same was as I do—we both love it, and we think it's very marketable to women these days."

"But that third vote?"

"Is a problem. But not necessarily a problem that can't be worked around. When we have a 2-1 split in favor of a book, we have a built-in waiting period of one month before we have our official vote. That way, it gives the dissenting partner—in this case, Cormac—a chance to reconsider their position in light of how the other two partners feel. Usually they reread the book, or speak to the author again, and we often have heated internal discussions among ourselves to see if we can sway the third vote. Sometimes it goes the author's way and sometimes it doesn't. It all depends."

Great. So my future in publishing is at the whim of that arrogant—albeit really good looking—man. Why do I keep going to that in my head? I'm so mad at him I swear steam is going to come out of my ears like one of those Looney Tunes episodes, yet I can't stop thinking about how good looking he was—or how tall—or how... *stop it, Tori, the guy was a jerk, who cares what he looks like?*

"Okay, so I'll get my official 'no' in a month, then?"

"You never know," Elissa tells me. She's still giving me the sympathetic eyes, almost like she knows her partner is a hard-headed man who isn't going to change his mind easily. "Cormac is what you saw of him, but he's also a good man. I promise. I wouldn't have gone into business with him otherwise. He can be convinced, it just might take a little creativity on your part."

I know that she's just trying to make me feel better, but it's not working at all. The month waiting period is nice enough, but based on how severely Cormac reacted to my book, I know which way this is going to go. So instead of just getting rejected outright, licking my wounds, and moving on, now I have to wait to get the answer I know is coming anyway. One thing I do know—it isn't Elissa's fault.

"Thank you," I tell her, putting my hand over hers. "For everything. Thanks for listening and for trying. Not everyone sees my vision."

"As a woman in this industry, I've learned that sometimes you have to make someone see your vision. You have to shove it in their face, even if they don't want it or don't like it at first. Sometimes that's the only way for people to take you seriously."

Shove it in their face. Interesting thought. Now, if only I could figure out a way to actually do it.

CHAPTER 4

Tori

The Next Day

WHEN I NEED TO LICK MY wounds—and they need some serious licking right now—I always go to the same place. Actually, *place* is the wrong word, because the location doesn't matter. It's more accurate to say that when I'm hurting badly, I always go same *person*. She's about to answer the door now.

"Mom!"

I give her a hug just like the one I gave her the first time a boy broke my heart—his name was Adam, I was twelve, and after he told me that I was ugly I gave my mom a hug like the one I'm giving her now. And just like that one, I held on for dear life, as though letting go might result in me getting sucked into some kind of vortex I might never escape from.

And just like that day, my mom told me to man the hell up. "Baby, you know I love your hugs more than anything else in the world, but you're cutting off my circulation."

"Sorry. I needed to squeeze."

"Something must be bad, you haven't squeezed me that hard in a very long time."

"I haven't had to. But today I need a good one. You could have squeezed me back, you know?"

"I needed to assess the situation first. Your squeeze was about a seven."

"You rank my hugs?"

"Only the ones like that—the panic ones that come without any words. I rate those and decide if you need a squeeze back."

"And seven doesn't make the cut?"

"Eight and above. You were close, but not sad enough for me to break your ribs like you almost broke mine."

Here's the thing about Mom—she's like two different people. Maybe that's where I get it from. When she thinks I need it, she can be the warmest, kindest, most understanding person in the entire world. I'll give you an example. That time when Adam called me ugly, my mom let me cry on her lap until I ran out of tears. She didn't ask me a bunch of questions, or tell me it was all going to be okay, she just let me empty my tear ducts like I needed to. Then she got up, made me my favorite tea (and yes, I was that kid who had a favorite tea), and then let me fall asleep on her lap. When I woke up and told her the story is when she gave me her other side—the hard-ass feminist who didn't let me cry any more, but told me that I didn't need some dumb boy to make me feel pretty. My two moms. I guess they helped raise two Tori's.

"Damn, I thought I was sad enough for a little love."

"You always have my love, baby. But I'm sure whatever it is you can tell me about over some coffee, because I need some before my class this afternoon. I can't take it anymore."

"Oh no, they gave you the undergrads again?"

"Let's just say that I might be at your place later looking for my own squeeze."

"Oh no, I'm so sorry."

Mom's a professor of psychology. She has the distinction as being the oldest woman ever hired for a tenure track position at the university. She started this process late, but leave it to Mom to grind through, taking names and kicking ass all the way to her newly minted Ph.D. But she's still the low woman in the hierarchy, so for the past three years she's had to teach undergrad Introduction to Psychology courses, and she can barely handle it.

"They're just so immature. It's like I'm a high school teacher."

"You basically are," I tell her. "I mean, think about it. Those kids are three months removed from going to their prom, for God's sake. It's no wonder they giggle when you talk about anatomy and human sexuality."

"Please, don't remind me."

I almost had a Ph.D., just like Mom. Only, to her disappointment, I didn't follow through with it. I'm what you call ABD—all but dissertation. I did all the course work, but I never actually wrote my dissertation. See, once upon a time I thought I wanted to be an academic, to follow in my mom's footsteps and be a professor. I lasted all but one semester before I realized that it wasn't for me. Teaching a few undergrad classes while working on my degree taught me two things: one, teaching wasn't for me. And two, I was good in front of people. It was the second thing that led me to a career path that my mom still doesn't totally understand.

"Are we getting coffee?" I ask.

"You should know by now that the answer to that question is always 'yes.' I'm driving."

We get to a coffee shop a few minutes later. The place is packed but we manage to get our cups and sit for a few minutes to talk. I'm trying to hide my disappointment from yesterday, but it's hard. That whole thing really stung. Maybe I was being arrogant—not as arrogant as that Cormac guy—but in my own way, thinking that I had that in the bag was probably not the smartest way to go into the meeting. I guess I figured my platform would carry me through, and that they'd accept me no matter what because of the huge audience I brought to the table, but I guess not.

"What's the matter?" Mom asks. She can see right through me. It's a mom power.

"What makes you think something is wrong?"

"Victoria, do you even need to ask? I'm your mother. Now just tell me. Is it something with your podcast or YouTube whatever?"

"No," I tell her. "My social media empire is growing. Everything's great with that stuff."

"Every time you say that I think of the Romans or something," she laughs.

"Say what? Oh, you mean the word empire? That's what it's called, Mom. And trust me, if you knew more about it you'd understand how successful I am in that world. It took me a long time to build up an audience like I have. It's not easy."

"I know," she tells me. "I don't mean to diminish your accomplishments, you know that. I just wish you..." She trails off. I know what she's going to say, she doesn't need to finish.

"What? Would have followed you to the classroom? I wanted to. I tried, but it wasn't for me. I had to follow my own path."

"I know. I guess I'm just being a mom. But we've had that talk a million times. What's going on with you?"

I tell her the story, start to finish. She didn't know that I was going for the meeting. I'm not secretive with my mom, but I don't exactly tell her everything, either. She did know that I was writing a book, but not that a fan had contacted me to have it published at her company. I tell her, finally, and then I tell her what happened during the meeting.

"That guy sounds like a typical smug man."

"I agree. But that smug man has a lot of power." *And blue eyes. Really, really blue eyes that I couldn't stop staring at, even when he was saying terrible stuff about my book.*

"I guess you'll just have to find other companies. I know a few that do academic publishing if you're interested."

"Actually, there's a part of the story that I left out." That's when I tell her about the whole second vote thing, and that seems to peak her interest.

"So let me get this straight. You get a chance to convince him that he was wrong, and if you can then the book will get published?"

"Exactly. That's what Elissa said. Something about a company policy they have."

"Well, then that's what you have to do. What's the plan?"

That's a great question, Mom. "I'm still working that part out in my head."

"I wish I could help you, baby." I suck down my coffee faster than usual. I'm hoping that the caffeine will at least give me energy to think, 'cause Lord knows I don't have it right now. I didn't sleep great, and I have to think of something I can say or do to get a deal, but it's just not coming to me. I take another big gulp and Mom notices. "Go easy. You're going to get jittery."

"I'm already jittery. At least I'll have some energy to go with it."

I know Mom wants to help, but I forget sometimes how judgy she can be about my life choices. It's not obvious, and it's not mean, but it's there. The daughter in me wants to just ask for help and hear some magical solution come out of my mom's mouth, but I know deep down she doesn't get the vlog, or the podcast, or even the book. She'd much rather I was publishing my dissertation on some boring topic no one would ever read, but that's not me. I decide to just change the subject.

"So... what are you teaching the future leaders of America today? Freud and his penis envy?"

"God, no. That was the first week, and it was painful. They seemed to like when I talked about his cocaine addiction."

"It's comforting to know that the most well-known psychologist in history was a druggie. It reminds me that I'm not the only messed up one out there."

"That's a very Tori way to look at things," she laughs. "No more Freud, though. We're going over the Stanford Prison Experiment."

"Wait, I remember. That was the one where they created a fake prison, right?"

"That's right. They made half the participants fake guards and the other half fake prisoners, to see how they'd treat one another."

"There was a movie on Netflix. It was really good. You couldn't do that today, right?"

"An experiment like this? No way. The ethical board wouldn't even let you suggest such a thing. Those kinds of experiments don't happen anymore, and probably with good reason."

"But you learned a lot from them, right? Even though you couldn't do them today?"

"We learned a crazy amount about human behavior—things you can't find out from other kinds of research. It's a shame we can't do things like this any more."

A lightbulb goes off in my head. My mom's words set off a chain reaction in my crazy head, and I jump up. "Drive me home!" I yell.

"Jesus, Victoria, you alright? I think that caffeine went straight to your head."

"It totally did," I say. "But that's besides the point. I just had an idea and I need to go home and think it through. Can we go?"

Mom gets up and drives me back to her place. I barely speak on the drive back because my mind is trying to work out the details of the slightly crazy idea I just had. After she parks I jump out, run around the other side of the car, and give her a big hug. "I love you. Thanks for the help."

"But I didn't..."

"Yeah, you did. I gotta go, I'll talk to you later. Enjoy your class."

"Bye."

I jump in my car and speed off. I need a pad and pencil. I have some brainstorming to do!

CHAPTER 5

Tori

Later That Night

I SET UP MY CAMERA AND GET ready to record. People have no idea how much time goes into a well produced YouTube video. It takes hours and hours to get it just right, but when it all comes together all of the sacrifice ends up being worth it. you do it's totally worth it. Tonight I'm not so sure if I should even be doing it, but here goes nothing.

I hit record and do my thing.

"What's up, *TorMenTors*, it's your girl coming to you with some breaking news. So, as some of you remember from the last episode of *Women on D*cks*, I dropped the news that I had just finished writing my very first book! I know, I'm as excited for it as you are. I know that I promised an update on publishing dates, tour info, and everything else you've been asking me for in the comments. I promise you, your patience will be rewarded, but I'm still working out some of the final details. As soon as I have the info you know I'll drop it here first. Stay tuned, 'cause some big announcements are coming in the next few days."

I click the camera off and feel like a total fraud.

Most of what I said is true, but a lot of it is just wishful thinking. The downside of making almost everything in your life open for public consumption is that you need to update people all the time, even when you want to keep things private. Oh, and you need to actually tell them the truth! I need to find a way to make into the truth, no matter what I have to do.

I had it all planned out, but you know what they say about the best laid plans. I upload the video to my channel. Little do they know that even though I won't have book announcement details, I will have an exciting new project to tell them about.

Sort of.

Seeing my mom gave me a crazy idea. It's so south of being sane that even I feel weird about it. There's no way anything could come of it, but I don't really have much to lose, do I? Elissa's words play in my head again, but that's not the only thing running through my mind. I hate to admit this, and it doesn't even make sense, but I keep thinking about Cormac—and not just how rude he was.

I keep thinking about *him*.

I hate myself for feeling this, but he's a hottie. Even when he was being douchey to me, I couldn't stop looking into those eyes of his. He's a beautiful man—tall, good looking, and I can tell that he's built underneath those clothes he was wearing. I have no idea why that, of all things, is what I'm thinking of right now. I have to focus though. The crazy lightbulb is still going off in my head and I need to decide if I'm strong enough to actually go through with it.

I think I'll be making a trip back to see Cormac tomorrow.

CHAPTER
6

Cormac

The Next Day

I MIGHT BE THE ONLY PERSON in the world who actually likes paperwork, which is good because I have a shit ton to do.

We've had a lot of new author signings lately—not nearly enough for Elissa and Cynthia's liking though, and not one who's the caliber of some of the authors who left us for the competition. The biggest loss was my ex, Maryanne. She hit the New York Times best seller list before dropping us like a hot potato.

But that's all past. What's done is done, and now it's time to focus on our company's future.

It's nine o'clock and I've already been at the office for a while. I started the day where I like to start my days—at the gym. I have a routine—I beat my body up, shower, then head to work to hammer out my paperwork.

My face is buried in a big old pile when I'm distracted by a knocking at my door. I'm not expecting anyone, so I'm not sure who this might... holy shit, it's *her*! It's Tori. What the hell is she doing here again?

If she's expecting an apology from me, she's crazy. She looks damn good, though. If only she could stand there and not speak, I'd give her a book deal in a second.

"Hey," she says all soft and sweet. "Cormac? It's me, Tori Klein." *Yeah, I remember you.* "Do you have a minute for me?"

I have no idea what she's doing here. We don't have an appointment, and her just showing up like this is totally unprofessional. "Hi Tori. What's going on? Did you come to see Elissa?"

"I came to see you, actually."

Me? "Listen, I've got my face buried in a pile of paperwork. We didn't have an appointment, did we?"

"Nope. No appointment. I just stopped by hoping that you were here."

I'm seriously confused. I'm not sure what the hell she could possibly want. I hated her book, and I wasn't exactly bashful about letting her know. Now she's standing here outside of my office without an appointment. Jesus, I hope she's not some crazy person who's about to go postal.

"Well, like I said, I..." Before I finish she invites herself in and sits down in the chair across from me.

"You asked me a very personal question the other day."

"I did. It seemed appropriate, giving what we were talking about." Knowing her type she's going to try to blackmail me for some kid of sexual harassment lawsuit if I don't give her a deal. I'd better tread lightly. "I didn't mean it a personal way, I was just..."

"I know why you asked me," she interrupts. "But I was wondering if you'd answer me a similar question. It's the least you can do."

I was a little harsh with her. I'll let her have her question. "Alright. Hit me with your best shot."

"Are you single?" she asks.

Am I single? Where the hell is this going? "Do you really think you should be asking me that?"

"I'm asking for a reason. I promise."

I just want this to end, so I give her what she wants. "I am. And you needed to know this for what reason?"

She practically jumps out of her seat. She's a little too happy. I've seen a lot of ways to insult someone, but celebrating their lack of companionship right in front of them is a new one, even for me.

"Why are you doing a little happy dance right now? Does my being single entertain you?"

"Forget that for a second. Elissa told me that if two of the three partners want to publish a book and the other one doesn't, that there's an official wait time of one month before any final decision is made. Was she telling me the truth?"

Why, Elissa? Why did you tell her that? "Well, technically yes, but I don't see how that..."

"Hold on," she says, putting her hand up and cutting me off just like I did to her at the meeting two days ago. "Let me just say my piece for once without you cutting me off."

"Okay. Fine. Say what you need to say. But then I need to get back to work. What is it?"

Based on the devilish grin making its appearance on her face, something tells me that I'm going to regret asking her that.

CHAPTER 7

Tori

Something tells me that I'm going to regret asking him this.

But, then again, I have nothing to lose at this point, do I?

I thought of a whacky idea at my coffee date with my mom, and I spent the rest of the day after that deciding whether discussion my idea with Cormac is going to spell career suicide. But I have to be realistic—if I just let things be he's never going to change his mind. Why would he? I mean, maybe Elissa could put a few good words in and try to butter him up some more, but the chances of that working out is pretty close to zero.

In other words, I have to try something, and that something might have to be a little extreme. Hence me inviting myself into his office and sitting across from him awkwardly right now.

He's looking over at me with those big beautiful blue eyes that look like the sea after a storm, and before I can start my sentence I'm lost in them. I snap out of it just long enough to get the five seconds of courage I need to say what I'm about to say. "So, I was thinking..."

"Okay," he answers when I don't follow up with any more words. I can hear the annoyance in his voice. "What were you thinking about? The evil of all men?"

I fake a smile. It's taking everything in me to be polite. "No, not that. I have a kind of proposal for you if you're interested."

I'm sweating.

Literally.

I can feel the hairs on the back of my neck standing up and my heart racing a little too fast—those are my early anxiety symptoms. I never let them show on the outside, but they always happen when I'm about to have a big moment.

"Alright," he relents. "I guess I was a little rude to you at the meeting, so the least I can do is let you run your new proposal by me. Give it your best shot."

Oh, Cormac, if only you knew what my best shot looks like.

"I have to preface by saying that what I'm about to suggest is going to sound a little nuts."

"Oh, please, don't let that stop you now."

He keeps taking shots at me, and he knows I'm not going to blow up on him because he has power over me. But I'm not taking the bait, I'm going to stay focused and just make him see my point of view. "In the interview you asked me how I could write a book about men and relationships without actually being in one?"

"I was just going by what you wrote in your book."

"I know. I didn't like it at the time, but then I realized that you had a little bit of a point."

"That must have really been painful for you to say to me."

You have no idea, Cormac. "Just a little bit. I was thinking, maybe I do need to have a more practical sense of what I'm writing about, and if I did, maybe you'd take my book a little more seriously when that final vote came around in a month."

"Where is this going?" he asks. He looks puzzled the more I talk. I don't blame him. He has no idea what I'm about to suggest, so most of what I'm saying has to be confusing to him. He'd better get used to making that expression.

"Since, you know, we're both single and everything, and since Elissa said I have four weeks to convince you that you're wrong about my book, how about you and I try a... situation together?" *Jesus, why am I being so vague? Maybe because I know what I'm about to say is going to sound like.*

"A situation? What are you talking about? Tori, I really need to get back to..."

Here goes everything.

"How about you and I live together as a couple for the next four weeks?"

There it is! I just pulled the crazy bandaid right off. Now I have to sit here awkwardly while his mind tries to process what I just said. He doesn't speak. He just looks at me and I can't take the building anxiety. I start saying words, any words, just so I don't have to sit in silence. "I'm still working out the details in my head—maybe you move into my place or I'll move into yours, it really depends on the commute. I mean, you know how traffic in New York can be, especially..."

"Woah, woah, wait a second! What did you just say? We live together? What are you talking about?"

"I warned you it was going to sound nuts."

"I didn't think you were going *that* nuts."

"Yeah, there were a few research case studies in the 1970's where scientists set up these experiments in a real world setting to observe gender roles and other aspects of couples. My mom told me all about them—I can probably get you the abstracts if you need."

"The abstracts?" he asks, his eyes all wide and crazy.

"Yeah. Like to the peer reviewed articles. And if my memory serves, the name of the researcher was..."

"I don't care what crazy experiments they did in the 1970's. What you're saying is beyond inappropriate." *Shit! I was worried he might react like this. He's giving me a look like I'm the main character in One Flew Over the Cuckoo's Nest.* "Why would you even suggest that?"

"I mean, so we can see."

"See?" he asks. "See what, exactly?"

"Well, I was thinking that maybe you could help me get some first-hand boyfriend experience—be my fake boyfriend."

The look on his face would be hilarious if he wasn't making it towards me. If only I had my camera to remember his expression forever.

"Tori, what you're saying to me—at least what I think you mean—it isn't only wildly inappropriate, it's also not a good way to convince me of anything."

Screw it. I decide to go all in at this point. What do I have to lose? "I think it will be good."

"Good?" He asks. "Good for who, exactly?"

"For both of us," I answer. He seems thoroughly unconvinced.

"Let me get this straight—you want me to live with you and

be a fake boyfriend. I'm not totally sure what that even means, but why would I ever do such a thing?"

That's when I catch it—the look he's giving me. I may not have had a lot of boyfriends, but I'm very intuitive. I see how he's looking at me, and his eyes are contradicting every word that's coming out of his mouth.

When I was little, my mom used to tell me what a great poker player I would have made, so I actually took the game up in high school. By the time I hit college, I was supplementing my non-existent income with a weekly pot I took off all the other kids—the guys, in particular—who underestimated my ability to bluff and read their faces. If this were a hand of poke, Cormac would be representing a straight flush even though he had no cards to speak of.

But like any good card shark, I'm not letting him know that I know what he's holding. Instead I'm going to play along.

"You should do it to prove me wrong." I tell him.

You see, the hand I'm really going to play isn't his obvious attraction to me, it's his even more obvious ego. Don't get me wrong, he's no stuck-up suit, but I can tell that he's used to thinking he's right. I'm gonna challenge him a little—I know he's probably not used to it.

"Excuse me?" he asks.

"It's easy to just tell me I'm wrong, but you only know guys from a friendship standpoint, you don't have any more experience with guys like most women do—unless I'm wrong and there's something you want to tell me."

"Ha ha," he jokes.

"Well, being that you like women, you have to consider the fact that I might be right about guys."

I can see that I'm making him tense—its exactly what I'm going for. "Is that right?"

I stand up like I'm ready to leave. Playing aloof is easy for me, but having him take the bait is something else. I might have pushed him too far—to the point where he'd rather have me than try to prove me wrong, but I hope not, otherwise my whole plan is out the window.

"Look," I say, trying to give off my greatest no-fucks-given vibes. "I get it. Right now you have all the power, so you get to think you're right, even if you're not. I totally understand. Easier to think that than actually test it out and see."

"Hey..."

"No, no, you're right." I hold up my hand and take a step away from his desk. "My idea is totally inappropriate. Sorry to have wasted your time and taken time away from your... paperwork stuff. Looks really interesting, btw. And hey, if it's any consolation, I wouldn't want to be proven wrong either."

That's the line that gets him. He literally jumps to his feet like I just challenged his masculinity in front of a room full of other guys. "Look, you have a lot of balls coming here and telling me that I'm wrong."

"Is that right? Well, then, since you don't wanna play along and test that theory of yours, why don't we just skip the month and say our goodbyes now? You know what? Even better, I'll take my big balls and shitty feminist nonsense—along with my million followers, by the way—and head a few blocks over to Mifflin, I'm sure they'd love to take my business."

That last part changes his whole expression. It really does pay to do your research sometimes, and I did mine last night. Mifflin Publishing is their biggest rival. Not only are they competitors, but word on the street is that Mifflin's been grabbing up all of Cormac's most popular authors, offering them better royalty deals and more money up front. On top of that they're known for taking chances on new authors who have big social media platforms.

I let my threat marinate in his egotistical little brain as I turn to walk out. *Five steps.* That's my guess as to how far I'll get before he calls me back. "Bye, Cormac. Sorry to keep you." One. Two. Three. Four.

"Tori, wait."

Four. Better than I thought. Men are so predictable. I had him the whole time. He thinks I'm hot, he has an ego that's easy to play, and he's insecure about losing another potential client to his competitors because of his own decision. Checkmate, Cormac.

I turn around slowly. He doesn't look as cocky any more, he looks like he's not sure quite how we got here—like he knows what he's about to say but doesn't understand why he's going to say it. I smile inside, and just wait and listen.

"Yes?"

"Don't go just yet."

I take a few steps back to make him think that he's in control. He's anything but. No need for him to know what's really happening, though. It's all working just like I hoped it would.

"Why not?"

He hesitates a second, his face scrunched and annoyed. I wait for him to lay down his king. It doesn't take long.

"I want to hear more about this idea of yours."

You sure do, Cormac.

CHAPTER
8

Tori

"HOW DID YOU EVEN KNOW I liked coffee?" he asks me. He doesn't know what to say and I don't blame him—he's still bewildered by my Jedi-mind-tricking him in the first place. He really looked sad to leave all that boring paperwork behind. You're an interesting one, Cormac, I'll give you that.

"A few reasons. First, most people like coffee, so I was playing the odds. And two, you'd have to be a caffeine lover to get through those tomes worth of paper you have piled on your desk and still stay upright."

"Fair enough," he says. "I do love coffee—but I don't need it to do what you walked in on me doing today. I actually enjoy the clerical side of the business."

"Who enjoys paperwork? Especially that much of it?"

"I know it sounds crazy to most people—Elissa and Cynthia

in particular—but I find a strange kind of peace when I'm sitting in my office, alone, working on something that I know will help the company but no one will ever see. I enjoy being behind the scenes."

I take a sip of my Americano. It's black, like Cormac's heart, but it's just the jolt I need to get through the rest of this conversation. "You're weird. I just wanted you to know that."

"Gee, thanks."

"Someone had to say it." I smile. He doesn't give me one back, but at least he knows I'm slightly kidding. "But that's your issue. And hey, do you want to know what would really help your company?"

"What's that?"

So easy, Cormac. You're so very easy. "Signing a hot, new, up and coming author like me. I bring a small army with me, you know?"

"I know," he says contemptuously. "Elissa mentioned that to me. But I can't sign someone just because they have a large audience behind them, Tori. Maybe my partners can make decisions like that as a cash grab, but I need to believe in what I'm putting out in the world. I have integrity when it comes to what I lend my company's name to. And rest assured, I do not feel that way about *Fuckboys*. And speaking of which, you know we could never publish that title, right?"

I practically roll my eyes at him, but I don't want to piss him off too much and lose the upper hand. I decide to go coy instead. "So that means you're publishing it and you want to work with me to change the title? Let me think." I look up at the ceiling and do my best fake thinking face. "Alright. I accept your offer! That was easier than I thought."

"You should be an actress, you know that?"

"I've been told that before. It's just years of practice in front of a camera. I can do almost any emotion I want to do."

"So you like to lie to your audience? Make them think you feel a certain way, but you're really just acting, is that it?"

"You have a special Marvel superpower for twisting words, you know that. All I meant was that if you have a successful YouTube channel and highly reviewed podcast, you learn a thing or two about projecting emotions."

"You can stop that, you know."

"Stop what?" I ask.

"Throwing your platform out every time you speak. I get it, Tori, you're popular. That isn't the problem at all. The problem is the work itself—I just don't believe in it."

I couldn't have transitioned any better myself. "Speaking of which, let's go back to the beginning of our conversation."

"You mean this crazy idea you have that you think I'm going to go for?"

I know you want to, Cormac. Why are you fighting so hard?

"Yup," I say. "That one."

"You have until the end of this venti quad to tell me more about it. That doesn't mean I'm even going to consider saying yes, you understand. But I still want to hear."

Of course you do, and I know exactly why.

"I'm so glad you asked. First of all, we wouldn't be, you know, actually dating. I'm not asking you to really be my boyfriend— more of what it's like if we pretend. Make it as real as we can."

"Okay." He says. "And remind me why again."

"Because I know I have something great here, and if you really believe that it's just some feminist nonsense, then why don't you put your money where your mouth is? Why argue in a board room when we can live out our own little social experiment and see who's right?"

He gets that look again—that did-you-really-just-challenge-me look, and that's when I know I have him. I got him to listen, I got him out of his office to coffee, and now I just have to Jedi mind trick him one more time into actually agreeing to the whole thing.

"Interesting," he says. I get excited when he does, because it means he's considering the whole thing. "And how—not saying I'm saying yes—but how would we—theoretically—keep track of who's right and who isn't? I assume this would just be between the two of us, right, so how would that work?"

"Well, we'd have to be adults. I'm not afraid to say when I'm wrong, but I don't know about you." I actually know exactly all about you and your giant ego.

"I can admit when I'm wrong," he answers. "I don't have a personal vendetta against you, you know that? If I reject a book—even in a preliminary vote—it's because I really feel strongly against it. It's not about you, personally."

Now he's practically quoting The Godfather—guys love that movie—'it isn't personal, it's strictly business.' "I get that, from your perspective."

"My perspective? It's not just..."

"Yes, it is. Look, I get it, you didn't like the book. But most of the book is what I've devoted my life to since college—women and their stories. I'm not some random YouTube star. My platforms are me. I'm not an actress playing some role in a movie you hated—this book represents everything I've dedicated the last few years of my life to, and all the stories that I was entrusted with by more real women than I can count. It is personal to me."

He takes a big old swig of his coffee. *Shit!* That means I'm losing time. Before he swallows, I realize that I'm approaching this all wrong. I'm not here to argue with him over what happened, or his opinion of the book. Of course he's not going to change his mind right here at Starbucks—if he was going to do that, I wouldn't need this crazy idea to begin with. No. The play isn't to bicker, it's to get him to agree to this idea of mine—then I have a month to prove him wrong.

"I get it. But this is a business. We can't make decisions based on how much a book means to an author, and we can make them based on subject matter—otherwise we'd say yes to ninety nine percent of all the books we get pitched."

I don't even respond. I just need to get back to the techniques that got me to the dance. "Like I said before, Cormac. You don't have to do anything—you have all the power here. But you seem to me like someone who takes his ethics and his integrity seriously, am I right about that?"

"Yes."

"So then imagine rejecting a book from a promising new author for no other reason than you didn't like the little bit of the book that you read. Is that ethical? What if it's actually a really valuable book to women, and you're denying them the chance to read it?"

"I think you might be exaggerating a little."

I decide to layer my attack. A good fighter works with combinations, not single shots, so I remember my three advantages here—he's a straight arrow with his integrity, he wants to fuck me right here on this table whether he admits it or not, and he doesn't want me taking my business elsewhere and making the New York Times bestseller list. Time for phase three.

"Maybe. Maybe not. But, look, what if you really are denying people my message?" I reach out deliberately and take his hand. I rest mine gently over his, and only for a few seconds. I swear he almost drops his coffee. As soon as my skin is over his, he makes this little kid face—like he just had his first kiss and doesn't know how to respond—and then I take away his lollipop as quickly as I rewarded him with it. "And what's even worse, what if you forced me to take it to Mifflin for a deal? What would you think if you looked back and realized that maybe you made a mistake, and that the book you couldn't wait to get out of your office is now a New York Times bestseller—soon to be licensed into a movie? Can you imagine that?"

My three-pronged attack has him thinking now—I'm hitting him in all the areas that matter to a man: his mind, his dick, and his bank account. It's just a matter of time before the last domino falls. He takes another sip. It's a small one. He wants to hear more.

"You should work in sales, you know that?"

"I'm a terrible saleswoman. Now ask me some questions about this whole thing—I know you have some." *See, Cormac, I'm really the best saleswoman there ever was.*

"I did actually have a few. If we did this—and that's a huge *IF*—how would it work? We move in together? Do we tell people? Tell me everything you have in your head and then I can make an informed decision."

"We'd have to move in together. The whole idea is that we spend enough time together that we can learn more about the opposite sex. We also should talk about the whole book thing, but not actually about the book itself."

"Huh?"

"What I mean is that we shouldn't just sit around debating

the book—we both know how we feel already. What we should do is talk about what's *in* the book—the content. Pick each other's brains a little."

"Pick each other's brains?"

"Yeah, like break down some of these issues so you see I'm not some man hating lunatic—and who knows, maybe you'll change my mind about guys being such pigs." *Fat chance, but you can try.*

He stops and thinks for a minute and takes yet another slug of that quad. The clock is ticking until he's going to get up and head back to his happy place of solitude and boring paperwork. I need to work fast.

"But what about... like... umm..."

I smile. "Use your words, Cormac. What do you want to know?" I know what he wants to know, and I know why he's stumbling over his words. He's not about to prove me wrong about guys at all—he's about to confirm everything that I already knew. But I'll play dumb, like the girls I'm sure he's used to being around.

"The sleeping arrangements. How is that going to work?"

"You mean like which end of the couch do you get?" I smile.

"Well, I guess you just answered me, huh?"

"I'm joking. We're both adults, Cormac. We can sleep in the same bed. That's how the sleeping arrangements will go. As long as you can keep it in your pants, we have nothing to worry about."

"Oh, please, Tori, don't flatter yourself."

He's overcompensating. Literally as he says those words his eyes drift from my face to my neck, and then as far down as he can see before the table we're sitting at cuts me off. "I'm not flattering myself, I just know men, and I know that the little head does most of the thinking for the big head."

"And what makes you think it's little?" He grins at me. I roll my eyes to take him down a notch.

"I'm sure it's very impressive, but the only 'sleeping arrangements' we'll be making is which side of the bed you want—as long as it's the left side, the right is mine."

"Left side is fine with me. Do we at least get to go out on dates?"

Huh? Dates? "What do you mean?"

"You know, dates. Like a real couple. Dinner, dancing, the movies maybe. That kind of thing."

The more he asks questions the more I realize that I haven't totally thought this through. It all sounded perfect in my head, but he's bringing up some valid points, and I'm not sure I have all of the answers. I have to think on my feet here. But honestly, the idea of being out to dinner or dancing with him doesn't completely make me want to vomit.

"Sure, yeah, we can do that. As long as we both agree what the date is going to be. It has to be a controlled situation."

"A controlled situation?" he asks.

"As in, we don't let things get out of hand and get swept up in the moment. I'm sure you've mesmerized a few women into giving up more than they wanted to with those eyes of yours." Did I really just give him a free compliment on his looks? This guy has some strange magic in his face, and I hate that it's kind of working on me.

"There you go, making assumptions again. I'm not some creep who tricks women into bed. I don't need to do that."

"Oh, I'm sorry," I say. "Someone thinks highly of himself, I see?"

"I'm just being honest, not cocky. I don't coerce women into anything. I never have and I never will. So our dates can be as 'controlled' as you want them to be, but if we're not at least acting like boyfriend and girlfriend then this whole thing is pointless."

I hate to admit it but he has a point. I need to unclench a little. If I'm going to be playing his girlfriend, then I have to at least be willing to *act* like a girlfriend in some ways.

"Fine, you're right."

"Thank you. Now, can we revisit this no-sex rule of yours?"

I almost spit my coffee out.

"We're not having sex, Cormac. I don't even want to kiss you unless we have to for appearances." Now it's my turn to put up a front. If he grabbed my face and planted one on me, not only wouldn't I resist, but I'd be all over him. But I'm not about to stroke his already too large male ego.

"I don't think that's true."

"Wow," I say. "Maybe you're even more arrogant that I thought. You think all women want to kiss you?"

For the first time in the conversation, I feel like I'm losing the upper hand. Our psychological Cold War is tipping in his favor on this issue, because this time he has my number. He leans forward, putting his cup down on the table and capturing me with those eyes. "No, Tori, I don't think all women want to kiss me, but I do know that *you* want to kiss me."

Holy shit. I just felt a fire light between my legs, and I'm totally thrown off my game for a minute. I take a drink because I don't know what else to do. I need a second to gather my thoughts. Holy crap, that was unexpected. But I regather myself quickly. He still hasn't said the words that I need him to say.

"Yeah, okay. Whatever helps you sleep at night."

"On the left-hand side of the bed, of course."

That one makes me smile. "So is that a yes then?"

"It's a *maybe* right now, and I can't even believe that I'm considering something like this, it's nuts."

"Totally nuts. But if you knew me better, you wouldn't be surprised that I'd come up with something crazy."

"Well I guess I'll just have to get to know you better, then, won't I?"

Dammit, he made me blush! That's going to throw off my whole I'm-not-affected-by-you-being-good-looking thing, but maybe he's oblivious to it. Probably not, my cheeks get really red. It's kind of embarrassing.

"So...is that a yes, finally?"

"One last question."

Uh! "Alright."

"If I said I'd only do this if you'd sleep with me at some point, what would you say?"

"Say?" I ask. "I wouldn't say anything. First, I'd throw this coffee at you. Then I'd punch you in your chauvinistic face, and then I'd tell you where you could stick it as I walked away from you forever and headed over to Mifflin."

The last thing I expect from a #metoo style rant is for the guy to smile. Like really, really smile. Like a happy smile. "Good," he says. "That's what I wanted to hear."

"Wait, I'm confused. You wanted to hear that I'd scald, slap, and curse you out?"

"I wanted to hear that you're not trying to sleep your way to a book deal. I can say fuck all to your feminism stuff, but what I can't do is move in with someone who's trying to use their sexuality to get a deal out of me. I've... let's just say I know how that story ends."

What was that? The plot just thickened a little. What does he mean by that? Do female authors proposition him all the time? I need to find out, but right now I'm just waiting for the only words I want to hear. He stands up and takes what I assume is the last sip of his quad that he's going to take. He seems energized.

"I'm going out with my brothers later on. I'll text you after."

He starts to walk away and I'm super confused. "Cormac, wait, is that a yes?"

"That's a I'll text you later and let you know, after I see my brothers."

Then he's gone. I'm not sure what just happened—if I got what I wanted or just blew the biggest opportunity of my career. But one thing I do know—I really want him to say yes, and not just for the chance to get a book deal.

CHAPTER 9

Cormac

"**B**RO, HAVE YOU LOST YOUR damn mind?"

That very judgy question came from Aidan after I filled him in on my coffee date with my favorite psycho feminist author.

Probably. I must have. Why else would I (sort of) agree to something so stupid? Actually, I know exactly why, but I'm not about to admit it.

Aidan and our youngest brother, Conor, agreed to meet me at Patty's Place, a bar three blocks away from where I work. As fate would have it, all three of us ended up working and living in Manhattan, so we have the chance to meet up from time to time when our schedules permit.

We also have the most stereotypically Irish names in the world—and it doesn't help stereotypes that we're having this conversation in a bar covered in green shamrocks. But proper representation of Irish American culture is dead last on my priority list. Instead, I need some advice. The funny part about meeting here is that I'm not even that much of a drinker—at least compared to Aidan and Conor—but after that whole thing with Tori today, I could use a stiff drink... maybe two. No more than three or four, I swear.

"I might have," I tell him. "Now that I'm thinking about it, I can't believe I'm even entertaining this shit. What in the fuck was I thinking?"

"I'll be the judge, let me see this girl." It's less of a question than a demand, so I take out my phone and Google her name. Holy crap, she really does have a huge following! Before I even finish her name Google autofills the rest. When I click on that about ten different websites pop up—her YouTube channel, her podcast on iTunes, her images—all of it. I have to check her out and do a little more research, but right now all my alpha male brothers want to see is what she looks like.

"Here," I say, handing my phone to Aidan. Conor leans over to steal a look also.

"Boom! Mystery solved!" he says, laughing his ass off.

"What are you talking about?"

"You asked yourself the wrong question before," Aidan says. "The question isn't what were you thinking, it's which part of you you were thinking *with*? And the answer is that shriveled up little pecker in there. Now it totally makes sense. I'd listen to any crazy shit that girl said to me."

"You're nuts. Yeah, she's cute and all, but she's not all that." I don't know why I'm lying so badly. She's fire. She's a dime piece.

I'm so full of shit it's coming out of my ears. Conor smells it right away.

"Okay, sure. Yeah, she's just cute. She's definitely not making my dick hard just from looking at your old ass phone." Conor's a savage. A really nice one, deep down, but the man has no filter, especially when it comes to discussing anything female related. "Don't be a hater, that girl's a smoke show, and I would have signed my tax return over to her if she asked me to. Now stop fronting and take a shot with your brothers!"

I wasn't going to hit the hard liquor quite so hard, but ... "All right. Fuck it. Let's do it."

"Atta boy!"

The bartender pours three shots of Tequila and in seconds they're burning their way down our throats. "Warm up complete. So let me tell you about this Tori chick."

"Hold on a second, her name's Tori?" Conor asks. He looks like he just saw a ghost.

"Oh shit, man, I didn't even put that together."

There's been a running joke among the three of us since high school, and I didn't even think of it until just now. Whenever Aidan and I want to mess with our baby brother we call him 'Snowball'. Not because he's delicate—he's the opposite—it's because of this girl Tori he dated in his sophomore year of high school.

We started calling him Snowball after he came home late one night, red faced and embarrassed, which was not like him at all. Usually Conor could give a shit what anyone thought of him, but that night he wouldn't even speak to us. He just ran into the bathroom and stayed in there for like fifteen minutes. When we shouted to check what was wrong he came out with an empty bottle of mouthwash in his hand, and left the bathroom a wet mess.

"You good?" we asked. He didn't answer, just shook his head back and forth all slow and weird.

And that's when he told us.

Apparently, Tori—who had a00 little bit of a reputation as one of *those* girls in high school—gave Conor head in his car after he took her to the movies. He made the mistake of giving her instructions on how to do it more to his liking, which apparently offended some sense of blow-job pride she had in herself. Not taking too kindly to him telling her how to do her job, she decided to get even, unbeknownst to Conor.

After letting Conor come in her mouth, high school Tori grabbed him by the face and kissed him, spewing all of his own cum back in his mouth, which mixed with both of their salivas and ended up dripping all over his shirt.

He never should have told us that story, because he was henceforth known to me and Aidan as "Snowball Delaney", even though my parents never got the reference when we said it.

Aidan laughs his ass off and orders another shot. "Fuck, Snowball, I forgot that girl's name was Tori. I always just called her the school whore, I thought that was her name! Cormac, listen to me, don't let your Tori blow you, alright, otherwise you might be Snowball the Second."

"I think I'm in the clear. Something tells me that this Tori doesn't do that. Girl's never even had a real boyfriend, at least according to her book."

"Wait, what?" Conor asks. "She wrote that shit in a book?"

"Yeah. She's trying to publish some man-hating nonsense and she needs my vote to get it through."

"And that's where this living together thing came from?"

"Exactly. I thought the girl was crazy at first—I still think she's crazy—but the idea of living with a hot chick and trying to change her mind about men is kind of intriguing to me. But could be a total disaster."

"Look on the bright side," Conor says. "She can't be worse than the last one—nothing can be worse than Maryanne!"

I was hoping her name wasn't going to come up. I haven't thought about her in a few months, and for me that's a record. She was a mistake—the first and only time I've ever mixed my personal and professional lives. That story I mentioned to Tori—let's just say she's the author of it. "Remember the last time you let your dick choose your books for you? How'd that turn out?"

They both laugh. It's funny if you're not me. It's funny if you didn't almost lose everything because of a fling with an author. A fling that became a relationship. A relationship that ended when I realized she was using me to get a publishing deal.

The crazy part is, I would have published her anyway. Maryanne's a great writer. Me and the partners were unanimous right away about publishing her debut novel—the first in a long detective fiction series. That book was a hit. Not just a hit in the literary world—it was a crossover hit. She made her career, and our company made a lot of money. We published the next two in the series, and each did better than the last. Netflix is shooting the limited series now. Unfortunately, Maryanne isn't with us anymore.

After the third book landed her on the *New York Times* bestseller list for six weeks in a row, it was time to renew her contract. We offered her a great deal, and at the time she was still my girlfriend. After we offered her the terms for a new contract, she took me out to dinner, broke up with me, and then had her agent reject our offer and inform us that she was 'moving on' to Mifflin, our biggest rival. Cynthia and Elissa were crushed, but I was crushed on both a personal and professional level. My partners didn't know that Maryanne and I were an item—and if they ever found out they didn't let on. When that whole thing ended I was good and messed up about it for a long time. She used me and my company to make her career, and once she got what she wanted she kicked us to the curb. That's about the time I started valuing professional ethics over emotion.

I look at Aidan. He jumps in to stop Conor before he goes too far with the Maryanne thing and I get pissed for real. "Forget her. Exes are exes. Let's leave her as our older bro's Voldemort and let's talk about this Tori chick instead."

I thank him with my eyes. I'll thank him with words next time I speak to him without Conor around. Normally I wouldn't care about an ex being brought up—we all do it to each other, and we all have some hilarious stories that we like to bring up to embarrass one another whenever we get together like this, but Maryanne isn't a joke—that girl ripped my still beating heart out of my chest like that dude in *Indiana Jones and the Temple of Doom*.

"This could be an epic, epic disaster," I say.

"Or," Aidan interrupts, "it could just be epic. You could change her mind about men, sling some powerful dick, and not have to do any of the shit real boyfriends have to do! You're looking at this all wrong."

I left the no-sex part out when I told them about this whole thing originally. My brothers—Conor especially—are kind of knuckleheads, and if I told them that I'm doing a lot of boyfriend shit without any of the boyfriend benefits they'd probably laugh at me, but I don't want to lie to them. I take a deep breath and get ready for the ridicule. Here we go. "Oh, right, I didn't tell you about that part."

"About what part?" Aidan asks.

"The only rule of this little experiment she concocted was that we can't have sex, or do anything physical."

Rarely are my savage brothers speechless, but right now the only communication I'm getting is stunned silence and two judgmental eyebrow raises. Conor breaks the silence. "Excuse me?"

"Yeah. I know. She said she doesn't even want to have to kiss me unless its required. You don't have to say anything."

"I think I do, bro. So lemme get this straight—you have to take her out, do shit around the house, all of that, but you don't get to fuck her?"

"She was pretty explicit about that part, and she's not the type to be easily swayed, so I'm gonna go with a hard no on that one. I don't get to fuck her. Or even kiss her, from what she's saying."

Aidan looks at me and cracks up. "Holy shit, you got played."

"How did I get played?"

"How?" he asks. "Oh, c'mon. You're the older brother, you're supposed to be the wise one."

"I guess I left my wisdom back at the office. Enlighten me."

"You just agreed to be a boyfriend without benefits. You're gonna cook for her, spend your hard-earned money taking her to fancy restaurants, and at the end of it all she can just say that you didn't change her mind and you'll be forced to publish a book that you don't want to publish."

When Aidan says it like that it sounds even more ridiculous than it sounded in my head. He's right. What's in this arrangement for me? Why did I even (somewhat) agree to it? She has all the cards, and she can play them however she chooses.

"Fuck, maybe I need to text her to forget all this. You're right, there's no upside in it for me at all."

"Unless..." Conor says, the smell of tequila already coming off him like it's a cologne.

"Unless what?"

"You're a partner in a prestigious publishing company."

"Right. I think I knew that already. What's your point?"

"My point, dick, is that you're probably experienced in the art of negotiation, yes?"

"Yeah. I mean, authors try to negotiate terms of contracts all the time."

"Well pretend that you're on the other side of that table. Negotiate terms with her. Remember, you don't even have to do this. You can just tell her no and it's over, there's nothing else she can do about it, right?" I nod. "So? Make sure that you get something out of the situation. If she won't bend on the sex thing, think of other things you want her to do and work that into the contract."

A contract.

Conor's the most brilliant idiot I've ever known. Most of the shit he says is as dumb as he is, but every now and then he catches lightning in a bottle. We'll negotiate terms and sign a contract!

"That's a damn good idea."

"Thank you," he says, doing a little fake bow.

"I've gotta give it up to you, Snowball, it is a good idea."

"Hey, fuck you!" Conor yells. "It's been a while, we're not bringing that Snowball shit back again."

"Umm, I think we just did." Me and Aidan belly laugh so hard people start to look at us. "But for real, I like that idea a lot. I'm gonna text her later and work out terms." I take my second shot.

"Don't get too drunk," Aidan says. "If you're gonna work this out correctly, the last thing you want to be is stupid drunk. You might say some dumb shit you regret, or forget to work something in that you really want."

"You're right," I agree, stopping myself at my second shot. "You're both right. You see, this is why I need my brothers."

"Great," Conor jokes. "Last round is on you."

"You got it."

Now all I need to do is think of what I want.

CHAPTER 10

Tori

S HOSHANA IS SITTING ACROSS FROM ME, looking at me like I just lost my mind.

Maybe I have.

I waited until we were done going over the notes for my next vlog to tell her about my rapidly unfolding book drama. She listened. She's really good at listening. Unfortunately, she's also good at asking a million follow up questions, a good deal of them inappropriate. But I guess when you tell your bestie that you're shacking up with a semi-random guy who's a partner in your dream publishing company, fielding a few questions is the least you can do.

"Wait, so you're going to bang the guy who owns the publishing company? What's his name again?"

"Cormac. Cormac Delaney. And I'm not banging anyone, Shosh, it's just an experiment."

"That's so crazy! I dated a Cormac junior year of high school. Did I ever tell you about him?" I shake my head. "Oh. Sad story. He had the smallest little baby dick—we're talking end of thumb length—and to add insult to injury he used to hum when we made out. It was so weird that I had to break it off."

"Wait, his dick or his humming were weird?"

"Both, actually. But the breakup was because of the humming—and because he was a little obsessive. They always go from boyfriend to stalker with me. I guess I just have that quality."

I look at her sideways. She says the craziest shit sometimes. "That stalking quality?"

"It's a thing. Look it up."

"Actually, I'm more interested in the humming. Like, how did it sound?"

"It's kinda hard to explain. I could show you but I'd have to have my tongue pretty far down your throat to get the sound just right. Wanna try it?"

"That's a hard pass."

"Fine, suit yourself. You'll just have to use your writer's imagination—think a seventeen-year-old with acne, a baby dick, and a soft muffled hum. That was my Cormac. I wonder what he's up to these days? You think he found a girl with a little tiny vagina?"

"Have you ever stopped to consider how often you bring up vaginas in casual conversation? It's, like, a lot."

"I'm sorry," she says. "I thought Ms. Feminist would be a little more comfortable talking about the female anatomy. Poser."

"I am a poser," I tell her. "I'm about to pretend to be a girlfriend to a guy I barely know—and all to get a book deal. What am I doing?"

"Back to your Cormac, right. You said he was a prick, didn't you? That he hated your book?"

"He is—I mean, he was. It's complicated."

"Is it? Did you like him or didn't you?'"

"Not at first. He was kind of an asshole to me. He made it seem like my book was a bunch of crap I'd made up out of thin air. But he seemed like less of a prick when we had coffee. I don't know. He's really hot, also."

"So you want this guy to be your fake boyfriend for a few weeks, but you don't want to have sex with him?"

"That's right," I tell her. "The spider webs are going to have to stay put a little longer. But it was the only play I had left. He was going to reject my book, I needed to act."

"And this was what you came up with? Why not just go to another publishing house? You always hear successful authors talking about how they got rejected thirty times before getting lucrative deals. You could be one of those rejects!"

"Gee, thanks."

"You know what I mean. I loved *Fuckboys*, whether some guy named Cormac hated it or not, but this is pretty far to the right of whacky, even for you."

"I know."

"You do realize why he got interested, right?"

"Yeah, because I exploited his ego and his fears."

"No, Tor. You're good but you're not that good. He said yes because he secretly likes you."

"I promise you he despises me—and the feeling is very mutual."

"That's just a guy thing. His words may say 'I hate you and

your stupid book', but I bet his eyes say 'I secretly want to be your fake boyfriend and have lots of very real sex with you.' Am I right?"

"No, you're not right." Except she is right. She couldn't be more right. She's so right I feel like she might not be my best friend, she might be some kind of supernatural creature sent to watch over me and give me sage-like advice. "I mean, maybe you're a little right. All I know for sure was that he was pretty close to agreeing to my deal when he walked out of that coffee shop."

"So walk me through the rules. I'm interested now. Are you sleeping in the same bed? Oh, Tori, tell me you're sleeping in the same bed!"

"Why do you want us to sleep together so bad?"

"'Cause he could be the one, Tor."

"And which 'one' would that be?"

"He could be like that guy in the old story—Merlin, or whatever. No, wait, Merlin was that shady magician." She looked at me all confused at that point, like I was supposed to be following her crazy thoughts. "Who's the one who became the king?"

"You mean King Arthur?"

"Yes! This Cormac fella could be like Arthur, only instead of pulling a gigantic sword out of a hole it's stuck in, he could stick his gigantic sword in..."

"Stop! Stop! Stop! I get it. God, where do you get these comparisons from?"

"Who knows? My mind is a strange and unexplored landscape. I think NASA's sending a rover in there. But enough about me, let's get back to your boy."

"He's not my boy."

"That's yet to be determined. So tell me the rules."

"I'm not sure of all the rules just yet. He keeps asking for more and more. He wants to hold hands, and go on dates, and..."

"To fuck you? Yeah, of course he does, Tor."

"Because he's a man."

"No, because you're a goddess in human form. We've been over this before."

Shoshana always tells me how beautiful I am and I never believe her. I don't want to be defined by how I look or how a bunch of horny men perceive me. So usually I just brush her compliments off because I don't really know what do with them.

That time I just gave her a hug. "Thank you. You're too nice to me."

"I know," she agrees. "Now, look, I'm going to need details. Lots of them. All of them, actually. The dirtier the better. Especially the ones involving his penis."

"You'll be waiting a while because I'm never going to see his penis."

"But you said he was hot?"

"Very." I didn't realize at first, but I feel myself smiling as I describe how good looking he is. I'd never say this out loud, but I like thinking about him—picturing the way he looked at me today, even as he was spitting venom from his tongue. Oh, that tongue. What that thing could do to me... I like thinking about what his body must look like under his clothes. "Yeah, he is, alright. Like... hot hot. Hotter than anyone either of us has ever seen in person."

"Well, holy shit balls. This just became much more exciting— for me, I mean. You have a lot of issues to deal with."

"Gee, thanks."

"You'll be fine. There are worse punishments than having to live with a hot guy who keeps asking to touch, kiss, and otherwise take the place of BOB. Just unclench that tight ass of yours and go with the flow. Let it happen."

We record for my blog, have some leftover pizza, and then Shosh goes on yet another date with some guy she met on an app. I swear, for a hot woman who runs a huge social media empire, she doesn't know where to find a good guy. She deserves better than the kind of creeps who always seem to find her. One day I hope she meets the right guy.

Now it's ten o'clock and, even though I feel like I'm a hundred years old for doing this, I'm about to pass out. It's been a long one. Just as I close my eyes, I hear my phone vibrating. It's been a long day, and who could possibly be so rude as to call me this late?

"Hello?" *Oh lord.* Of course it's him. "Yes? What? What contract? Are you drunk? Wait, wait, stop, you're slurring a little. Listen. Let's meet for breakfast tomorrow morning. You know the Colony Diner on Broad Street? Let's meet there at seven. You can explain then, alright? Good. Goodnight."

I hang up. He was definitely drunk, no doubt about it.

Maybe this was all a mistake. Maybe I acted too fast—again—without thinking of the consequences. I mean, Cormac's company is *the* most prestigious publishing company in the city, and they are *the* place to get your book out there.

We're not even living together yet and I'm already getting drunk dials at ten at night, babbling about some contract we should make together. I don't even know what he was saying, and I don't think he does either. I guess we'll find out tomorrow morning.

I close my eyes. I'm a terrible sleeper. Always have been. Usually I can't keep my mind still enough to actually fall asleep at a decent hour. I'm always thinking. About my work, my family, my work again, about anything you can imagine. But never thoughts like... like this.

As soon as my eyes are sealed I see him, Cormac, in front of me. Well, not really in front of me—more like, on top of me. He's not wearing that stuffy business suit, and he has nothing bad to say about me. In fact, he doesn't speak at all. He doesn't need to. His naked body hovers just over me, dripping sweat and smelling like pure man. He has a firm touch, reaching down and putting his hand on my face before he kisses me.

When I open my eyes, my hand is down between my legs. I didn't even realize I'd slid my finger inside of myself. All I remember is the feeling my body had when he put himself on top of me, pressing down, the smell of him filling my nose. All it took was the sound of that deep voice to hit me right where it matters.

I hate that I'm attracted to him when I find the rest of him so repulsive. Maybe living with him will cure me of that. Or maybe it'll make it even worse. Good Lord, Tori, what did you get yourself into?

We'll find out tomorrow.

CHAPTER 11

Tori

H E'S FIVE MINUTES LATE.

I was expecting it to be at least ten after how he sounded on the phone last night. I can practically smell him from where I'm sitting, but even hung over he looks fine as hell. He's walking towards the table and I notice how his particular style of disheveled really works for me. He's got a five o'clock shadow and his hair is all messy. All I think about as he walks towards me is running my hands through it.

That's not all I want.

What I really want is to find him hideous—to be repulsed by him and think he's a complete troll, but that's not the case at all. If I have a type, he's definitely it. After we spoke last night I couldn't get him out of my head, and I had some of the most intense dreams I've had in years.

Right now, I don't just want to get breakfast with him, I want to have him for breakfast.

He sits across the table, pulling his shades off and squinting like I'm shining an interrogation light into his eyes. "You look exactly like you sounded on the phone last night."

He ignores my commentary and plops his shades down on the other side of the table. He smells about eighty proof, and he's begging the universe for a shower. "Sorry about the call." He tells me in his gruffest, hung over voice. "I was out late with my brothers and it got a little crazy, as it can with them."

"Out on the prowl I take it?"

"Huh?" he asks. "The prowl?"

"You know, out looking to pick up women?"

"You really don't know me at all if you're asking that question. I'm not the picking up type—and last night was just catching up over some—actually, over way too many drinks."

Not the pick-up type? Yeah, right. You're all the pick-up type. "So you don't talk to women when you're out?"

"I didn't say that. I said I'm not... what did you call it? I'm not *on the prowl*. That sounds super predatory, by the way."

"Well, if the shoe fits."

He laughs. It looks painful for him to do but he gives me a genuine howl. "Trust me, it doesn't fit. We were just being brothers. In fact, the only woman who came up last night was you."

"Me?" I'm shocked to hear him say that. What was he saying? Was he talking shit? Telling his brothers about this crazy chick who made their brother a proposition? Now I'm curious. "What about me?"

"We'll get to that. Right now, I need coffee and waffles."

"Waffles?" I ask. "That's so specific."

"Well, I specifically need waffles, so it makes sense."

I smile. "Wait, not pancakes or French toast? Waffles?"

"Pancakes and French toast can fuck off—they're inferior tools for the job at hand."

"Which is?"

"The delivery of syrup and butter to my mouth. Only waffles can do that right, so I need some, asap."

He's funny. I fight smiling too hard because I want to keep the upper hand in our little Cold War—but the more he talks, the less he seems like that dickish guy at my pitch meeting and the more like someone who interests me. But I still have to remind myself of who and what he is.

This is just for my book, nothing else. Right?

"Excuse me." He waves at the waitress with this pained look on his face. She comes over looking frantic.

"Yes, sir."

"Are you our waitress?" he asks.

"I can be. I'm sorry, I have a bunch of tables. I was about to come over."

"No apologies. You're working harder than either of us are, trust me. I just need to get waffles into my stomach to soak up the remaining alcohol and stomach acid, and you're the only person who can make that happen."

He flashes a smile to her and she practically melts.

"I'll see what I can do, okay?"

"You're the best!"

"Oh," she says, finally realizing that I exist. "I'm so sorry, and for you?"

"I'm good for right now, thanks."

"Okay, sorry about that. I'll get those waffles as fast as I can."

"And a cup of coffee when you have a chance—a big one!"

"You got it."

As soon as she's gone, he turns the charm right back off, and goes back to being the good-looking hung-over guy. This time I laugh. "What the hell was that?"

"What?"

"Oh, come on. Giving that waitress those eyes so you can get your waffles quicker."

"I don't know what you're talking about, I just asked her politely and she agreed."

"Sure, okay. That's definitely what happened."

"Why don't we just get back to business at hand?" he asks. That sounds perfect to me.

"Fine. So, back to this me coming up at the bar last night? Tell me more. I assume it was about our potential arrangement?"

He runs his hands through his hair, and it's the sexist thing ever. I don't know why, but at the office he seemed buttoned up and self-righteous. I mean, he's still those things, but the sight of him with messy hair, a tee shirt, and a little vulnerability is something different. "It came up, I'm not going to lie."

Is it weird that I want to know everything he said about me? "And?" I ask, trying not to sound too desperate. "What did you say?"

"You didn't even ask me how many brothers I had."

"Oh," I say, a little thrown off. "Did you want me to?"

"Only if you're interested."

I'll bite. "How many brothers do you have, Cormac?"

"I'm the oldest of three." Then he leans in—really leans in, and for a second, I swear he's going to reach across and kiss me, but then I remember I'm fantasizing about a guy I'm supposed to hate. "There's a year between me and my younger brother, Aidan, and three years between me and my youngest brother, Conor.

Aidan is an electrical engineer and Conor has a degree in sports medicine. He works with a lot of pro athletes. We all live in the city."

"Three brothers all living in the same city—you guys are lucky."

"It just worked out that way. Conor travels a lot and we all have busy lives, so the three of us don't always get a chance to hang out like we did last night. But I can see from your face what you really want to know is what I said about you."

"Is it that obvious?" I ask.

"It's natural. Nothing bad, per say, I was just telling them about our little... what would you call it?"

"I'd call it nothing until you actually agree to do it. But if you need a name let's call it an experiment."

"I didn't say no. That's a start."

"I'll take it. So what did your brothers think?"

"They had some interesting ideas about the whole thing."

I don't think I like the word 'interesting' in that sentence, but I have to hear him out. "Oh yeah? Like what?"

"I was thinking about what they said, and they had some good points. Like, for example, what do I get out of this whole thing?"

"What do you get?" Shit, he finally realized—or his clearly much smarter brothers did—that there's really nothing in this for him. I'm going to make him spell it out before I give him anything.

"Well, the way I see it, you stand to gain a lot more than me in this situation, don't you agree?"

Of course I do, but I'm not gonna tell you that just yet. "I guess. How do you mean?"

"You could convince me to give you a book deal, but what do I get out of the whole thing? Especially with the... how should I say this? The limitations you put on the arrangements."

There it is. "Limitations? You mean me not trading my body for a book deal? I think that's a pretty fair demand."

"I don't want you to trade your body for a book deal, I already told you that. But at the same time—if it were organic, why put limits on ourselves?"

"Organic?" I ask.

"Yeah, like what if you actually liked me and didn't want to hold my hand or kiss me just for appearances? What if you were feeling me?" I'm feeling sick is what I'm feeling. The ego on this guy could fill this room. I don't mean to, but I giggle "What's funny?"

"You really do think you're God's gift, don't you?"

"Excuse me?"

"First the googly eyes at the waitress, then suggesting that I'm going to be 'feeling you.' I think you might already be in a committed relationship with your mirror."

I get a smile for that one. "I promise you, I'm not. But I do think if we're going to do this, then we need to make some modifications."

I don't like the sound of this at all. "Modifications, huh?" And I bet I know what those modifications are going to be.

"I think It's only fair."

"So let's do it this way. You list the modifications you're talking about and we'll go through them, one by one." I feel sick to my stomach. I think I know what he's going to say even before he says it.

"So don't flip out when I say this, okay?"

"Of course not." I tell him. *That might be the worst way to start a sentence, ever.*

"I wanted to address this whole nothing physical thing, but not in the way you think."

"Okay," I say with as much hesitance as I can muster. "So, like what, then?"

"How about hand holding?"

What? "Hand holding?"

"Yeah," he says. "I like hand holding." You're a complicated one, Cormac. I think about it for a second—it's not a huge ask, and honestly the idea of him touching me is kind of exciting, but I answer him by making a face like I just ate half a raw lemon with some raw garlic sprinkled on top. "I guess that's not sooo bad. If we're in public, that is, and you want to, go for it. I won't pull away."

"Is that supposed to flatter me?" he asks.

"Take what you can get, champ. This is a negotiation, right? Neither of us is just going to give in, are we?" He shakes his head. "Right, so be happy that you get to touch my hand."

"It'll be the greatest honor of my life, I'm sure. Let's step it up, now. How about kissing?"

Here we go again. "Absolutely not." I swear I'm protesting the hardest for the things I secretly want the most.

"You can take a second to consider it before shooting me down, you know? Fake it at least."

"Do you like when women fake it with you?"

"I don't know, it's never been an issue for me." His smug smile lets me know it's definitely been an issue for him before, he just doesn't know it. Every man thinks they can make a girl come. I had a whole podcast on this once with some other famous female YouTubers.

"That's probably not the case, just so you know."

"What are you talking about?"

"You'd be surprised how many women can't have an orgasm, it's a huge problem. One of my most popular vlogs was about that. Most men think they can bring a girl to orgasm, but most of the time she's faking it."

He looks like I just rocked his whole world. "No way."

"Way. Trust me."

"Like, for you too?"

Holy shit, he just got super personal! "We're not discussing my orgasms, Cormac. Sorry."

"Understood."

Just then, when I'm about to turn red out of embarrassment that I've never actually had an orgasm, Cormac's number one fan brings him his waffles and coffee.

"Thank you so much…"

"Debrah."

"Debrah," he repeats. His voice and face change again, and it makes me want to vomit.

"It was no problem at all."

Just as she's about to walk away and I'm about to hurl last night's dinner at how cute Cormac thinks he is, he reaches out and touches her arm. "Deborah, would you mind settling an argument between me and my friend here? It won't take long, I promise, I know you're busy."

"Sure," she says. "No problem. What's the argument?"

"My friend Tori, here, says that most women have never had a real orgasm in their life, and I said that wasn't true. She even spoke about it on some YouTube video she did, but I call bullshit. As a woman, which one of us is right?"

At first, I can't believe this guy has the audacity to ask some random woman he barely knows about their feelings on orgasms.

Actually, including me, that makes two women he barely knows. I'm about to jump in and tell this poor girl she doesn't have to answer him, but then I see her expression when she gets a better look at me. I'm used to that look by now, but I never expect it.

"Oh. My. God."

Cormac looks so confused when she says that. He doesn't realize what's happening, and I'm afraid it's going to break his fragile little ego.

"Hi," I say.

"What's going on?" He looks so very confused.

"You're Tori! Oh, sweet Jesus, I'm a Tor-Men-Tor!"

She leans over and gives me the biggest and most enthusiastic hug ever. She's squeaky and animated, and people start looking over at us. I love every second of it. I never get used to being recognized.

"It's really nice to meet you."

"Oh my God," Cormac says. "She knows you from..."

"Are you kidding?" Deborah yells. "I subscribe to her, like... everything! Her blog, her vlog, her podcast is like a must-listen every week on my way to work."

Cormac looks more pained than he did when he first walked in. I'm soaking it all up. "Well, isn't that... interesting."

"And just so you know—Cormac, is it?" He nods. "Clearly you didn't listen to The Big O."

"I hate to even ask, but..."

"It's the title of that vlog I was telling you about." I look back at Deborah. "My friend here isn't familiar with the online version of myself."

She turns to him, and her expression is literally priceless. "This is Tori Klein. She's like, one of the fastest growing YouTube feminist influencers there is. Her podcast is, like, everything." She turns back to me. "I seriously love everything you do. #slavestotheirdicks." Cormac looks like he's about to spit when she lets my hashtag fly, but he seems genuinely interested.

"Can I ask you a question I think I already know the answer to?"

"Yeah."

"Would you also buy a book that Tori wrote about..."

"Oh my God, yes!"

"Wait, I didn't finish my sentence."

"It doesn't matter what the end of that sentence is. This woman has inspired me to take control of my life and know my worth. I'd buy a copy of her laundry list if she published it."

I don't usually gloat, but my eyes are telling Cormac *I told you so* since my mouth can't do it right now.

"Thanks for your feedback, Deborah. And for the fast waffles."

"You got it. And the pleasure was all mine. I love you."

I stand up and give her a big hug. "Love you too. Fans like you inspire me."

"You're so sweet. I know you're having breakfast, but before you leave can I get a picture with you? Otherwise my friends will never believe this. We all love you."

"Awww, well tell them hi for me, and it'd be my honor to take a pic later—as long as you promise to tag me."

"Of course! I promise. #tormentorarmy."

She walks back to her other tables. I'm pretty sure I just gained the upper hand in our little negotiation.

"Does that happen to you a lot?" he asks.

"Not a lot," I answer. "But often enough. Don't let your waffles get cold, that would be a shame after all the politicking you did to get them."

"You're not wrong."

And he wasn't kidding about drenching them in butter and syrup. He goes through his ritual and I just sit there, waiting for him to finish telling me what exactly he's trying to change about our arrangement. After a syrup-soaked bite he finally speaks.

"Let's talk about the kissing thing."

"Is it a thing?" I ask.

"What I want to know is, what happens if you actually feel like kissing me? Which you might, by the way. Just putting it out there."

"Oh really?" I ask, shocked by how arrogant this guy is. "Cocky much?"

"I'm not cocky. Far from it. Cocky is believing that you have some kind of abilities that you don't have—and so far in my life, I've had no problem convincing women to kiss me... Or anything else for that matter."

"FuckBoy."

"What did you say?" he asks.

That literally came out of nowhere. It wasn't even a thought—it was a reaction, like when the doctor hits you on the leg and you kick up.

"Nothing. I was just thinking about my book." That was a totally unconvincing lie. I need to change the subject back to what we were talking about. "So before we go on, where is all this coming from? Your brothers?"

"I just think that we need some kind of contract."

"A contract? Like, you wanna consult an attorney?" I laugh because the image of that is pretty funny. I imagine the two of us sitting in a lawyer's office trying to decide on how many hand-holds per week he gets.

"Nothing official like that—just a more formal agreement before we go into this, so we both know what the other is expecting."

"I'm not expecting anything but what I said. But I'm guessing that you are. So tell me. Spit it out already." I reach into my bag to grab a pen and the notepad I usually keep to jot down ideas whenever I'm out, but I can't find the notepad. I must have left it on my nightstand. "Shit."

"What?" he asks.

"I need something to write on."

"Just use the notes app on your phone."

"I prefer actual writing. I'm weird like that."

"I'm shocked."

"Shut up. I need something."

"Here," he says, sliding a napkin across the table. "Write it on this."

"Alright." I test my pen on the napkin and it comes out fine. "So, what do you want?"

That's when he says it, as though he's known the entire time what he wanted to ask. "Three kisses," he says. "I want three kisses."

"Huh?" I ask, not believing my ears.

"I get to kiss you—or you get to kiss me, three times over the course of this little experiment. They can be short or long, whatever you feel like. They can be for show in front of friends and family, I don't really care. But I want three kisses from you over the four weeks."

"Wait, wait," I say, putting my pen down. "Let's put aside the request itself. Where did you get the number three from?" I ask.

He shrugs. "I don't know. It's a satisfying number. Like a genie that grants three wishes. I want three kisses. It just seems like a reasonable number to me. Not too many or too few."

"So it's like Goldilocks? Just the right amount of kisses."

He laughs. "Yeah, exactly."

"Cute," I say. "But that's a big old no."

"What? Why? Is it such a big deal?"

I guess it shouldn't be. The truth that I'm trying to hide from myself is that the idea of kissing him isn't just something that wouldn't bother me—it's something I keep thinking about the more I look at him. Even obnoxious, cocky, and shoving his face full of waffles he's still so hot that I keep forgetting that we're just going to be pretending.

"So, if I'm hearing you correctly, you want a three-kiss clause included in our little contract? Am I right?"

"A three-kiss clause," he repeats, smiling at himself like a happy idiot. "I like that, write that on the napkin."

"Slow your roll, there. I didn't agree. I was just confirming."

"Oh, come on Tori. Would it really be so bad to kiss me three times?"

I stop, frozen in his gaze. For a second, I forget where we are, or just what we're doing. Instead I only hear his question, and with razor focus I think to myself the most honest answer there is. No, Cormac, it wouldn't be bad at all. It would be the opposite of bad. I take a deep breath, afraid to be vulnerable.

"Alright, done."

"Excuse me?" he asks, looking confused at my change of heart.

"I said alright. Does this mean that we have a deal?"

This time it's him who stops and thinks—and he's *really*

thinking now. I realize that I'm holding my breath, hoping that he says yes. And just then...

"I must be out of my mind to be agreeing to this, but yeah, we have a deal."

"Yes!" I throw my hands up in the air like I just won something. "That's amazing!"

"Wait," he says. I start to worry he's going to change his mind, and that's when he asks something neither of us has really thought of. "Where are we going to stay?"

Shit. I hadn't thought of that. The idea of him at my place is just... no. But the idea of staying at his place is also unappealing. "I have no idea. Who gets the home court advantage?"

He thinks again, then takes the last gulp of his cup of coffee. "I have an idea—how about neither of us has the home court advantage? My partner, Cynthia, has a place in the suburbs that I'm sure she's paying someone to check in on while she's away. It's only a thirty-minute commute. She's going to be away for about another month. I'll offer to house sit for her, and we can move in there during the experiment. How does that sound?"

It doesn't sound bad at all. I already know from Elissa that Cynthia is into my book, plus she's a woman, so her house is probably more my speed than Cormac's anyhow. Why not? "Alright. I can have my friend Shoshana look after my apartment, and I can have my mail forwarded to Cynthia's address for a month. It's a deal."

"Great. I'll text her now."

"What are you going to say?"

"Don't worry, I have it all worked out. And we can figure out the sleeping thing another time."

I'm not sure I believe that he has it all worked out, but I'll give him the benefit of the doubt this time. I take out my pen and write as he texts. "So here," I say, scribbling as fast as I can. "Look this over."

"Jeez, your handwriting is terrible."

"Focus on what's important right now. And I'm writing on a napkin fast enough to land me in Guinness—so cut me a break, will ya?"

"Fair enough." He reads over our impromptu napkin contract, smiling the whole way. "Two thoughts I'm having right now. One, I'm crazy. And two, this is perfect. But are you okay with this? I know it's not exactly how you envisioned things, and book deal or no, I won't do this if you're not comfortable with everything we just discussed."

I'd trained myself to think Cormac Delaney was the biggest jerk in existence. I'm still not totally convinced I was wrong on that, but the more I talk to him the softer I feel towards him. And that last part, about wanting my consent—even though the whole thing was my idea—is enough to let me know that he—that *we*—are not so crazy for going through with this crazy idea after all.

"I'm more than comfortable. It's a deal."

"Good. I need to get to the office—boring piles of work and all that, you know?"

"Right. Enjoy that. Call me later on and we can figure some of the details out."

"You got it." He stands up and walks past me. I don't turn around, but I feel him stop just behind me. And then I feel something I don't expect—a firm hand on my shoulder. Right after, his mouth comes close to my ear, and I hear his deep voice whisper in my ear. "Who knows. Maybe I'll end up being a Tor-Men-Tor after all."

My whole body feels that whisper. His deep voice, the warmth of his breath, and the feeling of his body standing so close to mine. I didn't expect to feel anything but disgust, but apparently my body had other plans in mind.

Huh. That was unexpected.

Now I turn around without thought, watching the tall, muscular frame of his body walk away until he's gone.

I think I might not hate our little three kiss clause after all.

PART II
THE EXPERIMENT

CHAPTER 12

Cormac

Saturday, July 15th

IF CYNTHIA ONLY KNEW WHAT HER beautiful home was about to be used for!

Oh well, what she doesn't know won't hurt her, right? Unless we mess her place up, in which case I'll be the one doing the hurting.

Here's the official story—officially, I'm offering to house sit because I'm sick of the clutter and noise in the city and needed to clear my mind so I could work on my book.

Unofficially, I'm living with a rabid feminist who hates my guts and who'll be living here with me as my fake girlfriend.

Yeah. I'll be leaving that unofficial stuff out of any future conversations with my partner.

What I told her isn't a total lie—besides agreeing to be Tori's fake boyfriend, I actually am going to use this unexpected change in geography as an opportunity to work on a project I've been struggling to finish.

I make decisions on which of the thousands of authors who query us actually gets their book seen in print, but I've dreamed of being one of those authors ever since I was in college. I love everything about books—even though my brothers and I grew up struggling financially, Mom always managed to have at least a few books around the house for each of us.

It's actually the reason I got into this business in the first place. It wasn't for the salary, and it wasn't to reject authors trying their best to get published. It's much more of a self-serving reason than those. The truth is that I love getting to read great books before anyone else does. I get to sit across from authors and pick their brains about their processes, inspirations, and preferences.

I met Elissa and Cynthia when I was one of those authors—pitching an idea that wasn't ready to be pitched. They didn't think I was ready to be an author, but they were impressed with my knowledge of the industry itself—I knew all of the best-selling authors in every genre going back five years. I knew the process of getting on a New York Times or Wall Street Journal best selling list—I was like a walking savant when it came to all things publishing.

I was thirty when that book got rejected. I was crushed. I thought I'd never get close to a publishing agency again. Then, a few months later, right after I'd turned thirty-one, Elissa contacted me out of the blue and offered to interview me to be the newest partner at the same company that had turned down my book. The rest is history. Well, almost.

I still have dreams of being a writer—that never went

away—only I've been too caught up in life to ever see that process through. I've been writing a love story for years. I have the whole thing set—except I can't seem to finish the last few chapters. I either get the worst case of writer's block ever, or I'm just too busy reading other people's work to really make a dent in my own. At least that's what I tell myself. So I'm going to look on the bright side of things—maybe having a new house will give me some inspiration.

Speaking of the experiment, Tori should be here any minute now.

It's been three days since we drew up our contract on a napkin, and we've spoken every night since, mostly by text. Even when it comes to a whacked-out idea like this one I agreed to, Tori's attention to detail is insane. She wanted to know everything— which one of us was going to buy groceries, cook dinner, she even wanted to see my my damn Netflix list to see if our TV watching was going to be compatible. Big surprise, we like different types of shows!

But still, whatever I think of her book, I can see how the woman runs her own social media empire. I don't really know what that means, exactly, but I know how much work and detail it takes to be one of three partners keeping a business floating, so I can't imagine how she keeps a YouTube channel, a podcast, and all of her other accounts going all by herself.

And she added one thing to our contract I wasn't thrilled about, but I said yes just so we could do this already. She wanted to do some interviews with me to pick a guy's brain about some of the subject matter in her book. I had to agree to let her publish those interviews—anonymously—in her book, whether we end up publishing it or not. I'm not too excited about that part, but I'm interested in what she's going to ask me about.

We said noon, and it's eleven fifty-five according to my phone. I get a text telling me her ETA is about three minutes from now. There she goes again—details. Most people would have just said noon, but she wants me to know that she'll be two minutes earlier than she originally said.

She's good to her word—or she has the best GPS ever—because three minutes later she sends another text telling me that she's outside, and I go to meet her like a good fake boyfriend should.

"Hey there, sweetie pie honey buns." I wave and smile like we're some couple in a bad 1950's movie, all saccharine and overly energetic. "You find the place okay?"

"Thank God for GPS—I can't remember the world before it."

"There was a world before it?" I joke.

She gives me a look of death. If she were a superhero, she'd be shooting lasers out of her eyes to strike me down right here on the lawn. I'd be Rorschach to her Dr. Manhattan. As it is, I'm another fictional character altogether—Captain Fake Boyfriend—I have no particular powers except to stand here and wait for the vitriol I know is about to spew from her mouth.

"It's too hot for this. If you try to call me sweetie pie honey buns again I'm going to cut your balls right off and toss them out the window like that woman in the 90's."

"Lorena Bobbitt. Oh yeah, I forgot about her. If I recall correctly it was his dick, not his balls."

"Details," she says a little too convincingly. "Either way, you try a 'sweetie' on me again and something down there is ending up on the side of the road."

"I kind of like both my dick and my balls, so I guess it'll just be 'Tori' for our time shacking up together."

"Perfect. That works for me. Speaking of shacking up, how long have you been here?"

"Not long," I tell her. "Maybe a half hour or so. I just started putting my stuff down and getting the lay of the land."

"Haven't you been here before?" she asks me, looking sweaty and sexy as she wipes her brow.

"Sure, but only as a guest those times. I don't know the nooks and crannies of the house like that."

"Nooks and crannies?"

"Yeah, you know, the little details..."

"No, I get the metaphor, it's just bad. It's not an English muffin commercial."

I laugh. "Someone's in a mood, huh? That time of the month?"

"Did you really just ask me that?"

"Oh, right," I joke. "I'm supposed to be breaking your stereotypes of guys, right? So I should say what you want me to say. How about 'you're really beautiful when you're shitting over my super awesome use of metaphor.' That better?"

"You're such a dick. And yes, I'm in a mood and no, it's not that time of the month. It's this heat, it's insane."

Tori decided to spring this little experiment on me in the absolute dead of July in New York, and that means a few indisputable things: pulsating and oppressive heat, humidity that makes Long Island closely resemble equatorial Africa, and invasive tiger mosquitos that give no fucks about your silly *Off!* Repellant, or dumb ass citronella candles. As much as I love being outside, this time of year it's best to make friends with a cold drink and central air conditioning, otherwise you're risking a case of heat prostration and West Nile Virus from all the bugs.

"The central air is on inside."

"So let's stop talking on the lawn and go cool down."

We both stop right in front of the door like certain death awaits us inside—like we're vampires who need to be invited in. We look at each other awkwardly, and that's when it hits me—I barely know this woman, and I'm about to be living with her.

"Aren't you going to go in?" she asks.

"Ladies first."

"Don't pull that fake chivalry stuff on me."

"It's not fake, I'm just offering to let you go inside first."

"Why?"

"Jesus, woman, this little experiment hasn't even started yet and we're already having our first fight. Just go into the damn house already."

"Fine."

I'm amazed she actually gave in so fast—I had about six more comebacks ready if she didn't walk through that door. I sneak a look at her ass as she finally walks inside and it does not disappoint at all. Damn, she has a body to die for!

My pants start to feel just a little bit tighter than they did a few seconds ago. The truth is I'm ridiculously attracted to Tori. I don't even like admitting it to myself, and I'm sure as hell not going to admit it to her, but she's gorgeous, and she doesn't seem to know it.

Once we go inside, the sweet artificial cold of the air conditioning hits us right in our faces. It's a refreshing welcome to what's going to be our new home for the month.

"Oh my God, that feels amazing!" Tori stands a few feet

inside the living room, arms out to the side and eyes closed like she's having a religious experience. With her arms out like that her shirt lifts up just enough to see the tiniest bit of her skin.

"It sure does."

She finally puts her arms down and opens her eyes. "So what did you tell Cynthia about this whole thing?"

"That I needed to recharge my batteries and work on my book in a quiet setting that I just couldn't get in the city. I told her in exchange for letting me use the place, I'd watch over everything and get her mail and all that. It was an easy sell. I grabbed the key from the neighbor who was doing some of that stuff and now it's all ours."

"It is very nice of her to let..." She stops like she's just realizing what I said. "Wait. Your book?"

"Yeah, I'm writing one, but I don't really want to get into it right now."

"Fine. I'm not interested anyway, I was just trying to be polite."

"We can skip the pleasantries for now, let's just get unpacked."

"Fine by me."

We stand staring around the room like a couple of idiots, not knowing what to do now that we've officially begun our fake relationship. I've never lived with another person outside of a college roommate, and that was a very different situation.

"So," I say. "Here we are, huh?"

"Yup. Here we are."

"What do we do first?" I smile because this is so awkward. Talking about it was one thing, writing down terms on a napkin was something else, but actually being here with her is a whole new ball game.

"Unpacking seems a little too obvious. Ohh... I have an idea.

You feel up to doing our first interview?"

Shit! I wasn't even thinking of that. "You mean right now?"

"Now or never. Not really, we can do it anytime, but why not, you have something better to do on fake moving in day?"

Fair point. "I guess not. Yeah, that's fine, just let me roll all my stuff into the bedroom. You're welcome to join me in there."

"Sure," she says, taking her bags and following me. "This might be the last time we're in here together, so suck it up."

"Interesting choice of words."

"Don't be gross."

"Well, isn't that the kind of thing you want to ask me about?"

"Sexual puns? Not really what I do. You should try listening to an episode or two. Who knows, you might actually enjoy it."

"Podcasts are not really my thing," I tell her.

"Spoken like someone who's never listened to one. I think I can change your mind."

I bet you can, Tori—in more ways than one.

Recording
Session One

"I have an idea," she tells me. The look in her eyes is devious, and I know she's about to say something I'm not expecting. "How about I make these interviews into a podcast?" Yup, there it is.

"Say what?"

"Listen," she says, putting her hand on my leg. I'm not expecting it and suddenly I get really excited. "I know it's not part of our deal—but podcasts are most interesting than interviews anyhow—this way it can be more... conversational."

I think about it for a second. "Umm... that's a hard pass for me."

"Oh, come on, you'll be great."

"I'm not worried about that," I tell her.

"Then what?"

"I'm worried about a whole bunch of people hearing what I have to say about women and relationships."

She giggles. It's a little snarky. "Look, Cormac, I don't know how to break it to your clearly gigantic ego, but no one knows who you are, and I can keep you anonymous. Yes, I have a huge group of followers and subscribers, but there's not going to be any video—it's just your voice. I think it would be good."

"Good for you, you mean?"

"No, I meant good for my audience. They only ever hear a female's perspective. Mine and my guests. But it would be good to hear from a normal guy for once. I think having a different opinion might be refreshing."

"Refreshing, huh? Help your listeners?"

"Uh-huh."

"Well, how could my huge male ego say no? As long as you can promise it'll stay anonymous."

"It will," she says. "I have another idea!"

"I'm starting to get anxiety every time you say that."

"No, it's not groundbreaking, trust me, just an idea to help with the anonymity thing. How about we use a fake name when I refer to you?"

"A fake name? Like what?"

"I don't know, whatever you like. Pick a name, any name."

"Kylo."

She looks at me sideways. "Kylo? What kind of name is that?"

Then it's my turn to look at her sideways. "Oh, come on? Kylo. Like Kylo Ren?"

"You're not helping me any."

"Clearly you're not a Star Wars fan."

"And clearly you are," she jokes. "Whatever floats your boat Corm... I mean Kylo."

"That's better."

"Alright, then we can do this?"

After I agree, she sets up her mics and other equipment she has in one of her bags. We haven't unpacked our clothing or toiletries yet, but she's got a giant black bag of electronics unpacked. I have to admit, I have a little bit of a bias when it comes to the social media stuff. I'm not really a social media guy—I know it sounds old fashioned as hell, but I don't even have any of those pages. Well, actually, I have one that we can all access for the company, but I don't have any of my own. I'll have to check out Tori's stuff at some point. I did look at one thing she has online...

She finishes shuffling around and sets up the mic in between us. "I feel pretty important right now."

"That's your ego again," she says with a smile. "Are you ready? I didn't hit 'record' yet."

"As ready as I'll ever be. Do you have to do, like, an intro or something? Like on the radio?"

"Not yet," she tells me. "I just record the conversation, then later I'll record the intro and do my sponsorships."

"Oh, okay. Sorry for all the questions, I'm new to this."

"No worries. Here we go."

She presses a button and sits back. I guess this is how a podcast begins. "Welcome to another episode of the podcast, Tormentors. This is your girl, Tori Klein, bringing you another very special episode. Brace yourselves, ladies, tonight I have our first ever male guest, a good friend named Kylo. Why don't you introduce yourself to our audience?"

I lean into the mic. I feel stupid for some reason. "Hello, ladies."

"Kylo agreed to be on the show to give us a male perspective on some of the issues we love to talk about here. So, Kylo..."

"Actually, Tori, seeing as how this is an... unorthodox episode, would you mind if I start off asking you a question instead of the other way around?"

She looks at me but doesn't want to stop recording. She furrows her brow like she's interested and scared at the same time. "Okay, sure."

"Why do you hate men so much?"

Her eyebrows shoot up higher than I thought eyebrows could. She's not mad, I can tell that much—that look is more like someone who just accepted a challenge to debate.

"A little context here, ladies. Kylo here is something of a Tormentor hater. He thinks I'm a man hater. But, for the record, I don't hate men."

"Okay, fine, but you definitely hate aspects of them, right? I mean, don't you use that hashtag?"

"Which one, Kylo? I use a lot of hashtags."

"What is it again? #slavestotheirdicks? Tell me that's not a man hater hashtag?"

"Huh," she says. "I didn't know that you were a Tormentor."

"I'm not. I just looked at your pages."

"Sure," she says dismissively. "But that hashtag isn't man hate, it's just the truth."

"I don't think so. I think you're a dick hater? What did a dick ever do to you? And feel free to answer that in as much detail as you'd like."

"I'm not a dick hater. I just hate that dicks take over a man's identity. It acts as a sex organ, a second brain, a decision maker. Face it, men are obsessed with them."

"Define 'obsessed.'"

"Obsessed—like, thinking about it, and with it, all the time."

"I definitely don't think about my dick all the time. I mean, I'm thinking about it right now, but only because we're talking about it. Otherwise my thoughts would be fairly dick free."

"It's subconscious with you guys. You all don't even know that you're doing it."

"Oh, come on. How can you claim to know that men are thinking about their dicks at all times?"

"Have you ever worked in a school? Any school, it doesn't matter what grades or ages."

"Can't say that I've had the pleasure, no."

"Well, as my listeners already know, my mom teaches undergrads. Most of them are about three months removed from renting a tux for their prom."

"Okay."

"I'll give you three guesses as to what the desks in her lecture halls are covered in."

"I'm guessing survey says..."

"Ding Ding," she says. "Giant, veiny cocks. Always huge, and always multiple ones on each desk. The artistic depictions vary from kid to kid. Why are you laughing?"

"Because we all do that. I'm not saying it makes us obsessed, but we're all very accomplished dick artists."

"And that doesn't sound obsessive to you at all? You think when I'm bored at a doctor's office I like to draw my tits on the magazine table?"

"Okay, point taken. Great image by the way. Now tell me about the dick variation. I'm curious."

"She's shown me pictures. Some have balls and some are just free floating, like space cocks, not bound to any testicles and seemingly devoid of any gravitational pull."

I can't help but laugh out loud. "That was funny. What else?"

"Name it. Circumcised and uncircumcised, long and thin, short and fat, hair on the balls, hairless balls, about to go into some poor, unsuspecting male stick figure's mouth. Erupting with cum like a volcano—name it, I've seen it drawn by grown men who are paying a lot of money to get a degree. Stop laughing!"

"I can't!"

"My thing is this — men are always trying to get laid, right?"

"Usually, yeah."

"But they'll never draw pictures of vaginas. I've never seen one."

"That's 'cause we have porn. There's no need to draw pussies when they're right there in our pockets—figuratively speaking."

"You're gross, you know that?"

"Why am I gross? 'Cause I'm telling the truth?"

"No, you're gross because you're gross—and by 'you' I mean all of you."

"All men are gross? 'Cause we have a biological imperative to have sex and jerk off?"

"That's crap."

"It is not. Men want to have sex with as many women as they can to spread their genes. It's a real thing."

"Yeah if you're a male wolf. Humans have the power to fight against their genetic impulses—we're not animals."

"Look, I'm not saying that guys have the right to do whatever they want because of their biological impulses—far from it—I'm just saying that those impulses exist, whether women want to admit it or not. Any way you want to slice it, it's part of our DNA. Now, what individual men choose to do with those feelings and thoughts is a different story."

"Like jerking off way too much."

"Woah, there's no such thing as too much, first off."

"Why don't we let our audience be the judge of that. What's your number?"

"My number?" I repeat.

"Yeah, the most amount of times you've jerked it in a single day."

I stop and think for a second. "I want to say seven."

"Seven! Holy shit."

"I think seven. No less than six—I might be a little off. But it was definitely either six or seven times in a day."

"You must have been coming dust at that point."

"Pretty much. Basically, just a spasm that feels good for a second, followed by you feeling creepy and questioning your life decisions."

"As well you should. But, look, I'm not a prude, and none of my listeners are, either. We like sex, I just hate that guys are directed by their little heads and not their big ones."

"Let's go back for a second—you're saying that you don't find sex disgusting then?"

"Hell no," she says. "I find the idea of a guy touching himself pretty hot, actually, just not seven times a day to some gross porn on his phone. But given the right set of circumstances, why not?"

As soon as she says that, it's like I have no control over my body. My pants start to stiffen, and everything that I was feeling a second ago—sarcastic, nervous, unsure, all of a sudden just becomes an overwhelming feeling of being turned on. Hearing her talk about guys stroking themselves turning her on turns me on so much that I start to get hard. I don't even think about it, but as soon as I feel my cock start to rise, I put my hands over my lap.

I need to stop, but I can't tell her why, so I look down at my watch for effect. I don't want to interrupt the flow of this whole thing, so I type out a message on my phone and show it to her:

Can we stop?

She hits the button. "No problem. What's wrong?"

Nothing. Just getting hard as a rock, you? "Nothing," I lie. "I just need to head into work in a little bit so I wanted to have time to unpack. We can keep going later."

"Alright."

She starts to put her stuff away and I'm still as hard as I was before. I take a few deep breaths and hope this thing is going to go down before I stand up to unpack. Right now, it's not looking promising.

CHAPTER 13

Tori

I HAVE TO GIVE HIM props for his honesty.

We've been living together for about fifteen minutes and he just finished telling me about his masturbation patterns. He's more open than I thought he'd be, I'll give him that.

But now that we're done with our first session we have to actually start living together. We're just sitting here, staring at each other on what's a surprisingly comfy couch (good job, Cynthia).

"So..." I say hoping that he'll take some initiative. "Have you ever done this before?"

"Pretended to be someone's boyfriend so they can get a publishing deal? Nope, can't say that I have."

"No, dummy, not that. I mean, have you ever lived with a woman before?"

"Like a girlfriend?" he asks.

I raise my eyebrow. "No, like your mom."

"I would never live with my mom again. She was a boss—if my brothers and I ever left a thing on the floor or a dirty dish in the sink my mom would kick our butts and not let us leave the house until it was cleaned up. Love her to death, but I'd sooner move in with my knucklehead brother than live with her again."

"Sounds like my kind of woman. But about my question, though?"

He hesitates, like he doesn't want to talk about what I'm asking, but I want to know. "Yeah," he finally admits. "I've lived with a woman before. My last relationship."

"I'm guessing by the sound of your voice that it didn't go well. What happened?"

"Jesus, Tori, are you always this forward? We just met each other."

"I was just making conversation—I wasn't trying to make you uncomfortable."

I've never heard him be that snippy with me. I must have hit a sore spot. I don't want to push too much—yet. But maybe he's right, it might be a little soon to be swapping romantic histories. I know if he asked me the same question I really wouldn't want to discuss it, so I let the whole subject go. "Fine. Let's unpack, shall we?"

He seems relieved that I changed the subject. "I thought you'd never ask. And maybe later on we can do some boyfriend and girlfriend stuff."

I give him the side eye. "Cormac, I told you, I'm not..."

"Oh, loosen your sphincter, Tori, I wasn't talking about sex. But—side note—it is interesting that you keep bringing the conversation back to that."

"Stop it, I do not. It's you who keeps bringing it up, not me."

"Really? Have I ever looked at you—a woman I've known for about a week, and asked 'Hey Tori, you mind if I have sex with you?'"

"You don't have to. And no man says that."

"I don't have to?" he asks.

"It's obvious. It's all over your face."

"Are you saying I'm making sex face?"

"I am."

"And can I ask, what exactly does my sex face look like?"

"Like the face you always make when you look at me," I tell him.

"Now who's the arrogant one? I look at you and you assume I want to have sex with you?"

"Never mind, you're too much of a child to admit that you want me. I get it. It's fine."

"I don't..."

"Yeah, yeah, I know, it's all in my head, right? Let's drop it."

"Fine by me. And all I was going to say was that we should go out—maybe meet each other's friends. I know normally that would take longer than the first night of being in a 'relationship', but we're on the fast track here. What do you say?"

I breathe a sigh of relief. "I'm sorry, I just thought that..."

"Men are always thinking about sex, even when they're not thinking about sex? I know, you have a lot of biases to get past. I'll be patient with you."

"Excuse me?" He has such balls. "You're going to be patient with *me*? Are you kidding? I'm the one who should be taking the deep breaths."

"And what exactly have I done to you except hate your book

and agree to this crazy experiment? You act like I've been trying to sleep with you since we met."

"Yeah, I saw how you were looking at me during the pitch meeting. Maybe I'm not so experienced when it comes to relationships, but I'm not stupid. I could tell that you wanted me."

"Here we go again!" he says.

Things are starting to get heated. I can tell he's annoyed with me constantly bringing this issue up. I don't want to start off on the wrong foot. "Sure," I say randomly, "we can go out. But let's work out the sleeping arrangements first so we don't have to do it when we get back."

"Take the bed. I'll take the couch. And before you go on about fake chivalry, it isn't—it's just me being nice. I want you to be comfortable, and I'm no stranger to sleeping on couches."

That was sweet, and unexpected. I love that he's thinking of me. "Thank you."

"You're welcome. But if it's all the same, I'll still use Cynthia's husband's closet and drawers for my stuff."

"Oh, yeah, of course. Why don't we go unpack?"

"Sounds good. Should we text whoever about later?"

"Right. I forgot for a second. I'll call my best friend and producer, Shoshana. You'll love her, she's... different."

"I like different. Does she know about this whole thing?"

"Yeah, I told her."

"Alright, that's not the worst thing in the world. I'm gonna bring an old college buddy. He sure as hell doesn't know, so he'll be your first test."

"My test?"

"Yeah," he says. "To see how good of an actress you can be.

There's a bar in town that Cynthia took me to one time that's really cool. Strong drinks and live music on weekends."

"Sounds fun. Let me see what she's up to, alright?"

"No problem," he takes a step towards me. I don't know why, but at first, I think he's going to kiss me. The thought comes out of nowhere, and to my surprise, I don't step back or move at all. For just a second, I close my eyes and wait. Then I hear the sound of his voice.

"Can I take your bags into the room while you text Shoshana?" His hand is already on my suitcase, and I love that he asked me first.

"Yeah. Thank you. I'll message her now."

I take out my phone and hold it, but I'm not doing anything except watching him walk to the bedroom. The view isn't bad at all. He's wearing shorts that show off the ass I've never noticed before. His legs are muscled, and I can tell looking at them that he spends a lot of time in the gym. I catch myself watching until he's out of sight, and that's when my concentration comes back.

I don't feel like texting, so I step back out into the swampy jungle outside to call her. "Be right back."

"Alright."

Opening the front door is a terrible mistake. It's even more gross than it was when I first got here, if that's even possible. It feels worse, anyhow. I dial Shoshana's number.

"Hey. I expected your voicemail," I say when her voice comes through.

"I'm off today, what's up?"

Off. She never takes off. "Are you sick?" I ask.

"No. All my clients cancelled." Shoshana's an occupational therapist by trade. Even though I pay her pretty well to keep my disorganized life in order, she still sees a few clients, mostly home visits for kids with special needs. "I had three yesterday, but I guess things come up all the time when you have kids."

"Perfect!" I yell, a little too excited.

"Huh?"

"Today's the day," I tell her. "You know, move-in day."

Shoshana yells into the phone like I just announced I was getting engaged. She's the best cheerleader you could ever hope for, even when you don't really need one. "Would you relax? It's not that serious."

"It's very serious to me. Are you sleeping in the same bed? Did he ask to kiss you? I need to know everything!"

"Shosh, I promise I'll tell you more when there's more to tell. You have my word. That's not why I was calling."

"Alright, alright," she interrupts. "But can you at least answer those two questions?"

"What were they again?"

"Are you sleeping in the same bed, and did he ask to kiss you?"

"No and no."

"Well that sucks. I'm bored now."

"Shoshana, focus!"

"Sorry, sorry. What do you need?"

I explain the situation. I sound like the most selfish friend ever, but I need her to drop whatever plans she had and get to Long Island asap so we can go to a bar with this strange man who's now my fake boyfriend, and one of his friends."

"Done!" she says without missing a beat. "Is that all? I thought something was really wrong."

"You mean besides this situation?"

"Oh, stop, Captain Negative. If I remember correctly this was your idea to begin with."

"That doesn't make it a good one. It was just... necessary, but I don't actually want to live with this man for four weeks. We don't even really know each other, and what we do know about one another we don't like."

"Sexual tension."

"What was that?"

"You've been going a little hard for this project, don't you think?"

"Yeah," I say. "And we know why—because being published will help me bring my message to even more of my listeners."

"I know, I know, your book. But it's more than that, admit it."

"I will do no such thing," I say, wondering how we got on this.

"You don't have to, but I've known you the longest of anyone in your life outside of your family, and I've never seen you like this with a guy—even one you pretend to hate."

"There's no pretending going on."

"Oh, come on, you can't fool me. You're attracted to Mr. Publisher Man. You said he was really hot."

"He is, but that's not the point."

"That's always the point, Tori. But I'll let you get there on your own—that's what friends do."

"No. Friends get their ass on the parkway within the next hour so that they don't get stuck in gridlock traffic, so that they can accompany their best friend and her fake boyfriend to a bar."

"Done. Let me go. Text me the address and I'll GPS it."

"Thanks again, see you soon."

I go back inside and see that Cormac is diligently unpacking. He has no idea that in just a few short hours I'm about to unleash the force of nature that is Shoshana on him.

CHAPTER 14

Cormac

OF COURSE I JUST MOVED IN WITH an anal-retentive freak—and I don't mean 'anal' or 'freak' in a good way.

While she was outside I started unloading my stuff, and by *unload* I mean I started to drop my crap in the Cynthia's husband's empty drawers. I hear the front door close, and now that she's back in from calling her friend she starts to unpack. There's nothing unusual about that—it's how she's doing it.

When I look over to her side of the room her open suitcase tells me everything I need to know about this experience—there's not a thing out of place in that little box—her socks, her shirts, everything folded more neatly than I ever could—or than I ever would. I mean, who needs their socks folded so perfectly? They're matched, folded in half, and stacked with the others in neat little piles. As she unpacks, she takes each sorted pile out, never dropping anything, and putting everything in carefully thought out positions in Cynthia's drawers and closet. She looks like she's handling rare glass instead of some shirts and pants.

When she's done with that little ritual, that's when suitcase number two comes out—and that one is way bigger than the first one, by the way. "More clothes?" I ask.

"Nope." Once she opens it I see more shoes than I've ever owned in my life. Besides the sheer number of them, I'm impressed that she got all of them into that small space. No exaggeration—there might be twenty pair. I tried to count but stopped after she saw me doing it. "What?" she asks. "What's your problem?"

"No problem," I say. "But you have a few pair of shoes right there."

"Keen powers of observation you have there."

If she wants to play sarcastic tennis I have an awesome return of serve. "You know, for a woman who hates gender stereotypes so much, you have a *lot* of fucking shoes. It just seems a little too on the nose for you."

"You're right," she says, to my total surprise. "I guess some stereotypes are true." I can't believe my ears. Are we actually turning a corner here where she admits she's wrong about something? I get too excited for what I think is the first reasonable thing I'd heard her say since I met her, and then she ruins the moment completely. "You know, like you wanting to know if you could kiss me all the time. That's pretty stereotypical, don't you think?"

Uhhh! I should have known it couldn't just be a nice, easy exchange, that she would have to get me back. I guess I should pay less attention to her and do my own unpacking. I don't answer her back, I just smile and grab my bathroom bag.

I brought a few essentials—nothing crazy—but it looks like

she brought her whole medicine cabinet from home, along with everything in her shower, and she may have stopped at CVS for a few extras on the way over here. There are a million little lotions, body washes (what the hell is wrong with good, old-fashioned soap?), a razor (at least she shaves—you never know with these radical feminist types—probably thinks armpit hair is some kind of liberating act), and more things than I can even count. She even has this plug-in thing that makes the room smell like...

"What is that?" I ask.

"A scented plug-in."

"No, I know that. I mean, what scent is it?"

"Lavender," she says.

"Lavender?"

"Yeah. It smells good, right? I suppose you think that's a stereotypical female thing to say."

I throw my hands up. "I didn't say a word. All good with your friend?"

"All good. She's going to meet us there at 9:30. Who are you bringing, your brothers?"

"Hold your roll there, sweetheart. Meeting the family is another phase of this little game. We're still in phase one."

"Excuse me?" she says, her nostrils fuming like a Looney Tunes episode.

"I said, meeting the family..."

"Nope," she says indignantly. "Not that part."

"Which part then?" I'm pretending to not know exactly what she's talking about, but I do. I wanted to see if pet names were going to fly.

"Don't call me sweetheart, okay? While we're at it, don't call me anything except Tori."

"You know, boyfriends call their girlfriends things like 'babe' or 'baby'. And despite what you think, pet names aren't some male conspiracy to subjugate woman. They're..."

"What?" she asks.

"I was going to say that they're meant to be endearing. Some might even say sweet."

"Well I'm not a fan, but I'll meet you halfway. In public, and *only* in public, if you want to throw a 'babe' out there, I'll fake a smile. That's the best I can do, but don't push it."

"Fair enough. And in private, and *only* in private, if you get the urge to have crazy animal sex with me, I'll fake a moan or two. Best I can do. And feel free to push it as far you like."

She just looks at me — that look you give the crazy guy on the subway who whips his dick out while you're taking your morning commute to the office. She doesn't even make a comeback, she just rolls her eyes. "This is going to be a long four weeks." She turns her back and goes into the bathroom—probably to organize her fifteen little bottles of lotion.

While she's in there, I look over at her mostly empty suitcase and my eyes go as wide as melons. Look at what we have here! Sitting at the bottom of that suitcase is some of the hottest, skimpiest lingerie I've ever seen. That's shocking enough, but sticking just outside of the lace bra and panties is a big, fat dildo. Holy shit, maybe there's more to this girl than meets the eye. When I hear her coming back I look away and pretend like I didn't just find a huge fake dick in her suitcase. God, all sorts of thoughts start running through my mind at the same time.

"Almost done?" I ask.

"Pretty much." She looks over in my direction, then down towards her almost empty suitcase. Even though she doesn't realize that I saw, she realizes that at the very least I can see her lingerie. She scrambles to cover it up, slamming and then locking the suitcase so that I won't see—even though I already did. "Done, actually."

"Great. I'm going to run into the office to catch up on a few things. Are you going to stick around here?"

"Yeah," she says. "I'm going to get used to the place. Watch some TV. Maybe write a little."

"Make yourself at home—Cynthia's home, anyhow. I'll text you the address of the bar and we'll all meet there at 9:30. That work?"

"Perfect."

"Oh, and to answer your question, my old college buddy Maxwell is in town. He's been asking me to hang out for a few days, so I figured why not introduce him to my new girlfriend and one of her friends."

"You told him about me?"

"I sure did. The way I figure, if we can't convince someone who's never met you and never seen us together that we're boyfriend and girlfriend, then this whole thing is a waste of time. Wouldn't you agree?"

"You have a point... I guess. I mean, you have a point."

"See, sometimes I'm not just a dumb man. I hit a home run every now and again. I'm gonna run, remember to be convincing later."

"Don't worry, it'll be an Oscar worthy performance. Meryl Streep won't be able to hold a candle to me. I'll see you then."

"Alright," I say, pulling the front door shut. "Bye, babe!"

I don't wait around to see her response.

As I get in my car and pump the a/c up to high, I think about the bottom of that suitcase. Why would she bring such sexy lingerie here? I expected straight granny-panties, but I see that she's full of surprises. And that big fake cock? I wonder how many miles she gets out of that thing.

Maybe she's a closet freak. Or maybe she wants to be, but doesn't know how to tap into that part of herself. I guess I'll find out soon enough.

Heading to the office may occupy my mind for a little while until it's time to meet her at the bar. We'll see what happens tonight.

CHAPTER 15

Tori

I WAIT IN MY CAR, NERVOUS FOR no reason. I literally talk to millions of people each week on all of my social media platforms, but meeting my fake boyfriend's college friend at a bar is somehow filling me with anxiety. I take a few deep breaths and wait for Shosh.

Shoshana: I'm here. I just parked next to you.

I look up from the text and turn to my left. Nothing. Then my right. Shoshana is smiling and waving like a little kid. I wave back and smile. Shoshana's always positive. I'd never tell her this, but I envy that trait, no matter how much I make fun of it—like I'm about to. "Took your meth before coming here, I see."

"I'm high on life. Don't be a hater. Where's your man?"

"Don't call him that. He's not my man. He's... I don't even know what he is. But definitely not my man."

"Fine," she says. "Your fake man, then. Where is he?"

"Should be here any minute with his friend."

She perks up when I say that. "Friend? You didn't mention any friend? Who is he and what does he look like? Is he hot like Cormac?"

Shoshana's never met Cormac, but I—can't believe I'm admitting this—I stole a picture of him while we were in the house before he left. He was lying back on the couch in nothing but a tight-fitting tee shirt, and it framed his chest perfectly in white. His hair was messy, the way I like it, and he was leaning his head back. I took out my phone like a stalker and stole a pic. I was stupid enough to have left the sound on, so a giant camera 'click' sound came on.

"What was that?" he asked. "You taking pics of me for later?"

"There's that crazy ego of yours rearing its ugly head again." I was making fun of him at the time, but he was totally right. If only he knew. I texted it to Shoshana right after with a heart emoji in the text.

Back in real time, we're waiting just outside the bar. "I don't know if the friend's hot or not, but it's not like a double date situation. I don't think it is, anyway. He made it seem like this was... what did he call it? Oh, right, phase one. What does that even mean?"

"My dear, sweet Tori," she jokes. "So much to learn."

"So teach me," I tell her. "What's phase one?"

"I'm pretty sure he's talking about the phases of a relationship. I guess he wants friends to meet you before you meet his family. How it works is that you normally start with with lower risk situations and people and then build you way up to the important ones. Like, who's this friend?"

"Cormac said he was an old friend. He made it sound like they hadn't seen each other in a while."

"Exactly, see, low risk situation."

"Meaning?" I ask, not sure what she means.

"Meaning that—and understand that I'm not talking about you, specifically—if you turned out to be some crazy psycho stalker—like the kind who'd sneak a pic of a guy and text it to your best friend right on the spot..."

"Good one."

"Then you might be too crazy to introduce to someone more important—like his mom or someone."

"I see, so drinks with the buddy is like a trial run for a relationship? Is that what you're saying?"

"Exactly. See, now you're getting it."

"Speaking of the devil..."

Cormac pulls up with his friend. He's leaning out the window. Shoshana sees him and without missing a beat she says, "I don't want no scrubs."

"Huh?"

"Oh, come on," she says. "It hasn't been that long since we've done it."

"I get it now. He's..."

"Hanging out the passenger side of his best friend's ride, silly. But so far, he's not trying to holler at me. He looks pretty sexy, I kind of wish he would though."

Shoshana and I were roommates in college, and back in the day we used to be obsessed with 90's and early 2000's music. We used to do this thing where we'd say a line from a popular song whenever it made sense for the situation we were in. Then the other one would have to say what song it was. It's been a while, and I'm clearly rusty.

"Don't go chasing waterfalls," I say, and she gives me the you-fucked-it-up look.

"That doesn't fit. The moment's passed."

"Sorry. Didn't know you were the game judge."

"Well I am. Have it make sense next time."

We giggle a little as Cormac and his friend approach. "Hey."

"Hey yourself." Cormac walks from Maxwell's side to mine and gives me a big hug. Did I say 'big'—I meant 'bear'. He pulls me in tight to his chest and squeezes me. I let him hold me tightly and when I do, something strange happens inside of me. I start to like it. He feels warm, comforting, and despite the fact that he looked a mess before, he smells like a man. The hug feels like it goes on forever, and when he lets me go I feel cold. I'm not expecting that at all. When we separate, I breathe in a little deeper, like maybe I'll catch some of that amazing musk that was just coming off of him.

"Sweetie, this is the friend I was telling you about. Maxwell."

Sweetie. Well played, Cormac, well played. "Nice to meet you, Maxwell."

"Likewise," he says.

"It's funny, Shoshana and I met in college also. We were roommates."

"Is that right?"

Cormac has his arm around me, and I can't decide if I like it or not. The hug was one thing, but now his big arm is just draped across my shoulders. I don't pry it off—that would look strange, but I try to give him a look that communicates how I'm feeing. It fails miserably.

"Why don't we go inside and get a drink?" Cormac suggests.

"Great idea."

We all head inside. I can hear the music blasting from outside, but it doesn't sound live. I look around. "Where's the band?" I ask Cormac.

"They start at ten," he answers. "They're probably on their way or already setting up in the back."

We grab a table and the guys take our orders. I'm happy I don't have to push my way through the crowd standing around the bar. Maybe chivalry isn't so bad. I order a rum and Coke and Shoshana gets a Maker's Mark and Coke. As the guys go to get our drinks, Shoshana nudges me.

"He's gorgeous," she says.

"Maxwell?" I ask. "He's alright. You interested?"

"No, not Maxwell! I mean, yeah, he's attractive enough, but I'm talking about your... excuse me, your 'fake' man. Cormac is a Greek god."

"An Irish god, actually. And he's not bad, is he?"

"Not bad?" she repeats. "Come on, Tori, you see it as much as I do. That man is totally gorgeous." Shosh just stands there, deep in her weird thoughts, and then she blurts out. "I bet he has a huge dick."

"How did we get there?"

"I'm always there, Tor, I practically live there. I only vacation in the normal world. Anyhow, who cares? I'm just saying what everyone else thinks."

Typical Shoshana answer. "I can guarantee you that not everyone is thinking about Cormac's dick—or dicks in general."

"I'm just saying, nature tends to be proportionate. Big guy, big feet, big hands. If he had a tiny little dick I'd really be surprised. It's just a read—you can let me know."

"I certainly cannot let you know. We're just playing house, you know that—acting for an experiment. I will not be seeing his... thing... anytime soon."

"Can you just say it? C'mon. Real quick before they get back. No one can hear you, I promise."

"Nope. Sorry, not happening. I'll turn bright red."

"Stop being dramatic—just say it."

"Hey, look," I say, trying to distract her. "The guys are coming back. Too late."

"Say it real fast, right now, or I'm telling Cormac about that time at the dorm."

"You wouldn't dare!" The time at the dorm is the most embarrassing thing that happened to me in college. It's something I'd turn bright red about if the story was ever repeated.

"You really want to test that theory out?"

"You're so petty sometimes, you know that?"

"Guilty as charged. You're running out of time, they're getting closer."

I don't hear the music on the jukebox stop. It must have been louder than I thought. Or maybe they just shut it down to let the band set up. Don't know. Doesn't matter. All that matters is that I screamed out "COCK, alright, are you happy, COCK COCK COCKETY COCK!" just as the room got quiet.

I've never thought about dying, but if I could do it right then and there I would have. I turn red when I'm embarrassed. A lot of people use that expression, but my cheeks literally resemble a red Crayola crayon when I feel foolish and, before Shoshana motions to my face to tell me, I already feel the hotness.

"What the hell were you girls talking about?" Maxwell asks.

"Chickens," Shoshana says, jumping in. "You know. Hens and and stuff—Tori can never remember which is which."

"Oh, that's easy," Cormac says. "Cocks are the males, of course." He high fives Maxwell like a true bro, and they laugh.

"Thanks for the clarification."

"Anytime you need to know about cocks, just ask me." Repeat the high five and laugh. I feel like I'm at a fraternity party right now.

The boys brought us drinks, but I need something a little stronger to get through this. I grab Shosh by the arm. "Excuse us, guys, I think we need to pre-lubricate." They both laugh, and I realize what I just said. "Don't say it, you know what I meant."

I take her to the bar and order two shots of tequila. "What are we doing?" she asks.

"Getting brave."

"You don't need to be brave. You're not meeting the queen of England, we're just hanging out with some guys. Seriously, don't drink too much." The shot's down my throat and I'm ordering another before Shosh can go motherly on me. "Slow down, girl, seriously."

I should. I know she's right, but for some reason my anxiety is through the roof right now. Everything is coming into sharp focus now that we're out 'acting' our way through this. I speak for a huge audience everyday—I've even done huge meet and greets with live audiences—but meeting Cormac's friend is messing with my head. I figure a little liquid courage isn't so bad, right?

"Aren't you going to join me?" I ask.

"In getting completely blitzed? Nah, I'm all good."

"At least take the shot I ordered."

"I'm not really a shot girl. But I have an idea." Shosh takes her shot and pulls me back to the table where the guys are waiting for us. "Maxwell, could you be so kind as to drink this for me?"

He looks up at her with doe eyes—that's how all guys look at her. "You don't want it?" he asks her.

"See, I thought I did when Tori got it for me, but now I really don't, and I don't want to waste it. Do you want?"

"Sure, thanks." He takes it from her and downs it in one gulp. "Woo-hoo, that burns!" She winks at me.

We sit down and start talking. I'm feeling those shots already, and I can hear my words getting slurred. I try to hide it as best I can, but the room is starting to spin a little. Did I mention that I don't really drink a lot? Maybe two shots on an empty stomach wasn't the best idea.

We talk for a few minutes. Mostly I stay quiet because I don't want to sound like the sloppy drunk girlfriend and give a bad impression to Maxwell. This whole thing was my idea, so acting stupid in front of Cormac's friend isn't the best look.

Besides me being painfully self-aware of how cloudy I'm getting, I'm also aware of something else—just how fine Cormac is looking. I don't think it's just the booze, either. I think the alcohol is just shutting down the mental block I've had towards Cormac ever since that pitch meeting. But once the tequila starts to break down my defenses, I can really see how attracted to him I could be. He's literally tall, dark and handsome, and when he held me outside I could feel the ripples of his chest beneath his clothes.

He looks over at me and takes my hand. "Everything alright?" he whispers in my ear. My whole body feels it.

"Yeah," I tell him, feeling the warmth between my legs. "Everything is just fine."

Hmm. This is starting to get interesting.

CHAPTER 16

Cormac

S HE NEVER HAD HER DRINK.

"Here," I say, sliding the glass over to her. She smelled amazing when I leaned into her just now, and the smell of her is still in my nose. "Before the ice melts and makes it gross."

"Thanks." She takes it from me hesitantly and just looks at it for a few seconds, like she's not sure if she should have it.

"You don't have to," I tell her.

"No. It's totally fine." About five seconds later that glass is half empty. She went from not looking like she wanted it to doing a Nicholas Cage in *Leaving Las Vegas* impersonation. "Go easy," I caution, leaning in. "I'm not that bad to be around that you need to get so messed up."

"I'm fine," she tells me. "But thanks for looking out for me."

I do my best Daniel Day Lewis impersonation and fully

commit to my role of loving boyfriend. Maxwell is a Chatty, so he jumps in with about a million questions that I know she's not ready for. Not only didn't we rehearse any sort of origin story for our 'relationship', but she's looking, sounding, and yes—smelling—a little north of tipsy right now. I'm worried she won't know what to say. That doesn't stop Max from asking the question we've both been dreading.

"So, Tori, how did you and my boy here meet? Cormac was telling me how amazing you are on the car ride over here, but he didn't tell me much about how you two got together."

"That's my Cormac," she says. "Always forgetting the little details."

"He's always been like that. So you tell me instead."

We did not prepare for this at all, and now that it's actually happening I feel really stupid for not discussing it. Part of me wants to jump in and make up a story for Maxwell, but the other part of me—the part that's going to win out—wants to see how Tori navigates the bullshit river she currently has us paddling down with both hands. She wanted this, so it's on her to make it as realistic as possible. I'll jump in if she needs me, but I really want to see how she handles this.

She looks at me with glassy eyes for a second before turning away and smiling. Even though I've got no skin in this game, I get nervous when I see she's about to open her mouth and make up a story. Here we go.

"We met at a conference."

Her lie doesn't miss a beat. It flows right off of her... damn, have her lips always been that red? I know she's had a few, but she's looking really beautiful right now. I don't know if it's that she's finally relaxing or what, but I can't stop staring at her mouth.

"A conference?" Maxwell asks.

I see where Tori's going with this, and I jump in to help her but she keeps going before I can. "Like a publishing conference. Cormac goes to them all the time—they have them all over the country. They're opportunities for readers to get their books out in front of publishers."

"Oh, so you're an author?" he asks.

"Our girl Tori here isn't just an author, she's a social media mogul." It's Shoshana jumping in this time. "And I'm her... what would you call me, Tor?"

"My best friend," she says before cackling at her own joke a little too loudly. "Oh, you mean professionally?"

"Uh-huh."

"Shoshana is my manager. She's the producer of my podcast, she helps edit my vlogs, and she helps with book appearances and professional conference stuff. Basically, she's my eyes, ears, brain, and everything else. I don't know what I'd do without her."

"Awww," she says back. "Well I love every minute of it."

"Wait," Max says. "Are you one of those... what do they call them? Online personalities? Cormac you didn't tell me that part."

"Sorry, man, I didn't want to overwhelm you all at once. But yeah, Tori here runs her own empire. She's on YouTube and has a hit podcast."

"Wow, that's incredible," Max says. "I feel like I just met a famous person."

Tori waves her hands. "Nah, not famous. I don't get recognized or anything."

"Actually," I say, jumping in. "We were out at breakfast recently and our waitress nearly dropped our food on the ground when she found out she was serving the one and only Tori Klein."

"That's nuts!" Max says. "What's your podcast? I'll download right now."

"It's called..."

"Women on dicks," Shoshana interrupts. "Obviously it's not all spelled out or iTunes wouldn't let us on, but if you start to type it your phone should auto fill."

"You know, last time I typed those words into my phone it was for a whole different kind of search. Oh, this one?" Max turns his screen around.

"Yup," Tori says. "That's me."

"Perfect. Well, you just got one more download."

"Thanks Max, you're a Tormentor now."

"Huh?" he asks.

"That's what we call Tori's fans and subscribers. You know, like her name, only it sounds like they torture us."

"Ah, I get it now. So, Tori, you were saying? You were at a conference?"

"Oh yeah, right. So I decided to write a book a while ago—on the same topics I discuss on my podcast—so I started going to those conferences where authors can hook up with publishers and get some feedback on their work. That's when we met. I thought this man was so sexy that I didn't even bother pitching him my book, I just asked what he was doing after the event. He told me nothing, so I decided to make the first move and ask him to get a drink. The rest is history."

"Wow," Max says. "That's a great story. You'll have to tell your grandkids one day."

"Yeah," Tori says, looking at me. "Our grandkids."

The next hour passes quickly. Shoshana and Max hit it off, but more than that, they're both great at keeping the conversation going and the mood positive. It's not that I don't like to talk, but the more they talk the less lying Tori and I have to do, at least verbally. Physically, we're still lying our asses off. Tori's getting a little... friendlier than I ever thought she would with me. At first, I'm excited about it, until I realize that it's happening after a couple of drinks. I wasn't really paying attention, but I notice Shoshana tapping her on the leg and telling her to stop.

"Hey," I say leaning into her. "I saw you get up again but how many is this?"

"I think it's my third. Or my fifth. I don't know, who can count?"

"You need to go easy, okay. You should cut yourself off."

"Are you telling me what to do, just like a typical man?"

"No, I'm telling you what to do like a responsible human being."

I need to get her out of here before she says something that we'll both regret. I lean over to Max and explain the situation. "Go ahead, man, I got you."

"Shoshana?" I ask. "I think we have to cut the night a little short so that I can take our girl home. Think she's celebrating a little too hard."

Shoshana nods like she was waiting for me to say that. I get up, Tori on my arm and we go to my car. "Where are you taking me?" she says, all slurry.

"Home," I answer. "I'm taking you home. And I know you don't like me very much, but please try not to throw up in my car."

I don't think she'll be throwing up because she's asleep practically as soon as the passenger door shuts. A million questions are running through my mind. Is this normal? Is she secretly an alcoholic? Did something happen? I have no answers, but I don't need them right now. All I need to do is get her home, safe and sound.

Back at the house I carry her—literally—out of the car and up to the front door. Once I get her inside, I head straight to the bedroom and lay her down on the king-sized bed. I take off her shoes, put the covers over her, and grab my iPad so I can write a little while I watch out for her. I made sure to put her on her stomach just in case she vomits in her sleep. She reeks of booze.

Just as I start to walk out of the room, she wakes up—sort of. Her eyes are open a little and she's talking to me, but she's clearly still out of it. "You alright?" I ask. I'm waiting for her to jump up and run into the bathroom, holding her mouth to keep all the throw-up inside, but that's not what happens. She starts talking to me.

"Cormac?"

"Yeah, Tori? Are you alright?" I go to the side of the bed. Her body is down and her face is turned to the side. Her eyes are glassy and her speech is still a little hard to understand.

"I think so," she says.

"Good. Get some rest." As I get up she reaches up and grabs my arm. "What's the matter? Do you need me to get you something?"

"I think I might," she says. "Come here." She motions like she wants me to lean in. I can barely hear her, so I dip my head, and before I know it she reaches around the back of my head and plants one right on my lips. She smells eighty proof. I think we just had kiss number one. I pull back after about a second.

"Woah, what are you doing?"

"Kissing you, silly. I just wanted to say that it was really sweet of you to give me the bed and all."

"I appreciate that, but we won't be kissing anymore right now. You're not in your right mind."

"I think I might need you to get undressed and crawl under these covers with me."

She's beyond drunk, and the last thing I'd ever do is get into bed with a woman as blitzed as her, no matter how hot she is, or how much she claims to want me. That's just not going to happen for a whole host of reasons. I pull the covers up around her and dislodge her very weak grip on my arm. "Ask me that again when you'll remember asking me."

Before she can even answer I hear the snores. I get changed, grab my iPad, and crawl up in the oversized lounge chair that's sitting in the corner. I cover myself with a large blanket that I found in the linen closet and open my screen.

What a weird night this turned into.

Sunday, July 16th

THE MORNING COMES quickly.

I must have passed out around midnight or so. I clear my eyes and the first thing I feel is the soreness from having slept for hours in a sitting position in this lounge chair. I push myself up out of the chair and walk over to Tori, who's still lying in her clothes from last night. I reach down and gently shake her shoulders.

"Wake up, sleepy head."

Her eyes open slowly, and when she finally focuses on me she jumps like she's startled. Sitting up, she clears her eyes and looks at me with a disoriented stare. "Where? Oh, right. Cynthia's house."

"It's our house for the next few weeks, remember? How are you feeling?"

"My head," she says, rubbing her temple. "It's killing me, holy shit. What happened?"

"You're a lightweight, and you drank way too much. That's the simple answer. There's probably a longer, more satisfying one, but the explanation I just gave is the shortest route to the truth."

"The bar, right? Your friend. What happened?"

"What's the last thing you remember?" I ask.

"Telling the fake story about how we met. Then this."

"Wow," I say. "There are a few things in between."

"Like what? Did I say something or do anything weird?"

"Besides kissing me in a drunken stupor? Nope, just that. Oh, and now that I think about it, your car is still at the bar. I'll take you to get it later."

"Wait, what!!!"

"Sorry, I wasn't speaking loud enough, was I? I said, your car..."

"Not the fucking car! The other part."

"The kiss?" I ask, playing coy. "It was sweet. Our first. Not quite how I imagined—in my fantasy it was a little less... boozy."

"You kissed me when I was drunk?"

"No." I tell her, getting serious for a minute. "I'd never, ever do that. *You*, however, kissed *me* while you were drunk. 'Ambushed' might be a better way to put it."

"And what did you do?"

"Pulled away as soon as I realized what was happening. I swear."

I hope she knows that I'm telling the truth. She may not think the world of me—or of men in general—but I'd like to believe she doesn't think I'd be even remotely sexual with her without her consent. "I feel stupid now," she says, rubbing her eyes. "I really can't believe I did that."

"Don't feel stupid," I tell her. "I've done much dumber and more embarrassing things after I've had a few, trust me. And, hey, you just checked one off the box, right? That makes two more to go."

"Oh yeah, I forgot. Wait, you put me into bed?"

"I just took off your shoes—figured you didn't want to sleep in those heels. Then I pulled the covers up so you wouldn't be cold."

"And where did you sleep?" she asks.

I point at the chair that's responsible for my next ten chiropractic appointments. "Over there in that thing."

"Why'd you sleep there?"

I'm not going to mention the part where she asked me to violate her one and only rule of the house—first, she wouldn't believe me. And even if she did, she'd be even more embarrassed than she already is. "Just in case you needed me to hold your hair back in the middle of the night, or something. I didn't want anything bad to happen to you."

She smiles. "Cormac, I don't know what to..."

"I have to go into the office." I cut her off because I know she was about to say something that would have been hard for her to say, and I don't need praise or an apology. I just wanted her to be okay. I put on some clothes quickly and grab my bag. "I recommend a shower, you smelled about eighty proof last night, and I'm guessing a long night's sleep in the same clothes hasn't improved things any. Just my two cents."

"Thanks. I'll keep that in mind." I start to walk out when she stops me. "Cormac?" she calls.

"Yeah?"

"You're a really good fake boyfriend, you know that?"

I smile and head to my car.

CHAPTER 17

Tori

I'VE NEVER TAKEN SUCH A LONG SHOWER in my life. It was totally necessary, but I might have used up all the hot water for the next week. But it felt good. The steam cleared my head and the smell of my favorite body wash replacing the smell of liquor was just what I needed. A shower isn't enough, though. A half a bottle of Listerine later and I swear that I can still taste the alcohol.

I can't believe I kissed him with this mouth.

I can't believe that I kissed him at all.

When I'm done getting last night off me, I text Shoshana to come over. We need to talk.

I hear her knock on the door about an hour later. My hair is still a little damp and I'm still a little embarrassed about how I might have acted at the bar last night. I suspect that Cormac might be leaving some things out of his version of last night to spare my feelings. Shosh won't pull any punches with that kind of thing though. If there's one thing of many that I count on her for, it's her honesty.

I open the door and she has on that disapproving mom look that isn't like her at all. "Fuck, I was so worried about you. I thought we were just having a nice night out and you turned into Kim Basinger in Blind Date."

"Never saw it."

"What? How dare you!"

"I'm sorry. You know I'm bad with movies."

"It's a 1980's classic. Bruce Willis plays this guy who has to take Kim Basinger out on a blind date. She ends up drinking, but she has this genetic thing that makes her super sensitive to alcohol, so she starts acting crazy and doing things that get both of them in deep shit."

"Jesus, I didn't do that kind of stuff, did I?"

"No, you were just white girl wasted. All kinds of sloppy."

"Fuck." I rub my head and feel really silly. It's not just embarrassment at what I might have done or said, but I always wonder if someone's going to recognize me and pull out their phone. The last thing I need is to be on YouTube looking the fool.

"What the hell even made you drink like that?" Shosh asks. "It's not like you at all."

"I was nervous, for one."

"You? You're around 100 times more people than that every day on your channels."

"That's my audience," I tell her. "It's not the same. And I wasn't nervous because of the people, I was worried about..."

"About what?"

"Being convincing. I was obsessed with Max thinking the

relationship was real, even though it really didn't matter. I don't know how to explain it. That, and the way Cormac and Maxwell were acting—bro-ing out and high fiving at every stupid sexual innuendo. It reminded me of the frat house. It reminded me of..."

"Trevor," Shoshana says. "I knew it!"

I don't even want to speak his name out loud. It was bad enough just being vaguely reminded of him last night. "Yeah. Look I don't want to go there right now, but I promise I'll control myself from now on. I'm sorry I left you high and dry. I got nervous. This whole thing felt so... real all of a sudden. I got really scared and tried to drink the feeling away. Clearly it was a mistake."

"No worries, you know me, I get along with everyone. Maxwell was super nice. Not my type at all, though."

"No? I didn't know you had a type?"

"I don't, not really," she agrees. "But that's just my polite way of saying he didn't exactly wake my vagina up from the slumber its been in recently. And if you can't wake her up, then we've really got nothing to talk about." I smile. I love her crazy metaphors. "Oh, speaking of which, it's about time your hibernation came to an end. It's summer—time to wake up and fuck."

"I think we've been down this road—and recently. I'm not fucking Cormac. He's not my type."

"Oh yeah? Too tall, right? Too muscular and handsome. Too much swag and self confidence. Too much stability and brains. I get it, he's a total loser."

"Alright, look, I'll give you all of those things. He's hot, okay. And yes, he makes a great living, dresses well, is sexy as hell. Oh, and I forgot to tell you."

"What?" she says, looking all fake mad. "What did you forget to tell me?"

"Well, apparently I kissed him in a drunken stupor that I can't remember no matter how hard I try. And trust me, I've been trying since he told me."

"You kissed him and you don't remember? That's tragic. Not sleeping with such a sexy guy who you're living with is even more tragic. We're talking Macbeth level of tragedy here."

"This isn't going to make sense to you—it might not make sense at all—but me not wanting to sleep with him has nothing to do with how hot or not hot he is. It has to do with the fact that this isn't real. What kind of feminist author would I be if I got my first publishing deal by screwing the guy who runs the publishing company?"

"You wouldn't be screwing him just to get a deal. Look, if you don't want to sleep with him then don't. I'm not trying to pressure you, I'm just saying that you're missing a golden opportunity— and one that you created!"

"And what opportunity is that?"

"To be in a relationship. However contrived it might be, it's something. I've read your book, Tori, more than once. It's perfect—except for one thing."

Here it comes. "That I've..."

"Never experienced it yourself. Not for a long time, any how. And—I'm sorry to go there—but Trevor doesn't really count, and we both know why."

"So, what do I do, then? Make out with him next chance I get? Throw myself all over him? Not argue when he tells me that he doesn't think my book is good enough for his publishing company?"

"No," she says. "No to all that. I'm not telling you to be a woman you're not. Be you, Tor. Be the strong, intelligent, confident woman that a million people listen to and watch every week. Be the woman who started #slavestotheirdicks and #tormentorarmy. All I'm saying is give him—and it—a chance. At the very least it'll make your book stronger."

I've got to give it to the girl, sometimes she knows exactly what she's talking about. "Oh shit."

"What?"

"My car. It's still at the bar. Can you drive me there really quick? I need to go do a few things."

"Of course. And consider what I said."

"I always consider what you say, Shosh. Always."

After I give Shoshana the biggest hug ever, I change into real clothes and throw last night's outfit in a plastic bag that I'm either going to take to the dry cleaners or burn outright, I haven't decided which yet. That's when I get a text that dings from across the room. It's Cormac.

Cormac: Even though you were sloppy drunk, you're still one of the most beautiful women I've ever seen. I'd never take advantage like that, but it took all my self control not to climb into bed with you.

I read it twice.

Then I read it twice more.

I forget my own mental blocks, and remember Shoshana's advice. I just let his words sink in, and when they do, they make me tingle in all the right places. He thinks I'm beautiful? I know I shouldn't care what some man thinks of my face—it shouldn't matter at all, but for some reason it does—it feels really nice.

Tori: :) Thank you!

Cormac: Don't make any plans for dinner tomorrow night. It's time for the next phase.

Tori: Meeting your family already? Didn't I embarrass you enough last night?

Cormac: You didn't embarrass me. Let's call this phase 1.5. Something in between friends and family.

Tori: Okay? And what's that?

Cormac: A date. A legit date. A romantic dinner, just you and me. I know a place. I promise I won't order for you :)

A date. I know those were part of our negotiations, but I'd say yes even if they weren't. Something changed last night, but I don't know what. After the way he took care of me and watched me show a bad side of myself without judgment makes me look at him in a new light. I'd love to go out with him, even if it is pretend.

Tori: I'd love to. Text me the time and place and I'll be there.

"Who's that?" Shoshana asks.

"Sorry. It's Cormac. He wants to take me out."

"You said yes, right?"

"Of course I said yes. What kind of fake girlfriend would I be if I said no?"

CHAPTER 18

Cormac

L
A *FONTINA* IS A CUTE LITTLE ITALIAN PLACE that I've always
wanted to try.

Elissa and Cynthia have told me about it for years. It's one of
those places that has the ambiance you need when you're trying
to close a big-time author. I'm not the wining and dining type
when it comes to my professional life, but in my personal life
there's nothing I enjoy more than a quiet dinner with a woman
I'm dating—or, pretend dating, in this case.

I left work at eight and picked up Tori at Cynthia's house so
that I could take her out properly. I feel like one of those guys
in a romantic comedy or something— I picked up flowers and
everything. You should have seen her face when I handed them
to her! She looked at me with that strange, uncomfortable
condescension that you'd give your dog when they come over to

you with a dead bird in their mouth—you're happy they know how to retrieve, but you are kind of freaked out at the same time.

I don't mind, though. I'm not even doing all this for the experiment. Something just tells me that she's not used to being treated nicely by a guy, so I'm happy to do what I'd normally do, even if she thinks I'm just trying to prove her wrong about men. Whichever way this whacky thing goes, at the very least, maybe I can show her that not all guys are total assholes.

When we get there, the hostess seats us at a candle-lit table right by the window. The atmosphere in the place is very romantic, and it's the perfect place for a date night. It's dressy, but not too dressy. The food is fancy, but not pretentious artwork food. The lights are dim enough to set a mood, but not dark. I hope she likes it.

"When was the last time you were on a date?" I ask her right after we order a glass of wine.

"Wow. We're jumping right in, are we?"

"We only have four weeks, Tori—that means we're on the accelerated getting-to-know-you program."

"You're right. And it's been a while. A long while. How about you?"

"It's been a few months, at least. I want to say it was April the last time I went out with someone. This girl Jennifer. It was a disaster!"

"How come?" she asks, smiling.

"You're going to think I'm lying to you if I tell you, but I swear it's the truth."

"Try me."

I smile just remembering this craziness. She's definitely going to think I'm making this up. "She tried to get me to join a cult."

"What! No."

"See, I knew you'd think I was lying, but I'm telling you. What was it called again?" I close my eyes and try hard to remember. "Oh, yeah! The Path, that's it! There was a pamphlet and a website and everything. Girl was crazy."

She starts to laugh. Really, really laugh. Her entire face changes when she smiles, in the best way possible. "How did that even come up?"

"Well I 'met' her on this dating app."

"There's your first mistake," she says. "I always tell my listeners to meet guys in person first. You never know what you're going to get when you swipe your way to a date."

"Tell me about it. I deleted that shit, canceled my account, and wrote a pretty pointed email to their 'contact us' section about vetting the lunatics who have profiles on there. But, anyway, we agreed to meet up for an early lunch before I had to go to work, and everything was fine... at first. She had this weird energy, though, I should have known something was up."

"Weird energy, like how?"

"Like eye contact that went on longer than it should have. You know what I mean. Like, you'd look away, then look back and she'd still be looking through you."

"Oh, that's uncomfortable."

"Now I realize that she was probably studying me to see how susceptible I'd be to her pitch to join The Path."

"I'm sorry," she says, laughing hard. "Every time you say The Path I die!"

"I know, right? You'd think they'd get more creative with the names so that it sounded less cultish. But anyway, it was a normal lunch, normal getting to know you chit chat, all that stuff. But now I realize she was asking me questions to see if I was attached, or had a family. Once she realized it was just good old me, she went in for the hard sell."

"Oh no. What did she say?"

"She did this, I shit you not." I take my napkin and fold it in half like it's a piece of paper and I slide it slowly across the table towards Tori while making a weird face and intense eye contact. *"Have you ever felt like a sheep without a flock? Have you ever wondered the answers to life's most burning questions? Well, if you have, it's time to consider getting on The Path.'"*

"No! Oh my God, I don't know what I'd do. That's hilarious."

"It is now," I tell her. "At the time, I was a little scared."

"So what did you do?"

"I left."

"You told her you weren't interested and left?"

"Nope. I just left. Once I realized what was happening—and trust me, it took a minute, because who the hell gets solicited into a cult on a first date—I just stood up and left. No words, no nothing."

"Did you at least leave money for the food?"

"Hell no," I joke. "That was the only time in my life where being a gentleman didn't even enter my mind. I felt bad, but let The Path pick up the check. I'm sure they had plenty of money from all the scamming. That was my last date until right now."

"How come?" she asks.

"As cliché as it sounds, I just haven't met the right woman. Weird, cultish ones aside."

"Okay, so let me ask you something else, then. Am I asking too many questions?"

"Never. We're getting to know each other, right? We should be asking questions."

"Okay. Well, if you did find that perfect woman—the one—what would she have to be like?"

"The physical attraction has to be there. No question about that. There has to be a fire when we look into each other's eyes. We have to want to tear at each other's clothes the second we're alone, and to want to slip away to rip each other's clothes off when we're around people. I know it sounds shallow, but that's a must. I want a girl who looks at me like I'm her dinner—who wants to devour me, who wants my hands all over her body at all times, who feels empty when I'm not inside her."

"Oh. My."

"Sorry. Did I go to far with that answer?"

"No," she says. "You went just the right amount, and please don't apologize. You just surprised me for a second, is all."

"In a good way, I hope."

"In a very good way. What else besides the physical attraction?" she asks.

"In and of itself it isn't enough for a serious relationship. A two-week fling, maybe, but not much more than that. For a relationship there has to be more substance there, otherwise..."

"It'll fizzle out?"

"Exactly. That flame burns hot and then burns out—especially when the girl can't hold a conversation, or has zero personality. There's an expression I'm sure you've heard before, but it's true—show me a hot woman, and I'll show you a man who's tired of having sex with her. Sorry. I know how that probably sounds to you, but it makes my point. There has to be more there, and so far, I've only found three women who've ever had that it-factor."

"Only three?"

"Only three. And even those three didn't last."

"How come?"

"That's a hell of a question."

"I'm sorry if that's too personal."

"It's not that, it's just that it's a conversation for another day. Too much to say here. Every relationship is just a story, like a book. They have characters, arcs, and the serious ones have a beginning, middle, and hopefully no end. Each one is a story. But the good news is that I'm currently involved in a committed fake relationship. It's going really well."

"You shouldn't make me laugh."

"Why not? You're beautiful when you smile."

"Stop it."

"Stop what?"

"You know what."

"Sorry. I can't help it sometimes. I didn't mean to make you uncomfortable."

"You didn't. I just want to hear the rest of it. What is the 'more' that needs to be there for you to be in a committed, serious relationship?"

"Before I answer that, let me just say that commitment is never an issue with me. I'm always one hundred percent in whatever kind of relationship I'm in—and monogamy is like a religion for me."

"Really?"

"Why do you sound so shocked?"

"I don't know. Something about what you just said struck me as shocking."

"Because you think all men cheat, right? We all chase women around like we're hunters and they're prey? Something like that?"

"Something like that."

"Don't feel bad—in some cases you're right, but in other cases—like my case—you're not. I've known a lot of guys, from high school to today, who've cheated on the women—or men—that they're in relationships with. Some of those dudes even brag about cheating to their friends. One guy in college told me 'if you're not cheating, you're not trying.' I think it's disgusting."

"Ewww."

"I agree. You can't conflate guys wanting to have sex a lot with guys being automatic cheaters—there's some cross over there, but they're different behaviors."

"What makes you so different then? How do you fly on the side of the relationship angels when guys around you are bragging about cheating on their significant other?"

"I have no idea. The way I was raised? Seeing guy friends lose amazing girls because they couldn't keep their dicks in their pants? All of the above? Who knows, who cares? It's just the way I am. I love women, I love having sex with women, but I'm not a piece of shit just because I have a penis. There are good men out there, Tori, and they don't always look like what you think they look like. Sometimes they look like me."

"I guess it was how you were raised."

"It is," I tell her. "One hundred percent. My mom is the strongest person I've ever met. She had to be with the piece of shit sperm donor of a father I had. He left my mom with three little boys when I was seven."

"I'm so sorry, I didn't know."

"It's okay. I only vaguely remember him at this point. I know what he looks like from pictures, but I have no strong memories of doing anything with him. My younger brothers don't remember him at all. He just up and left one day. When I got older my mom told me that he started another family in California. So I probably have a bunch of half siblings running around the west coast somewhere."

"So your mom raised three boys on her own? No step father or anything?"

"She got remarried when I was a junior in high school to really nice guy, but by that point most of the raising was done. She worked two jobs at crazy hours so she could have money for the things we needed and be there for us to spend time. She's the most amazing person I've ever met, but she had to be tough so that we stayed in line—thus the smacking upside the head part."

"I didn't realize..."

"What? That I was raised by a woman, and to respect women? I'm full of surprises, Tori. I'm not what you assume I am."

"Interesting," she says.

"What's even more interesting is that you didn't really answer me before. When was the last time you were on a real date?"

"And by 'real' you mean?"

"Don't do the debate club thing on me—let's be real with one another. You know what I mean—a date. Like this. Where a guy asked you out, paid for dinner or some other activity, all that. Maybe you kissed him at the end of it, maybe you didn't. When's the last time that happened?"

"That's an easy one. I just honestly didn't want to say the answer before 'cause I know you'll make fun of me."

"I promise you I won't."

"College."

I'm not believing my ears. "No fucking way."

"Yes, fucking way. Well, actually, maybe there was one after my undergrad. Oh yeah!" she says, remembering. "There was that guy Thad, but he was an asshole. I didn't like him at all. I forgot about him—tried to take me roller skating of all things. It was weird and awkward."

"Well his name was Thad—that should have been your first clue." She laughs. "But seriously, college? Why do I find that hard to believe?"

"I don't know, you tell me."

"Because you're hot, Tori. Do you know that? Like, really know it?" Let's add that she's not used to getting compliments to the growing list of things I can tell no guy—or very few—have done for her. Everything I do that most women like, she reacts to in the weirdest way. I tell her she's hot and she looks like I just tried to give her a wet willy.

"I don't know how to answer that. I know guys have said that to me, but I don't like to look at myself like that."

"How come? You're beautiful. There's nothing wrong with admitting that, is there?"

"No," she says. "I just always wanted to be more than that, you know? Not just another pretty girl. You probably wouldn't understand, you're a guy."

"Hey," I say, reaching across the table and taking her hand. "Anyone who thinks that you're just another pretty face is an asshole. Look, did I think you were hot the second I saw you? Yes. And did I like your book?"

"I think we both know the answer to that one."

"Regardless, I have respect for you. I don't think you're just some pretty girl with a bad book, not anymore."

She looks at me really closely. I can tell her guard is still up—something tells me it's always a little bit up. "Really? You respect me?"

"Like I said, I think it's really attractive when a woman knows what she wants and has the courage to pursue it, no matter what obstacles she faces along the way. There's nothing sexier than that, and there's nothing I respect more."

"Thank you, Cormac. That means a lot."

My hand is still over hers. As we talk, they start to move together so that we're almost holding hands, and when I feel her fingertips on the base of my palm my whole body gets electrified. It surprises me because it's just a touch—a simple feeling of skin on skin, but from her it means something more.

"You're welcome. I have a crazy idea."

"What's that?"

"How about we order actual food and talk about stuff that doesn't touch deep into the recesses of our personal psychology? I know it sounds crazy, but when has that stopped us before?"

She smiles. "I love that idea. And I'm starving!"

"Good. Then let's order."

CHAPTER 19

Tori

I'M A SUCKER FOR SOME GOOD, crispy calamari and eggplant parm.

I'm really enjoying being out with him—and being out, in general. I can't tell if he's genuine, or doing it as part of the experiment, but Cormac really seems to want to know me. The real me. I'm not used to how that feels, and it's making me look at him in a whole new light. I hope I'm not just being played because he wants something from me.

"Wait, you and Shoshana do what?"

I tell him about our little game. "Shoshana and I have always been obsessed with everything 90's and early 2000's—music, movies, all of it."

"Slow down," he says, taking a sip of his wine. "That's a long time period you just crossed. Now, are we talking Nirvana or N'Sync?"

"Do I look like an N'Sync girl? I mean, Shoshana dragged me to one of their shows once."

"Dragged you?" He's giving me the skeptical eyes. I think he sees right through me.

"Okay, maybe 'dragged' is a little aggressive. I mean, they were really good dancers, and the music was catchy."

"Date over. Actually, scratch that, experiment over. I can't be with someone who bumped to 'Bye Bye Bye' back when Justin Timberlake had that bright yellow Eminem hair."

"Oh, I loved me some Eminem back in the day. He was sexy. I guess he still is, but I haven't seen him in a while."

"I think he had a drug thing. His hair is brown now, it's not the same."

"I loved Nirvana, too. Rest in peace Kurt. I'm guessing you were more of a rock guy?"

"I'll level with you," he says. I like when he smiles, it makes his face even better looking than it already is. He's looking good tonight in this lighting. "Was 'I Want it That Way' a damn fine pop song? Sure. Did I download the single? Maybe. But if we're talking full album downloads, we're going with anything Nirvana, Green Day, Pearl Jam, Alice In Chains, Smashing Pumpkins— those are my bands."

"I can see you as a Pumpkins guy. You have a little darkness to you."

He smiles again. "In high school, especially. I went through this emo rock phase where I wanted to be Billie Corgan. I wore his black "Zero" shirt and wrote shitty poetry that I thought was going to be hit songs one day. I even tried to start a band, it was a disaster."

"Wait," I say laughing. "You were in a band? I can't see it."

"Oh yeah. I play guitar—badly—so I figured all I needed was a drummer and a bassist and we'd be on the radio in no time. But all we ended up doing was smoking a lot of weed and listening to existing bands. We never really wrote much now that I think about it. I wonder why we didn't get picked up by a music company?"

"Yeah," I say. "That's the mystery of the ages right there."

"I know, right!"

"Is that where it started?" I ask.

"Is that where what started?"

"Your writing. You said when we first moved into Cynthia's place that you were working on a book. Did you always want to be an author?"

"Kind of," he tells me. "I mean, I don't think I ever used that word when I thought of myself, but I always wanted to be a *writer*, if that makes sense."

"It makes total sense."

The waiter brings our food over, and the smell is overwhelming. We eat and talk, and as we do I forget that this is an experiment. Right now, we're just two people—a man and a woman—enjoying a meal together. I haven't wanted to escape, or be mean to him, or defend my book at all. I've just been having a good time, and it feels great.

"That was delicious," he says after the meal winds down.

"It was." The waiter takes my plates and asks if we'd like to see a dessert menu.

"Of course we would!" he says enthusiastically.

"Very well, sir," the waiter says. "I'll be right back."

I lean towards him. "I saw that chocolate cake on the other table over there and it looked so yummy!"

"Get it," he tells me. "Get two. One to stay and one for later when you get a late-night craving."

"You must want me to gain twenty pounds. Then what would you think of me?"

"I wouldn't care at all."

I give him the head tilt and the eyebrow raise. "Bullshit," I say. "If I gained twenty pounds, you're telling me that you'd still want to do this experiment with me? That you'd be asking about kissing me, and sleeping with me? There's no way."

"Why are you saying that?"

"Because men don't like women who aren't thin. We live in the same society, right? Don't tell me all of your girlfriends have been thick or heavy."

"Wow," he says, looking offended. It takes me by surprise.

"Wow what?"

"You know, we're here, having what I think is a good time, and then you say something like that."

He looks genuinely upset. Usually when we banter it's just that, but it looks like I touched a nerve when I said that and I'm not sure why.

"Look, I'm sorry, I didn't mean..."

"Yes, you did. You always mean what you say, Tori. Who the hell hurt you so bad?"

"Excuse me?"

"That has to be the only explanation. Nothing else makes sense. I've thought about it a lot."

"Thought about what, exactly?"

"The fact that you have such extreme views on all men. That has to come from somewhere. Because you're too smart and too cool when it comes to everything else—but on this subject you think... simplistically. What the hell happened that made you form these opinions?"

The waiter comes back, holding the small dessert menu in his hands. He places one in front of each of us. "I'll be back in a moment to take your order."

I stand up. "You know what, that won't be necessary. I'm not that hungry anymore. I'll meet you out front."

I didn't want the night to go like this, but I walk away from him. We're like oil and water. He thinks one thing and I think the other. So much for having a normal good time. So much to surrendering myself over to the experience.

CHAPTER 20

Cornac

I SLEPT ON THE COUCH.

That's where we agreed I'd sleep, anyhow, but it felt worse than I thought it would. Maybe it was the position I was sleeping in, or maybe it was the way things ended last night. We didn't speak a word to each other on the way home, and once we were here we just went to neutral corners.

But I have a day in front of me—a stack of interviews, contract negotiations, and meetings—I can't let this little experiment get in the way of real life. She didn't say a word to me as I got ready this morning, and that was honestly fine with me.

I decide to stop at Starbucks on my way into the office to get as large of a cup of coffee as they have, but seeing the line I'm already regretting my decision. It must be at least ten or more people deep. I look down at my watch and see that I'm already twenty minutes late, and counting. Fucking traffic from the suburbs into the city is a nightmare. I check my phone and see that I have two—count them, two—texts from Elissa asking me where I am.

Cormac: Traffic from Cynthia's place. Sorry. Be there soon.

Elissa: I'm going to start the first author meeting so that we don't get backed up.

Cormac: Okay. I'll be there as soon as I can. Sorry.

Alright. I need this line to move. I've been here five minutes already and I think only one person has put their order in. "How hard is it to make a fuckin' cup of coffee for all these hipster assholes?" Another one of those moments where I let my mouth say things that should probably stay inside of my head. I look around to make sure there are no Brooklynites with long beards, flannel shirts and fake glasses to get offended. I think I'm in the clear—everyone in here is wearing some kind of suit.

"The world needs hipster assholes." The female voice from behind me is familiar. Too familiar. "They're some of my most loyal readers."

Oh. My. God. I turn around and there she is—my ex, Maryanne—standing there in all her crazy glory. I don't say anything back. I just kind of stand there like I'm seeing the ghost of girlfriend past. She smiles. Of course she smiles. "What? Now you've got nothing to say? That's not the Cormy I know."

Cormy! Leave it to her crazy ass to formulate a nickname no one else has ever called me in my life.

I cringe inside when she calls me the name I hated even when we were together. My mom almost punched her in the face once when she heard how this woman bastardized the name she gave me.

"Hello Maryanne, how are you?"

"Better than you, it seems. You look like you've had better mornings."

She still looks good. But then I remind myself what she did to me and any effect her face or body may have had on me instantaneously vanishes. "Bad night last night."

"Oh, I'm sorry to hear that. Bad night's sleep? You have rings under your eyes."

"Yeah," I say, still staring a bit, like this is some weird dream I'm sure to wake from at any minute. "Something like that."

"You always got them when you didn't get a solid eight hours."

Don't reference our relationship, you awful...

"Yup. I always did." I hate that this is happening. If it wasn't for the arbitrary Long Island Expressway traffic I wouldn't have to see this woman right now. The universe hates me this week. "So what brings you this way?" I know exactly what brings her this way. That's just the kind of mindless question you ask your ex when you randomly run into them at Starbucks. She's here because our biggest rival—the publishing company she jumped ship to sign with—is around the block.

"I have a meeting."

Of course you do. Thanks for lazily trying to spare my feelings. That was almost nice of you. "Right. That makes sense."

I'm usually good at speaking to people—I pride myself on it. Even though I'm blunt, usually I can keep a mindless conversation going for as long as it needs to, but this exchange of words is painful. I want to euthanize this talk before it suffers any more— take it behind the barn and shoot it in the head. It's only humane.

"You wish I wasn't here, don't you?" she asks.

"Kind of," I don't expect to be that honest, but then I remember that I have absolutely zero incentive to be nice to her. "Or me. Or any other scenario that doesn't involve trying to make small talk with my ex girlfriend who used me to make her career."

"Oh, wow, that again. I must have really hurt you that you're still thinking about all that."

All that? You mean the year we spent together?

"Don't take this the wrong way, but I'm going to turn back around now and pretend that I'm just standing on an annoying line for coffee, instead of standing on an annoying line for coffee while debating the revisionist history of a failed relationship with my ex. If I have to choose, the former is just a little less painful."

I turn around, somehow stupidly assuming that would be the end of it. I know Maryanne well enough to know that she won't just let it lie—she has to get the last word in. "Revisionist history? Huh? Interesting way of putting it."

I turn around again. She missed the eye roll that happened right before, but it happened. "Look. Don't take this the wrong way, but it's just an accident of the universe that you and I find ourselves standing face to face. I don't want to fight with you but I also don't want to get into things I've been trying to let go for months now. I'm really not trying to be rude, but I just want to get my caffeine and get to work. Can we just do that without talking to each other?"

I expect her to go into straight bitch mode. That's what she used to do when she was challenged. But that was a while ago. Instead she surprises me.

"That's fine. We don't have to talk."

"Thanks. I'd say that it was good seeing you, but I don't want to lie to you. Good luck with your meeting, okay?"

"Thanks. And I hope you get a better night's sleep. She must be keeping you up."

She. Why go there? Is she jealous? And why am I about to play along? 'Cause I'm a petty asshole, that's why.

"It's not her," I say, playing right into the small amount of insecurity she just showed me. "I just had to sleep on the couch. Fucked up my back and neck."

"Oooh. What did you do to get the couch? Must have pissed her off."

"Apparently I can do that without even trying."

"I remember," she says. "The line's moving by the way." The line starts to move. I guess the manager came up front and started cracking some barista heads when they saw the store has about forty angry and sleepy customers. I take a few steps forward and move our painful conversation about ten feet closer to a trenta caramel macchiato with six shots. "Whatever you did, just say you're sorry. It helps. Even if you think you were right."

"Thanks, I'll give it a try."

I order and take a step to the side to wait. It's probably too much to hope that Maryanne is going to decide that she really doesn't want coffee and leave so I don't have to keep talking to her. Nope, here she comes. All I can hope is that they make my drink faster than they've been making them since I got here. We stand in silence for a few seconds. I think about asking her about her new book, but stop myself. I don't want to know. I really don't.

I hear the barista call out my name. It's the sweetest sound I've heard in a long time. I grab my cup so fast that I forget to put on the sleeve. "Shit!" I put it down and shake my hand out.

"Here." She hands me one of their cup sleeves. A small act of mercy.

"Thanks."

"What are horrible ex girlfriends for?" Her joke falls on deaf ears. I wish I was far enough away from the feeling of what she did to me to be able to joke around, but I'm not. She smiles and then stops. "Listen, maybe I'll text you sometime and we can get dinner and talk books or something?"

She's so fucked up. Talk books? Dinner? She thinks that I want to talk about the very thing that came between us? You've got to be kidding me. Hearing how delusional she is reminds me that her leaving me was the best thing. It was painful—in some ways the memories still are, but if I'm being objective it was the best possible outcome for us.

I don't want to be confrontational any more—I just want my coffee and to get the hell out of here, so I decide, despite myself, to just be fake and end this quickly—it's the path of least resistance.

"Sure. You still have my number, right?"

"I do."

"Great. Thanks for the sleeve. Have a good meeting."

"You too."

I walk out stressed. Of all the gin joints.

Life isn't so smooth at the moment.

CHAPTER 21

Cormac

THAT WAS A LONG DAY AT THE office, but I'll take a month of long, unproductive days over running into Maryanne again, even once. She's nuts if she thinks I'll ever text her. I wish things like that didn't cloud the entire day, but for me they did. We ended up seeing four authors, and each one felt flat to me. Most likely they weren't flat and I'm just in a shit mood. That's what Maryanne can do to someone. She's like a dark cloud that can hover over your head, shitting poisonous rain down on you.

I stayed later to do a mountain of paperwork that's been building up. I'm almost done with it when I get a text. Oh no. I'm hoping it's not... *her* again. I rub my eyes, prepare for what I'm going to write if it is her, then open my screen. But it's not Maryanne—it's a different her—one I'm strangely excited to hear from after everything that happened last night.

Tori: Sorry for last night. I said some things I shouldn't have. I didn't mean to ruin our nice dinner. Can I make it up to you?

I stare at my phone like I stared at Maryanne at Starbucks before—only in a good way. This stare isn't horror, it's happy surprise. Since we've met, Tori hasn't given me an inch. I write back right away because I know that was a hard text for her to send.

Cormac: I'm sorry too. How about we both stop doing that and just talk to one another? And what did you have in mind?

Tori: I'll tell you when you get home.

That last texts feels very girlfriend-ish. I don't hate it.

Cormac: Alright, just finishing up some paperwork. I should be home in less than two hours. Who knows with that traffic!

Tori: Okay.

I decide to go full boyfriend on her.

Cormac: You want me to pick up some Chinese on the way home?

Tori: Oh my God, you read my mind! I'd love some.

Cormac: See, I'm psychic like that. Text me your order and I'll stop.

Tori: You're the best. See you soon.

Wait, am I seeing things? Did she just end that last text with a heart emoji? Things are looking up!

THE TRAFFIC WASN'T nearly as bad as I thought it would be— small blessing to end the otherwise shitty day. I stop by this little hole in the wall Chinese place that got surprisingly good reviews on Yelp when I looked before. I got the wonton soup and lo mein, and I got Tori her chicken chow mein and fried rice. Now I'm off to bring it home and see what she has in store for me.

She might be a little right about the stereotypical male thing, because when she said 'I'll make it up to you' my first thought was a blowjob. Now, my rational brain realizes that the odds of walking in to Cynthia's home to a scantily clad Tori, on her knees, mouth open, holding a sign that says "I'm sorry, just keep walking forward" might be a bit of a stretch, but I can't help but go there. I almost crashed twice thinking about it.

I walk in the front. No naked woman. No mouth. No promise of a blowjob. I just see a very neat looking house. She steps out, looking a mess. "Hey."

"Hey. How are you? The place looks great."

"Thanks, I cleaned it up for you—for us."

She must have been hitting the liquor cabinet while I was at work because she looks like a housewife from the 1940's—I'm surprised there isn't a steak dinner and a glass of iced tea waiting for me. I have been keeping the place a little messy. At the office I'm buttoned up, but at home it's a different story. Let's just say I'm not the neatest of human beings. I know it's been driving her nuts because she's the opposite—and a part of me has let it go 'cause I secretly like pissing her off, but now I feel bad that she spent however much time today cleaning up after me.

"Shit, I'm sorry. I meant to pick up those clothes and clean those dishes. You didn't have to..."

"I wanted to. A little peace offering after last night," she says. "Plus, I was sick of looking at the mess. That might have had something to do with it too."

"Just maybe."

"Just a little bit. How was your day?"

I almost blurt out what happened at Starbucks, but I pull myself back. She doesn't need to hear about all that right now. She probably doesn't need to hear about it ever. We're not real, right? It's not like we have some unspoken agreement when it comes to being completely honest and open about our pasts. "Long. It just felt really, really long. You know those days?"

"I know them well. That's how it feels when you're trying to get through the perfect edit on a vlog—when you're stuck somewhere in the middle of it and you're not sure where to go, and you just have to sit there, messing around with the right shots, lighting, and graphics until you have something that you're proud of. Then you edit the crap out of it later to make sure you clean up the mess you left on the page." She smiles, deep in thought, not even looking at me when she's saying that.

"One day I might know what that feels like."

"Oh, right," she says. "Fiction or non-fiction?"

"Fiction. Don't tell Cynthia or Elissa, but I prefer it to non-fiction. Books about real things remind me too much of college. Fiction takes me someplace else. It's an escape."

"I get that. Let's sit down and eat. You can tell me about it."

When we start talking about books I don't even feel the bags of Chinese food weighing down on my fingers. It's a little bit of a sore spot. No matter what I think of her book, part of me is jealous of her, and all the other authors we see, for even having finished books. It's been a dream of mine for a very long time and I just can't seem to pull the trigger.

The dining room table is already set—plates, napkins, all of it. She really became a house wife for the afternoon—but that's not something I'd ever say out loud to her. We'd be fighting in no time, and I've had enough fighting for today.

We sit and eat for a little while, and all I want to know is if this is what she meant by making it up to me for last night. That's when she tells me we're taking a trip Wednesday.

"I was thinking we could hang out and then go on a date in the city."

"I love that idea. I have a few things to do at work, but only in the morning. We can meet after—walk around or something. How does that sound?"

"Perfect. It's sounds perfect."

She's so beautiful that sometimes I forget that we're basically playing house. I feel bad because, at the end of the day, I still really don't love the content that she's trying to put out into the world. But when we're together—at least over the last few days—I don't feel like we're playing, and I don't think of her as that crazy feminist who writes that garbage. Maybe I do need to rethink her book. If Elissa and Cynthia liked it, maybe it's me. The only difference is, of course, I'm a man, and I'm going to have a different perspective on the whole thing.

"I have an idea," she tells me. "We we can flip the switch a little—how about while we're in the city you tell me a little more about *your* book."

I'm really surprised. "Yeah? You really want to hear about what I'm working on?"

"Yeah, of course," she says. "Why not? I mean, if you were my real boyfriend you'd tell me all about a book you were writing, right?"

"I guess I would."

"So, you can tell me. We have to make this as real as possible, don't we?"

That's when she stands up. I sat back down when she told me to, so I'm half expecting a slap from above as she stands right in front of me. But there's no slap. She reaches down and puts both of her Chinese food smelling hands on my face as she leans in and kisses me. Her lips are soft and warm, and I feel my cock harden again—faster this time—the second I realize that she's kissing me. It lasts only a few seconds, but it's definitely not a peck, and the last thing it feels is obligatory. It feels like a place I want to move to—an island where I close my eyes and this happens all day.

She pulls away, slowly. "Thank you for agreeing to this whole thing."

Then she starts collecting all the paper plates and dishes and puts everything in garbage bags.

"You're welcome," I mutter under my breath.

Kiss number one felt amazing. Kiss number two just felt fucking electric.

And here's something I know for sure—one more of those is just not going to be enough!

CHAPTER 22

Tori

I NEED SHOSHANA.

I asked her to come over to Cynthia's place after Cormac left for work. She's going to sample my shitty attempt at home made coffee. I haven't made my own cup in a long time, and apparently Cynthia is quite the enthusiast—she's got like five different machines, all of which are kind of intimidating. I'm standing in their kitchen trying to decide if I need an advanced degree to use them.

There's a regular one. A French press. A Nespresso Machine, a Keurig single serve, and something that looks like it cost about five thousand dollars in the William Sonoma catalog. I'm not touching that thing with a ten-foot pole. I guess I'll go with the good old regular pot, and we'll pray to the caffeine gods that I don't screw things up.

Shosh texted me that she's grabbing some breakfast pastries on her way. I hear a knock on the door and let her in. "Delivery," she jokes.

"Tell me you got..."

"Cheese danish? Duh! Do you not understand that we're psychically linked at this point in our relationship? What did you think I was going to bring, muffins or something basic?"

"No basic bitch muffins. And I love you."

"You don't," she jokes. "You only use me to get cheese danish—that, and my video editing skills. It's an unhealthy love, but it's the best thing I have going right now so I'll take it. Wait, I don't smell the coffee you promised, what's going on? Did you back out on your end of the deal?"

"What's going on is that I just realized that I'm in my late twenties, I'm a hot shot on social media and —hopefully—a soon to be published author, but I can't make a cup of fucking coffee."

She breathes a deep and very fake sigh. "Aren't you lucky your girl is here to save the day once again? I swear, between making you coffee and bringing you your favorite pastry on the same day—I'm expecting you to put out at the end of this breakfast."

"I'd give it up to you anytime you wanted, Shosh, you know that."

"Like you had to tell me." We laugh. I love Shoshana. She makes life a better thing. "Now show me the equipment." We walk into the kitchen and I show her all the machines. She opens her eyes as wide as I've ever seen her open them. "What in the hell is that thing?"

"I'm not sure. But I think whatever it is, Elon Musk invented it. It might be listening to us right now and mining our data, so don't speak ill of it."

"Yeah, we won't be touching that very advanced piece of technology. Let's kick it old school today. I'm gonna take this pot, fill it with water, dump it in the top of this." She grabs the old-fashioned percolator and plugs it in. "Then I'm gonna put grinds... oh, wait, do we even have grinds?"

I look around the room. Nothing. I open up all the cabinets until I find an old Maxwell House can of ground coffee sitting in one right above the sink. "Jackpot." I open the lid and smell. "This might not be the freshest thing in the world. God knows when she opened this."

"I'm surprised that she even has this pot with that... thing, over there. But it'll do. Most ground coffee is stale before you even open it, anyhow. Best way is to grind your own beans, and right before, using a spice grinder."

"Look at you, my little coffee savant. You're like Rain Man."

"I know some stuff. I have my moments."

"I hope you know how to make this dry brown dust into a cup of something that'll wake me up."

"We'll see. Even I have my limits. I assume she has cream and sugar?"

"Assume nothing in this house."

"Okay. Check the fridge while I try to work some magic over here."

I open the fridge and look through some of the groceries that Cormac brought home the other day. I see a fresh, unopened carton of half and half. "Cream, check." I look on the counter. "Sugar, double check. We're good."

She pushes the button and I hear all these cool sounds coming from the machine as black goodness starts to drip down from the top of it. "And the percolations have begun! Why does the lady who lives here have all that stuff in the fridge? Weren't they going to be away for a while?"

"Yeah, they get back around when our thing ends. And Cormac got the half and half and all the other groceries."

"He's a domestic man, huh? That's sexy. He might be a keeper after all."

"You wouldn't think that, right? He comes across like a total... man."

"Here we go," she says, rolling her eyes.

"No, no, I'm not going to say what you think. What I was going to say was that he comes across like everything he's not— he's not really cocky or mean. He's got some surprising layers to him."

"Layers? Oh my God, Tor, you're catching some feelings for mean old Mr. Publisher Man, aren't you?"

"I didn't say that. I just said that he's a little more complex than I gave him credit for at first."

"I'll tell you a secret. Are you ready? Come in closer, I want to whisper it to you—whispers are always more important than when you say things in a regular voice. Are you ready?"

I lean in. "Yeah," I say. "Lay the secret of life on me."

"Okay," she whispers. "I. Think. You. Really. Like. Him. A. Lot."

I hear the last drips of coffee filling the pot. "The coffee's done, grab the accoutrement, will ya? And if I liked him like that I'd tell you."

"It's too early for French words—and you do like him like that, you're just too stubborn to let yourself admit it. I know you too well. I need to investigate a little further though. I'm going to need to ask you a question or two."

"Should I take a deep breath?" I ask.

"You should always take a deep breath when I ask you if I can ask you something. Question one—do you have feelings for him?"

"I told you no."

"Yeah, but you were obviously lying. Just like you're lying now."

"Why do you think I'm lying?"

"Because I know you, and when you know someone you should be able to tell when they're lying—especially if that person doesn't lie very often."

"Are you calling me a bad liar?" I ask.

"I am," she says. "And trust me that's a good thing. So, yes to my first question?"

"But I..."

"Second question—have you... you know? Done the deed?"

"God, Shoshana, no. We just kissed twice."

"Holy shit monster—did you say twice! You mean there was another one after the drunk one, and you didn't tell me?"

"There was also a totally sober post Chinese food one, yes. So now we only have one more to go."

"Okay, now you lost me."

"It was this thing we worked out before this experiment began. It's hard to explain, but I have to kiss him three times. It was an arrangement."

"I'm going to need you to spill the tea on that one, please."

"No tea, just something we worked out. He put this three-kiss clause into our contract."

"Wait, wait, what contract?"

I've never said this out loud to anyone, not even Shoshana. She knows we have this experiment going on, but she didn't know about the contract, or the clause, or any of the specifics. Saying some of it out loud now makes me hear what she's hearing. It does sound a little scandalous.

We make our coffee—lots of half and half and lots of sugar—then we pop a squat at the dining room table to finish talking. I take her through everything—I even show her the napkin we wrote the contract on. She doesn't react exactly how I think.

"Okay, it makes sense now."

"Wait, that's it? I thought you'd be shocked."

"I'd be shocked if you told me you were shaving your head and playing bass in a death metal band. Outside of that, I'm pretty open. Now tell me about these two kisses—were they just to check off the ones you 'owe' him, or did you want to?"

"No, I wanted to—both times. Although I guess I can't really know what I wanted while I was wasted, but I'll assume it happened like he told me. I know that I was thinking about kissing him at the bar before I got drunk. Last night, though, I really wanted to kiss him."

"This changes everything, doesn't it? It's one thing to play house, it's another to kiss a guy and mean it."

"I'm just... I'm not sure those kisses meant the same thing to him that they meant to me, or that he feels anything at all. In that way, he's a typical man—roll your eyes if you want to."

"Not this time," she says. "I know what you mean. Guys are funny when it comes to that stuff—they can do it without emotional attachment. Some of them, anyhow. I don't know exactly why that is, but sometimes it's hard to tell if they're feeling the same thing that we're feeling."

"It is. Guys suck sometimes."

"More than sometimes, in my experience. But when they're

worth it, they're really, really worth it, Tor. The only question is—is Cormac is worth it?"

"I don't know, Shosh. What I do know is that the lines between fantasy and reality are blurring for me, and I don't want to get hurt if I let myself fall for some guy I barely know. What if he doesn't feel the same?"

"Well," she says, thinking about my question. "Did it feel like he meant it when you kissed him last night?"

I stop and think about it, but only for a second. It's not the kind of question that needs a deep analysis—I know what the answer is, and it both excited and scared the shit out of me. "He meant it. I know he did."

"Then that tells you all you need to know. What are you two doing next?"

"We're hanging out in the city tomorrow. Probably after walking around a little we'll go to a nice dinner."

"Well then, sounds like you're going to need a new outfit. How about we go shopping?"

I love my best friend.

CHAPTER 23

Cormac

I'M NOT HATING LIVING IN THE suburbs, but there's no place like New York City. We agreed to meet by the office and then we took an Uber to downtown. It's late afternoon, and the city is buzzing with people. I wouldn't want to be anywhere else right now.

We're walking around with no particular destination in mind, and out of nowhere I see something.

"Oh, do you want a hot dog?"

"Huh?" she asks.

"I love dirty water dogs."

"Ewww."

"Ewww? Are you serious? Long hot dogs in water on the street is one of the best things the city has to offer. How dare you? And you call yourself a New Yorker?"

"Oh, I didn't know sticking disgusting tubes of meat into my mouth made me a good New Yorker. My bad. But you eat the meat for me, okay?"

"Happy to," I say. "Wait…"

She giggles, and I can't believe I didn't catch the joke as it was coming. She must have me distracted. When she giggles her face looks so sweet.

"I'm all good," she jokes. "I will take a pretzel, though. I love those. I'm a salt person, for sure."

"One oversized and over salted New York City pretzel and one dirty water tube of meat, coming up! C'mon," I say, taking her hand. "Let's cross."

Crossing streets in Manhattan should be its own Olympic sport. It's a dangerous and thrilling game of dodge-the-taxis. It takes just the right timing, but we get across to the nice man who's pulling hot dogs out of water. The smells of sauerkraut, onions, and a host of other things that are impossible to tell from one another get more intense the closer we get, and my mouth is practically watering.

"My good man, I'll have one dog and one pretzel, please." Everything smells amazing when you're hungry. I could eat a horse right now, but I'll settle for one of the best hot dogs there is. She takes a big bite of her pretzel, full salt and all. "Looks like I wasn't the only hungry one."

"This is the first thing I'm eating all day, so stop judging me."

"Hey, no judgement here. Do you. I love a girl who can eat her weight in salt." She has some rock salt on her face, and I reach out and rub it off gently with my hand.

"Thank you. And I want brownie points for letting you call me a girl without going all feminist Rambo on you."

"Brownie points granted. I like it when you don't scream at me. I could get used to it."

"I'm not a bitch, you know."

It's a really weird thing for her to say, but that's not what gets me. It's the way she says it—like maybe she's heard that word thrown her way one too many times.

"I never thought that you were." That's a little bit of a lie.

"Oh, c'mon, when I went back at you during my pitch meeting, you didn't let a 'bitch' fly in your head?"

"Well, maybe a little bit, but I don't really use that word a lot. I had a few other adjectives running through my head, but 'bitch' wasn't one of them. You're not a bitch because of you defending your book. And you're definitely not a bitch because you write... I don't even know how to classify it."

"If I remember correctly it was something like radical feminism drivel. Something like that."

I smile. "Something like that, yeah. But something tells me you've had people think of you that way a few times before, haven't you?"

"You should see the comments section in some of my videos. 'Bitch' is the nicest thing anyone says about me."

"Trolls."

"They should be studied. They're like their own species. They never have a picture of themselves, and leave the most hateful comments in a bunch of random videos."

"Does YouTube take them down?"

"Only if someone reports them or they violate community standards, but otherwise those guys living in their parents' basement can click away with their Cheetos-fingers."

"That sucks. Don't read that stuff. And if you do, definitely don't internalize any of it. In real life those guys are exactly what you think they are—losers who have nothing better to do with their lives than hate on others who are way more successful than they are."

"Thanks for that," she says, her big blue eyes looking up into mine. "So," she says, changing the subject, "when does Cynthia get back from her trip?'"

"Not too long from now," I tell her. "Just about at the end of our experiment. Another few weeks or so."

That word is starting to bother me. It's an experiment, for sure, but with each passing day it feels less and less like that, at least to me. It's hard to tell what she's feeling.

"How do you think your partner would react if she knew what we were really using her house for?"

"Knowing Cynthia as well as I do, part of her would laugh hysterically. The other part of her—the partner-in-my-firm part of her—would be horrified."

"Are you ever going to tell her the truth?"

"Eventually, maybe," I tell her. "But I'm not in any rush to tell her we're playing house at her house."

"Is that what we're doing?" she asks. "Playing house?"

"I mean, a little. Isn't that what you wanted to do?"

"I wanted to set up a situation where you could show me a different side of men."

"Right. How am I doing with all that?"

She smiles. The breeze blows her hair in front of her face, and I move it gently to the side. "Not bad. Not bad at all."

We keep walking with no destination in mind. That's the best way to walk around the city, and I'm enjoying just being here with her and talking. We make our stop at the New York Public

Library, which I have to confess I'd never been to before—the only time I'd seen the place is at the beginning of Ghostbusters! But it's majestic, and walking around those stacks with her really did inspire me. After we look around for a while we do a little more walking.

"I'm still hungry," she says. "You want to grab an early dinner?"

I look at my watch. "It would be a really early dinner, are you sure?"

"Yeah, screw it. We can always get Chinese later if I'm still hungry."

"Wow, you really love your Chinese food, huh?"

"What self respecting New Yorker doesn't?"

CHAPTER 24

Cormac

W E FIND A LITTLE PLACE TO EAT during our walk.
If there's any sure thing about the city, it's that there's always
ten places to eat within a short walk from wherever you are.
That, and lots of cabs honking and nearly running you over as you
cross the street. Manhattan is a complicated place.

After we sit down and order some appetizers, Tori jumps into
a subject I never thought I'd discuss with her.

"So, tell me what your book is about?"

"You mean the one I can't seem to finish?"

"Oh, come on, don't beat yourself up."

"It's not just the time," I tell her. "If you told me that I'd have to
wait ten years, but at the end of those ten years I'd have the perfect
novel, I'd happily wait."

"I hate to tell you, Cormac, but there is no perfect novel. It's a
myth. Don't chase it or you'll never finish."

"You sound like you're the one who works at a publishing company."

"You're right," she laughs. "But what I really know—at least after having gone through it—is how difficult it can be. Even though a lot of my book is transcriptions of conversations on my podcast and YouTube channel, I added in a lot of images, original thoughts, and new material that took a long time to put together. I can't imagine writing a whole book from scratch. So don't beat yourself up."

"Sometimes I just stare at my computer. I used to bullshit myself and believe that I was just too busy to get it done. I'd tell myself I had too many clients, or too many meetings to do my own work, and that little self delusion worked for a little while. At least I felt like I had a legitimate reason for not finishing. But then I got so fed up with always telling myself that that I took a day off every two weeks to work on my book, and you know what happened?"

"What?"

"Nothing. Nothing at all. I'd turn my phone off, open my computer, get a drink, and be lucky if I wrote a paragraph after a few hours. It's just frustrating."

"Tell me something. How far along are you?"

"Not sure. Maybe seventy percent of what I wanted to do."

"Well that's great! Seventy percent has the finish line in sight. The way you were talking about it I thought you had like your name and a title and nothing else."

I snicker at the idea. Sounds like something I'd do. Write my name on a Word file and call it a 'book' that I was working on, but luckily, in this case, I have more than that. "It's an almost-book."

"An almost-book?" she asks.

"Yeah. Like, it has a crust forming. It's pulling away from the pan, you know, but still too gooey in the middle to take out of the oven. It's an almost-book."

"See, you're funny. You need to put some of that in your book. It's fiction, right?"

"It is. This may shock you, but it's a romantic comedy. Like Crazy Rich Asians—only not Asian people, and not even close to the plot of that book at all."

"So... it's an almost-book that's not at all like Crazy Rich Asians?"

"Exactly. You're getting it."

We both laugh. I usually don't like talking about my book to other people—it's kind of a sore subject. In fact, there are only five people who know I'm even attempting it. My partners, my brothers, and now Tori. When I first met her, it was the last thing that I ever would have told her, because I know she would have ripped my ideas to shreds, but now I feel comfortable telling her. Not just comfortable, it's helping to talk through it with her.

"You still didn't tell me what it's about, though."

There it is. The question all authors dread. *What's your book about?* I'm sure Tori's gotten this question too. It isn't that we don't like talking about our book, but it's the question itself. There are too many ways to answer it, but I try my best to be a good sport about my own non-book.

"Ummm..."

"I know, we all hate that one. I mean, what's the basic plot?"

"That I can answer. It's a rom-com with two main characters—a guy and a girl—total opposites. Each of their friends knows that they're into one another, but they can't seem to see it. They kind of don't even get along. It's a little John Hughes meets... I'm not even sure."

"But not Crazy Rich Asians."

"Nope," I joke. "Definitely not that. No rich people and no Asians in the book."

"It sounds good," she says. "Now all you just have to finish it so I can read it."

"Tear it apart, you mean."

"No." She stops walking and looks at me pretty seriously, like I might have just said the wrong thing. "Why would you think I'd do that? Just because you did it to me?"

The answer to that question is 'yes', but I don't want to admit it because now I feel like a dick. "Sorry. I thought that maybe you might."

"I have an idea," she tells me, her face softening a little from a minute ago. "How about we not think the absolute worst of one another? Does that sound like a deal?"

"I don't think the worst of you now. Not the real you. Not the you I'm getting to know, I'm sorry."

"That's the funny thing, Cormac."

"What is?"

"They're all the real me. The feminist author at the pitch meeting, the vlogger, the podcaster, and the girl you ate Chinese take-out with who kissed you. They're all me, all bundled into one complicated package. The greatest danger in the world is seeing only one story—seeing a person for only one thing."

"So how do you see me, then? Because you sure as hell didn't see the whole complicated me when we first started this. Actually, I'm not sure there is a whole complicated me, I'm just saying."

I get a smile. It makes her look even more beautiful than she already does. "Of course there is, you know that. And no, we don't ever see one another for who we are from a distance, I realize that. I thought that you were just some big, good looking, jock type who likes beers and football, and hanging out with the guys."

"Wait, go back."

"What?"

"Go back a second. You thought I was what?"

"A big jock."

"Not that part. You thought I was good looking?"

She looks away. I swear, for a second, that she's blushing. "Well, you are."

I throw my hands up in the air like I just won something—maybe that football game she thinks I love so much. I don't have the heart to tell her I'm a baseball guy. I'll let her keep some of her male stereotypes.

"What?"

"Winning!"

"Oh, come on. You know you are. I'm sure you got all the girls in high school and college, right?"

I laugh. And I don't mean a little snicker. I laugh so hard that I'm thankful I don't have any liquid in my mouth. "Are you serious? That's what you think of me?"

"Well, kind of, yeah. I mean, you seem really sure of yourself."

"I am."

"And you're good looking."

"I am, at least according to you a second ago."

"Shut up. You know what I'm saying."

"Ready for the shocking truth? I never had a girlfriend until my junior year in high school. I weighed about a buck twenty-five, soaking wet, back then. I had bad skin and I was pretty shy and into comics. Trust me, no girl wanted any part of me."

"Really? Don't bullshit me."

"I'm not, I swear. I'll be happy to have my parents delve into the old leather-bound family albums to show you some of my high school photos. I was a dork, and a tiny one at at that."

"So what happened?"

"Well, a growth spurt end of sophomore year helped. I sprang up over six feet, but it was that awkward height because I didn't have the weight to go with it, so I just looked like a stick. By senior year I actually listened to my parents and saw a dermatologist to get my skin cleared up. I still read too many comics, though, so that might have been a little bit of a girl repellant."

She laughs. "I was into comics also."

"DC or Marvel?"

"Marvel, of course. DC is trash."

"Complete trash. Except for Batman. He's always been cool. Sometimes Superman, too, but it depends."

"Look," she says. "I would have talked to you in high school. Hell, if you'd talked to me I might have dated you in high school."

"Come on, now who's bullshitting. You're way hotter than I am. I'm guessing you didn't have boyfriends because, well, you're a hater, but with your looks you had to have been asked out all the time."

This time it's her turn to laugh. Unfortunately, she did have liquid in her mouth. It gets everywhere. "Oh my God, I'm so sorry."

"No worries." I look down and my shirt is soaked in a mix of water and spit. "I'm taking that as a no, you didn't get asked out a lot?"

"Wait, let me dry you off."

"It's all good, don't worry."

She gets up from her side of the table and starts patting at my chest with her napkin. At first, I'm a little embarrassed because everyone's looking over at us, but then something else happens—my pants get a little tighter and my dick starts to twitch. I'm the biggest pig in the world for this turning me on. Crap, maybe she does have a point about us men. She's trying to wipe her water-spit combo off my freshly dry-cleaned shirt and I'm taking it like some kind of kinky foreplay. I'm a sick bastard.

"It's all good, don't worry."

"I'm really sorry. And no." She sits back at her side of the table and I try to pretend we're not getting looks from everyone around us. "No boyfriends. Not until college. And even then, just one."

"How come?"

"Believe it or not I was a little hard to get along with."

"No!" I say sarcastically. "Not you, Ms. Warm and Fuzzy. I won't believe that for even a second!"

"Shut up," she jokes. "Look, I'm sorry, I am who I am. I have a well-honed bullshit detector and really high standards. I can't apologize for that."

I notice that the more we talk about this the more she's nervously sipping her wine. The same thing happened when we went to the bar that night. Outside of then and now, I've never really seen her drink at all. "No one's asking you to apologize for anything. We're all who we are. But there has to be something else to it. Forget high school, a lot of people don't have relationships in high school. But college? Why only the one guy?"

There it is again. Another sip from her glass. Granted, it's only wine this time, but still. This must be a bad topic for her, but I'm still interested.

"Can we talk about literally anything else?" she asks.

"I'm sorry. Didn't mean to upset you."

"I'm not upset." Cue another sip of wine. "It's just... a time I'd rather not remember."

"Bad experience?"

She looks at me with a little more intensity than usual, and even through glassy eyes I already know the answer to my question. "Let's just say that the guy—he wasn't exactly what he presented himself to be."

"You mean he was really a woman? Oh my God, are you a lesbian and didn't know it? Now everything is making sense."

"You're such an asshole. I'm gonna spit this wine all over you just like I did the water."

"You wouldn't dare!"

"Try me."

"Alright, alright, I tap out." I pause before I continue. "Can I ask you one more thing without getting spat on?"

"Only because you used the correct past participle of spit correctly."

"Is that the time when you... how do I ask this? Is that the time when you..."

"Started to be a little distrustful of men? Yeah, it is."

"Just because of one douchebag?"

"No, not just because of him. I mean, yeah, because of him at first, but it went deeper than that. I started to see and hear about other girls around me experiencing the same kind of things I had with my ex. One after the other, to the point where I started wondering about guys in general. How could so many women have so many bad experiences and there not be some relationship to the fact that it's always with a guy? I figured that there had to be something there."

"You know what I've been meaning to ask you? How did the whole podcast and YouTube thing happen? How did you become the person our server almost fainted at when she met?"

She takes a deep breath. "So you know how you called me out on never having been in a real relationship?"

"I think I remember that," I say jokingly.

"Well I was in one—a serious one—in college. High school stuff doesn't count."

"God, I hope not. Lord knows I don't wanna be judged by my few high school girlfriends."

"Me either. But I had the one really serious boyfriend in college."

"And let me guess—it didn't end well?"

"That's the understatement of the century. It ended bad—like, real bad."

"And I'm guessing you don't want to tell me any of the details?"

"It's not even that I don't want to tell you about it, it's that I don't want to think about it myself, and it doesn't matter anymore, right? It happened. What matters is what happened to me after."

"And what was that?"

"I changed. Big time. But not just that—every relationship should change you, right? For good or for worse. But what happened was that I started seeking comfort from other women—hanging out with Shoshana and some of the other girls at the dorm way more than I was when I was with him. And that's when it started to happen."

"What?" I ask.

"I started listening to other women's stories. I told them what had happened to me, and they told me similar stories. I realized that we were all around twenty and still had horror stories of our experiences with guys that went back to middle school."

"Yeah, I was a dick in middle school. Kids can be mean, guys especially. I'll give you that."

"At lease you didn't give me the 'we mature later' line. I hate that one."

"I was thinking about it, then I realized it's a piss poor excuse for being an asshole. Immature doesn't have to mean being a bad guy."

"Exactly. And the stories ranged, obviously, from really dumb stuff to some really intense things I can't even repeat."

"Jesus."

"I know. I started asking other girls — ones in my dorm, ones I was friends with or had classes with, then eventually I just went up to strangers. You'd be surprised how open some people will be when they want to get something off their chest."

"So where did the social media stuff come from?"

"The podcast came first, and it's still my bread and butter in terms of my income. It drives my YouTube page likes and subscriptions. It all started with the podcast. I'd heard of them before, but I started listening to one. Then before I knew it, I was listening to all the old episodes and became annoyed when I caught up and had to wait. I started seeing them blow up, but that's not why I started my own. I've never been after fame or money. For me it was always about capturing these collective female experiences and sharing them so that none of us would feel like we were going through things alone. That's how I felt when everything happened with my ex—I felt alone. I wanted to save other women from that feeling by being able to share and listen to what others are going through. It was never about fame, and it sure as hell wasn't about hating men. If I hated men I wouldn't be here with you now."

Hearing those words changes everything, almost instantly. It changes how I see her book, but it also changes how I see her—she's not some man hater, she's a woman who wants to help other women.

"Wow," I say. "I um... I didn't realize that's why you did all this."

"It's not totally your fault," she says. "I got cutesy with the name. I mean, "Women on Dicks" probably sounds like a porno you've seen."

"More than a few times."

She laughs. "But when you get the meaning—that it's about women talking about exes and things they hate about guys and relationships—it all makes sense."

It does all makes sense, and I'm glad she finally felt comfortable enough to tell me. "I hope that maybe—just maybe—I've shown you a different side than what's his name. Experiment or no experiment, I don't want you walking around thinking we're all like that guy just 'cause there are a lot of bad apples."

"I don't think you're like him, Cormac. Not anymore."

"Good." I look deep into her eyes, and for the first time I see vulnerability. "'Cause I really don't want to get spit on again."

"Well I'm getting a little buzzed now, so you never know."

"Please cut it off after that—I can't take another night of worrying you're gonna pull a Janis Joplin on me in the middle of the night."

"I'm NEVER doing that again, don't worry. I don't think I've had such a bad headache in my entire life. But I am feeling it a little."

"Oh yeah? And how much are you feeling it?"

She leans forward. "I have an idea."

"I'm all ears."

"Forget the food. Are you up to finish our talk for the podcast? I have some stuff I've been meaning to ask you—if you can handle it, that is."

"Is that a challenge?"

"It sure is," she says. "You up for it?"

I raise my hand and grab the waiter. "I'm sorry," I say as the guy comes over to our table. "My girlfriend isn't feeling great, we're gonna skip dinner. Just the check, please."

She looks at me, and I swear for a second that I see something that isn't just comfort or vulnerability.

I swear that I see desire in her eyes.

RECORDING SESSION TWO

Aᴏᴏ FTER WE SETTLE THE BILL AND head back home, Tori runs right for the recording equipment. I have to hand it to her— she's driven and focused, and I'm curious what she's going to ask me next. After she's set up, we get into position.

"Are you ready for me to record?" she asks.

"Ready."

"Okay. And... go."

I jump in before she has a chance to do her thing and surprise her with a question of my own. "Hey, can I ask you something?"

"Sure, go ahead."

"Have you interviewed many men for your show?"

"You'd be lucky number one," she says. I'm a little shocked.

"Really? I thought maybe you'd have a few more than me."

"Two things with that," she says. "We thought about having a weekly spot for guys to come and discuss their points of view on some of these issues, but we couldn't find enough guys who wanted to participate. Also, when we did have a guy on the show, they didn't like how bluntly we talked about things. You'd be surprised how many guys are bashful with talking about sex on record—especially for a book that's going to—hopefully—be in stores forever."

"Nice little pitch you did there," I joke.

"I'm glad you appreciate it. Just remember it in a couple of weeks from now."

"Noted. Now, back to these total pussies who don't want to talk sex with you..."

"Total pussies? Please define."

"Oh, come on, stop being a researcher for a second, you know what I mean. We all know a pussy or two."

"Whether I know what you mean or not, just define it for me."

"A pussy. A beta male. A soft man. A guy who's a bitch. You know, a pussy."

"Don't you get the irony of being called a pussy?"

"Irony?"

"Yeah, the irony of it is that men use it to describe other weak men."

"Right. So what?"

"So—if you want to do that, then you should call them testicles."

"Sorry, Tori, you lost me there. What are you saying?"

"Let's have an anatomy lesson, shall we? A pussy is probably the single strongest part of a woman. A fucking human being can come out of it, for God's sake. That's not weak, my friend, that's powerful. Balls, on the other hand? Have you ever hit a desk corner, nicked your sack, and almost doubled over in pain?"

"Nice touch, Tori. And yes, many times."

"You're proving my point. Women can have babies, and men can't even tap that area without wanting to go to the hospital and complaining that their stomachs hurt. Pussies are powerful, balls are weak, end of story. You're using the wrong word to describe each other."

"Alright. I'll give you that one. You earned it."

"Why thank you, Kylo, you know how to make a girl feel special."

"Don't you mean 'woman'? Don't want to demean yourself by using sexist terms like 'girl.'"

"Eh, I'm okay with it. I'm taking that one back, like 'bitch'— we should own our own words. I can call myself a girl if I want to—but you can't."

"So, since I'm lucky number one, what would you like to hear from a guy's perspective?"

"I think our female audience would like to know about sex. How often do you think about it?"

"You mean like, per day? Per hour?"

"Let's start with per day and then we'll scale down if we have to."

"Oh, we'll have to, trust me. And I'd say I think about sex... at least ten times a day. Probably north of that, I've never actually counted."

"Wow."

"But you have to remember what you're asking. Thinking about sex can mean any time the subject comes up. That can be talking to a beautiful woman, such as yourself, or listening to another guy talk about it, or seeing a sex scene in a movie I'm watching, or listening to a sexy lyric in a popular song. There's context, is my point. It's not like I'm just sitting at my desk watching porn on my phone."

"Nice transition," she says, smiling. "I was just about to go there."

"Go where?"

"To porn—that was my next question."

"Now we're getting somewhere!"

"What kind of stuff do you watch? What do you like?"

"My tastes vary. It depends on my mood."

"Okay, fine, you don't want to reveal your fetish porn favorites. I get it, people are listening. So how about this—tell our listeners what it feels like to walk around with a hard on. I think every woman has wondered about that one."

"Walk around? Like, literally?"

"What do you mean?"

"You don't walk around with a hard on. In fact, the last thing you do is walk around."

"You know what I mean."

"So the question is 'how does it feel to have a hard on?' Is that more accurate?"

"Sure."

"It feels amazing. Until it doesn't, that is."

"And when doesn't it?"

"After about ten minutes, if you don't take care of it."

"I'm sorry, 'take care of it?'"

"Yeah, you know? Take care of it—like, yourself. Or, preferably, with a woman lying next to you. Either works. The problem is when you don't take care of it. That's when you get a wicked case of blue balls."

"I always thought that was a myth. Something guys said to get girls to... take care of them."

"Trust me, it's very real. And it fucking hurts after a while. Like a soreness."

"Interesting. So, that's a pretty seamless transition to what I really want to ask you about, and what we've been dancing around this entire time. Sex."

"Yes! It's about damn time we got to the good stuff. Lay it on me—figuratively speaking, of course. Or maybe literally. That's totally up to you."

"Keep dreaming. I have some pointed questions, if you don't mind entertaining me."

"I live to entertain you. Go ahead."

"Number one: why do so many men skip foreplay and try to jump straight to sex?"

"Not all men skip foreplay. I love it, myself, so maybe I'm not the right guy to ask."

"No, actually. That might make you an even more interesting guy to ask. Tell me the opposite, then. What is it about foreplay that you like?"

"Even though I'm not ever going to try to speak for all men, I can at least take a stab because I have a lot of friends and two younger brothers, and we all talk about the girls that we've been with. I know a lot of guys see foreplay as a waste of time—they just want to get to to the good stuff, you know?"

"You and euphemisms. 'The good stuff?'"

"Most of the guys I know see the other stuff as things you do in high school with your first girlfriend before you actually start having sex with grown women. But like I said, that's not how I feel at all."

"I appreciate you trying to offer an explanation, but now tell me how you feel about foreplay—why you feel so differently from the guys you know?"

"For me, it's almost all about the foreplay. And trust me, I'm not just saying that to sound like the best guy ever—I mean it. Look, don't get me wrong, the sex is the best part of the whole thing, but I almost love the build up just as much."

"Interesting."

"You're saying that a lot, you know. I thought you thought of me as some caveman."

"I do. You are. But that doesn't mean that you can't have a moment or two of being interesting here and there. Right now is one of those moments."

"What's interesting about what I'm saying?"

"Who's interviewing who here?"

"Just asking."

"You answer me and maybe I'll answer you. Be specific. What do you like the most about foreplay? Don't leave out any details. And before you go into your euphemisms again, use any language that you like. Be as vulgar as you like."

"Okay, just remember you said that, Tori."

"Noted. Go ahead."

"To me, a woman's body is one of the most beautiful things in the world. Her shape, the feel of her, the smell of her. And being with a woman uses every single sense—sight, touch, smell, all of it. Foreplay is where you get to experience each of those at the same time. I love the taste of her mouth—the way her lips and her tongue make their own sort of flavor, and how that flavor passes from her into me. I love to savor that taste."

"Hmmm..."

"Interesting?"

"Maybe. Keep going."

"The next thing I love to savor is her smell—and the magical thing is that every woman smells differently. Her hair, her skin, every part of her has its own smell that you take in when you breathe her in, and it stays inside your nose. But as amazing as those both are, they're not even the best part."

"What's the best part then?"

"The touch. The feel. The way her skin against mine makes me feel. Her cheek against mine. Her hands running through my hair. Her soft breasts pressing into my chest. The feeling of her is everything. Then, of course, the payoff. The sex. The thing that's ten times better when you experience everything else that comes before it—the main course to some pretty amazing appetizers."

"Wow."

"What? Did I say something wrong? You said to use whatever language I wanted."

"No. You didn't say a thing wrong—not at all. That was... unexpected."

"Well I'm glad to surprise you. I meant it."

"I know. I can tell when someone's not being truthful. I know you meant every word of that."

"Do you want me to keep going?"

"I really do, Kylo. But not on here. I'm shutting my mic off now."

CHAPTER
25

Tori

"WHY DID WE STOP?" HE ASKS. "Did I say something wrong?"

It's a valid question, but I'm not going to answer it, even though that answer is 'absolutely not, Cormac, you said everything right.' I'm done talking, and I'm taking a hiatus from thinking. I don't know what's come over me, but all I want right now is his body.

He's sitting where he sat during our last interview—across on the other side of the couch from me. His eyes are sparkling, and after listening to his words, I see him differently. My body wants his like a starving woman wants a plate of food, and since I've just shut off the rational part of my brain, that's exactly what I'm going to get.

I pounce on him, and bury my face deep in his neck. He smells amazing. That musk of his gets me every time, only this time I'm going to do something about it. I start sucking on his neck hard, and I half expect him to pull me off and ask me what the hell I'm doing, but he only does half of that.

He does pull me off, but only to flip me over and end up on top of me on the couch. One of my arms and legs are draped off the side, and he positions his body between my legs. As soon as he does, the fact that I'm dripping wet becomes acute to me, and I start to become aware of my entire body in a way I'm not used to at all. I'm an intellectual—I use my brain for most things, and my body is always just kind of there to carry my head around. I've never been this aware of every sensation before—every nerve ending, all the little hairs on the back of my neck, and the throbbing that's happening between my legs. It's all coming into sharp focus as he takes his turn and buries his face in my neck.

The pressure of him feels incredible. I wrap my free arm and leg over his huge back and squeeze as I pull him down even closer, until there's no space between our bodies. He keeps working his mouth over every inch of my neck, using his lips and his tongue perfectly. The heat in my body is growing with every second that passes, and pretty soon I'm going to need him to take this to the next level.

I don't have to wait long. I feel his hand descend from the side of my face, along the side of my breast, past my hip, and over between our bodies. I'm wearing a skirt that he lifts up easily, moves my soaking wet underwear to the side and puts his finger deep inside of me. I gasp. I haven't felt this in so long that it takes a second to get used to, but, once I do, I never want him to stop.

He keeps his finger moving slowly in and out of me, and with his thumb he circles my clit in slow, powerful strokes. Once he

starts doing that, I can't sit still any longer. It's like I'm possessed—
my body starts to move beneath him. My back arches and I make
the kind of noises you only hear in movies. I never want him to
stop.

He leans his face next to my ear while he fingers me. "How
does that feel?"

"Amazing. It feels amazing, Cormac. Don't stop."

"Oh, I don't plan to."

"Oh, fuck!"

He sits up and takes off his shirt, and that's when I get my
first full view of his upper body. He's a Greek god. He's not even
flexing and I can see his pecs and six pack right in front of me. I
reach out and put my hands on his chest so that I can feel him,
and it feels like he's chiseled out of stone.

He puts his face next to my ear. "I've wanted to fuck you since
the first time I ever saw you. You're the most beautiful woman I've
ever seen in my entire life."

That's all I need to hear, because I know that he really means
it. "Fuck me, Cormac. Right now!"

He stands up from the couch and finishes undressing. His
shirt is already gone, which only leaves the clothing that's hiding
the good parts from me. He takes off his pants quickly, like he
can't wait any longer to have me. His underwear follows, and that's
when I get a good look at what I'm about to experience. I don't
have a lot to compare it to, but I don't need experience to know
how massive he is. "Are you ready?" he asks.

I sit up and take my clothes off. Normally I'd feel self-
conscious sitting here as naked as the day I was born in front of
a man I don't know that well, but Cormac doesn't give me any

weird feelings like that. I feel comfortable. More than comfortable, it feels perfect.

He stands me up and turns me around. I fall on my hands and my ass goes up in the air. In seconds he's inside me—his strong hands using my shoulders for leverage as I feel his long, hard cock penetrate me again and again. He slides his hands to my hips. He's so big!

I close my eyes and relax my body completely. He can do whatever he wants to me right now.

We're shaking the entire couch. With every single thrust we move a little more, until we're both off balance. He pulls out and I turn around and put my back against the back of the couch. He takes my ankles and spreads me open slowly before dropping to his knees in front of me.

His tongue hits the right spot, and he makes these small circles with it, making me even more wet. Before I know it, his finger slides back inside of me as he worships me with his tongue, making me sweat. He lays me down on my back again and puts his giant manhood back inside me. It slips in with no effort at all, and he fucks me faster and harder than I've ever experienced.

"Are you close?" he asks. "I want to make sure you come."

Normally I'd just fake it, like I used to do with my ex, but he's broken down all of the walls I built to keep men at a distance, so I tell him the truth. "I've... I've never."

"What?" He's still inside of me, moving in and out really slowly while his body hovers over mine and he looks deep into my eyes.

"I've never come before. Not like this."

"Well, we'll just have to do something about that, won't we?"

He stands up, and I don't know why. My body feels empty and cold without him on top of it. "Where are you going?"

"You'll see."

He lifts me up like I weigh nothing and carries me into the bedroom. He lays me down on the bed and then walks to the closet. After rummage around for a second, I see him take out my suitcase and throw it down on the ground. Then I realize what he's doing. *How did he know? Eh, who cares?*

He's got BOB in his hands—in all his huge, vibrating glory. "This might be able to help in that department."

Cormac comes back to the bed and lays down next to me. He looks around for how to turn it on. I grab it. "Here." With a click of my fingers, the light buzzing sound begins to fill the room. Cormac gets this huge, mischievous grin on his face, like he just discovered a new continent. He puts BOB next to my leg and climbs back between my legs.

In seconds he's back inside me, and we're going at it again. It feels incredible. But it's nothing compared to what I think is about to happen when I feel him reach over. He sits up, still inside me, and as he thrusts in and out, he places BOB right over my clit and I feel like I'm going to explode.

He keeps fucking me, looking down into my eyes with those beautiful blue orbs of his while he does. His left hand is on my breast, playing with my sensitive nipples while he rubs BOB over me gently. I feel the intensity building. At first, it's a slow burn, but quickly it becomes an inferno, and my entire body gets involved. I feel hot, flushed, and there's a happy pressure building by the second between my legs that's about to give way.

Cormac turns up the speed on BOB, and my body follows along on the ride. It's happening so fast now that I know it's going to happen any second. Oh, my God, I can feel myself starting to shake. I'm about to...

"Oh, fuck!!!!"

I come so hard that I feel like I'm in a trance—some Buddhist monk level meditative state where I lose all sense of self, and all I'm conscious of is the exploding happening inside of my body. It only lasts a few seconds, but when it's over I have the most satisfied feeling I've ever experienced in my life.

When I open my eyes, I see Cormac ready to explode himself. He pulls out, and now it's his turn to experience the kind of pleasure I just did. I sit up and take all of him in my mouth. He's huge, but I fit every inch of his throbbing hardness inside, all the way to the back of my throat. I can feel the little spasms his cock is making as I use my mouth to bring him closer.

He leans back and grabs my head as I blow him. He's moving around like a wild animal, screaming my name as his cock fills my willing mouth. It doesn't take long. "I'm going to come so fucking hard right now!"

He pulls himself out of my mouth a split second before he explodes all over me. All over my chest, my hands, and even on my face. His whole body tightens as he shoots his hot cum all over me.

He collapses next to me. We're both breathing like we just ran the New York City marathon, only instead of soreness and pain, all I feel is happy and warm.

"I guess we made all three?" he says.

"What do you mean? All three of what?"

"Kisses. You met the quota we agreed on."

I stop and think for a second. "I don't think I did, actually. We didn't kiss."

"We didn't?"

"Think back for a second."

He sits up and stares at the ceiling for a few seconds. "You know, you're right. We just had some no-kiss sex."

"I think we did."

"And you know what that means, don't you?"

I know what he's going to say before he says it. And for once, I'm happy about that.

"Yeah, yeah," I joke. "I still owe you one."

"You sure do."

CHAPTER 26

Tori

Thursday, July 20th

S o, I THINK I'M IN LOVE with orgasms.

I never understood the big deal before.

Now I get it. I really get it. In fact, I got it twice last night thanks to the magic of Cormac's fingers, tongue and that amazing cock of his.

I finally understand what the expression 'post coital bliss' refers to, because I totally feel blissful right now. The room still smells like a combination of sex and that man musk that comes off of Cormac—I love that smell, he should bottle and sell it. Every woman in the world would buy it.

I really never thought that I'd end up in bed with him when we started this whole thing. But then again, there were a lot of things I thought of differently before I met him.

Right now he's in the shower, and I'm being super lazy, taking my sweet time to stretch out my arms and legs in what might be the most comfortable bed in history. Seriously, I'm not this kind of person, but I could literally lie in here all day.

But I can't actually do that—I have a vlog I want to do, so I have to get my butt up and get ready as soon as Cormac's out of the shower.

I head into the kitchen to make myself a cup of coffee now that Shoshana showed me how. A little caffeine can go a long way in the morning. Not that I need it—I'm still high off of last night. The smell of him is still all over me and when I close my eyes I can see him on top of me. I stand next to the coffee maker and picture it, reliving every moment. I don't want to open my eyes, I just want to live inside that memory for as long as I can.

I do open them when the loud vibration of Cormac's phone rouses me from my remembering. He must have left it out to charge. I look down and see the text. Who's texting him first thing in the morning? Jesus, listen to me—I'm having girlfriend thoughts. I don't mean to be nosey but I can't help but look down. I read what's on the screen.

Maryanne: Great seeing you the other day. I loved reconnecting. You looked great. I loved our talk. You said you wanted to get dinner? How about you come by my place tonight? Let me know. I'll get some wine and we can talk about my new book like we discussed.

What the holy fuck is this? I can't believe my eyes.

In the time it takes for the rest of the hot water to drip itself into the pot, I've re-read that message about seven times. Each time my heart rate gets faster and faster, and I feel a range of emotions from frustration to anger to curiosity. Who the hell is Maryanne? Why is she getting dinner with Cormac? And he looked good? Who is the woman?

I check myself when my internal dialogue shifts from girlfriend thoughts to petty jealous girlfriend thoughts. I take a deep breath as I pour my coffee. First of all, Tori, you're not his girlfriend, you're just his fake girlfriend. Second, you had sex once—and no matter how amazing it felt—and it was amazing— you're not in an actual relationship with this man. And third, you secretly read his texts on a phone that he left in here right before he slept with you.

I'm not convincing myself of anything. I wish the rational part of my brain was working, but all I'm feeling is jealously. I know what I should do. I'm going to drink my coffee, and when he gets out of the shower I'll talk to him about it. Or maybe I shouldn't. Jesus, I don't know what to do. Is this what relationships are like? Confusion, suspicion, not knowing how to act in different situations? Uhh...

I leave my cup of coffee. I don't want it any more. I get dressed as fast as I can and head out the door before he's even out of the shower. I called him a coward, but I'm the one who feels like a coward right now. I should have stayed and said something to him—asked him what the text was about? Asked him who Maryanne is, and asked why her text sounds like there's more going on with them than just friendship. But I don't. I walk out, angry and jealous and wondering why I ever started this experiment in the first place.

I have one last recording that I need to do with him, but right now I don't want to think about it. I just feel like crying. God, this is so not like me! I'm every female stereotype that I hate right now, but I can't help the way that I feel. Before I back out of the driveway, I take out my phone and text him so he doesn't think anything's wrong.

Me: Hey. I had to run out. Have a meeting this morning. Let's do the final interview tonight.

Now all there's left to do is obsess over my crazy thoughts of him and this chick Maryanne. How the hell did I let myself get here?

CHAPTER
27

Cormac

L AST NIGHT WAS AMAZING.

I'm the first to admit that I was wrong about everything I thought about Tori. She showed me a completely different version of herself last night, and it's a version that I love being around.

She doesn't know this, but I'm going into the office today to read the rest of her book, only now I'm going to look at everything with fresh eyes and a more open mind. If I like what I read, I'm going to offer her a publishing contract.

I'm not telling her any of that though. I want it to be a surprise.

Cynthia has one of those cool showers with jets on all sides of you, so I spent a little extra time letting the steaming hot water hit every part of my body. I have to get one of these at my place. When I step out, the bathroom is a white cloud. I towel off quickly and open the door to see... an empty bedroom?

"Tori?" I call out. Maybe she's in the kitchen. "Tori?" Nothing. I dry off completely, throw on my boxer briefs, and look around the house. She's nowhere to be found and I start to worry. I was only in there like fifteen or twenty minutes, where the hell could she have gone?

I forgot that my phone was charging in the kitchen. There's a text on here from... Maryanne? What the hell does she want? She can wait. I scroll down looking for a text from Tori. There it is. Oh, she had a meeting. I text her back.

Me: No worries. I understand. And yeah, tonight is perfect.

When I'm done, I go through my other texts. There's one from Maxwell, saying that he had a great time the other night and telling me for the second time how hot he thinks Shoshana was.

Me: I'll put in a good word. Btw I have to tell you about last night with Tori. Hit me up.

Then I look at my last text, from the woman herself. I read it twice, and by the second time I realize how crazy that bitch really is. She's twisted every part of the conversation we had the other day at Starbucks. Dinner? Talk about books? She thought I actually wanted to see her again after I spent the whole conversation last time telling her the opposite.

Me: I'm surprised you wanted to see me again after our tense coffee encounter.

It's pretty early in the morning, so I don't expect her to write me back, but I see the bubbles at the bottom of my screen. Guess being a bestselling author leaves her more free time that I thought. About two seconds later my phone vibrates.

Maryanne: Of course I want to see you again. I want to talk about my newest book. I was thinking of using your company again, if you'd have me.

Holy shit. The audacity of that woman. She used me, broke my heart, got famous off the resources and opportunities that we gave her, and then jumped ship to our biggest rival. Now she wants to come back? Was she using me the other day when we were in line at Starbucks?

But, at the same time, the businessman in me is interested in her offer. What if she really wants to come back to us? We're at a low point in terms of famous and bestselling authors, we could really use Maryanne and the revenue that she'd bring in. But that would mean having to be around her all the time. I'm not sure it's worth it, but maybe I need to at least hear her out. What would Elissa and Cynthia think if they found out that a New York Times bestselling author offered to go with our company and I turned her down without consulting them?

I hate that I'm going to say this, but I write back that I'll meet her at the bar we used to go to tonight at eight, and I'll hear her out. Then I remember that I have to text Tori and cancel our recording. I feel like shit doing that, especially after the amazing night we had, but I don't think that I have much of a choice. I need to exorcise the ghost of Maryanne once and for all. I text Tori:

Me: I hate to do this, don't hate me. I need a rain check on the interview if that's okay. I have a meeting with a big potential client tonight so I won't be around for dinner. So sorry.

I hope I'm not making a huge mistake by going tonight.

CHAPTER 28

Tori

I DIDN'T THINK I COULD FEEL ANY WORSE than I felt when I left Cynthia's place.

Turns out that *rock bottom* is just an expression, because I feel much worse after the text I just got.

I decided to come to Shoshana's instead of hiding out at some coffee shop or something. I decided to save the sobbing for the far more dignified location of the inside of my car, which is currently parked in her driveway.

I text her that I'm here. I don't mention the part where I'm in complete hysterics right outside of her front door. She'll find that out soon enough. I knock on the door, and Shoshana gets to start her day off with a closeup of my ugly cry face.

"Oh my God, what's wrong?"

"I'm not sure where to start."

"Well, start by getting your butt in here."

I sit down on her couch and bury my face in my hands. I don't know what's come over me. Well, actually, I know exactly what's come over me—first it was pettiness and jealously, and now it's just straight jealously.

"Look!" I say like a crazy woman, holding my phone up and showing it to Shoshana. She looks at me like I'm as crazy as I am.

"Okay? Wait, it'll be like a game. We'll call it 'why is my best friend losing her mind?' —there's no prize at the end, except your sanity, of course, and there's only one player—me—but it still might be fun."

"This is no time for joking. Did you see?"

"*Aaaand* the game is over, never mind. Ummm... let me look again in case there was some subliminal message kind of thing that I missed. It's possible, I'm always the last to..."

"Just look!"

She takes the phone from my hand and scrolls a little through the texts before looking at me, once again, like I'm a character in Cuckoo's Nest. "I looked. Three times. I'm really trying here. All I'm seeing is that he canceled an interview or something tonight. Does that matter?"

I compose myself. I can't be this woman for too long. I'm still upset, but I stop the tears long enough to explain—and explain I do. I tell her about the text I found from this Maryanne person, and about his last text.

"I thought it was all in my head until he sent that last one."

"Walk me through it again."

"I'm thinking Maryanne is an ex, or maybe a woman he met. I don't even know. She said that she wanted to meet him tonight, so I texted him asking if we could do our last interview instead. I've been recording a podcast with him that I'm going to transcribe like an interview into the back of my book. May post the podcast, I don't know. We only have one recording session left and I asked him to do it tonight. Then I left because I didn't want to confront him about the whole thing after last night, and then..."

"Wait—pause crazy rant a second. Last night?"

"We had sex. Like... we really had sex. Crazy sex. Animal sex."

"I see," she says in her softest voice. "Listen, I'm going to listen to the rest about the text and all that, but then you're going to backtrack and tell me all about said animal sex. This isn't a request on my part, mind you, it's a friendship demand! Now, go on."

"So," I say, jumping right back into what I was saying before. "I texted him to do the last interview for the book, and he said yes. Then, right after, he texted me a second time and said he had to meet a client or something and that he needed to reschedule our interview."

"Right?"

"Come on, you're not stupid Shoshana. Put two and two together. He's obviously meeting this Maryanne tonight. I finally let my guard down and let myself feel something for Cormac. Then I slept with him. It was amazing, and the next morning I find out he's seeing another woman."

"Alright, I see the issue here." She moves over right next to me so that we're practically shoulder to shoulder. "A few things. You're doing that thing you do again."

"What thing?" I ask.

"Assumptions. You're making a lot of them. I mean, yes, what you think is happening is a possibility, I'm not gonna lie to you, but I don't think it's very likely. I think you might be connecting dots that don't actually connect."

"You should have read her text to him, Shosh. This Maryanne..."

"I know, you said it was flirty."

"Flirty. Thirsty. There are more adjectives that I could come up with, trust me."

"I'm sure you could—you're an amazing podcaster and author after all. You have command of all those cool adjectives the rest of us struggle with. But you didn't see what he wrote back to her, right?"

"No. I left."

"Okay, so let me walk you through some of your assumptions, 'cause there are many. I don't actually have a PowerPoint presentation ready, but you're smart, you can follow me."

I smile. Just a little. I can't help it when I'm around her. "You really think I'm being nuts."

"Hold please." I furrow my brow as Shoshana reaches for her own phone.

"What are you doing?"

"Hold, please!"

"Sorry, Jesus."

After a few clicks I hear the song playing. "Now there's no time for our usual game, and technically this is an 80's song, but still."

I almost start cracking up as I hear Ozzy Osbourne's voice screaming out of Shoshana's phone.

"...I'm going off the rails on a crazy train!"

"Very funny."

"Wait, wait, they haven't even gotten to the solo yet."

"Shut up." I'm laughing. I can't help it. I know she's right, that I'm being a little emotional and over the top, even for me, so I try to pull it back and listen to what she has to say. "Alright, I get it. Go on with what you were saying. I need your logic right now."

"And I need to get to the guitar solo, but whatever." She puts her phone away, and without missing a beat goes right back into her explanation as to why I'm strapped firmly to the crazy train. "What I was saying is that two and two don't always equal four. Sometimes they do, but in this case, you might be off. Maybe there actually is a new client. Maybe there isn't but he doesn't feel like doing an interview about gender, so he's going out with friends and didn't want to hurt your feelings."

"You really think it's one of those things?" I ask. "They sound a little implausible to me."

"I'm not saying one way or the other, all I'm saying is that it could be something you're not thinking of. But you have it set in your mind that he's out gallivanting with some hot ex who wants to bang him."

"Did you just use the word 'gallivanting'?"

"I sure did, and I'll do it again if I have to."

"Please don't, I'm begging you."

"I won't," she jokes. "But only if you don't act crazy anymore. What you need to do is talk to him directly. You've never had a problem being direct—you're one of the most straight forward, confrontational people I know. I've never known you to shy away from speaking your mind. What's going on?"

"I don't know. It's... it's him. He does something to me that I've never felt before. I'm different around him—more submissive, more likely to get emotional, more..."

"Like a typical woman?"

I look up sharply. I don't like the sound of that at all, but I have to admit, she's right.

"Kind of. I'm not used to it."

"Cormac really must be different, because..." she clears her throat. "He makes you feel... he makes you feel... he makes you feel like a natural..."

"Stop singing right now. Damn, you're on a pop song roll today."

"I don't know why, it's just flowing out of me. Your problems are super musical, you know that? If they ever make your relationship story with Cormac into a movie I've got the soundtrack set!"

"You're nuts, you know that?"

"I know. But I'm also your best friend, and I've been where you are more than you have. I'm telling you, take my advice, you need to go communicate with him directly. It's the best way to find out what's going on."

She's right, and that's exactly what I'm going to do. Maybe we can do the interview after he's back from wherever he's going— which is definitely not to go see an ex. I take out my phone to text him.

Me: I need to hit a deadline. Can we finish the podcast stuff after you get home later? I promise it won't take long. Cross my heart.

He writes back right away.

Cormac: You got it. Maybe around ten or so? I'll let you know when I'm on my way home.

Me: Perfect. See you then.

Shoshana's right. I'm just not used to having a guy as great as Cormac turned out to be in my life, and I'm sure as hell not used to all this relationship stuff. I'm just emotional. Post-coital. A new girlfriend who's being a little jealous.

"Alright, I texted him."

"Good," Shoshana says. "Now, about that animal sex?"

CHAPTER 29

Cormac

WHAT THE HELL AM I THINKING?

I must be out of my mind. I should have turned her down flat when she sent me the most random of all random texts. It was rough seeing her in the line at Starbucks, so I don't know why I agreed to this drink. Actually, I'm lying, I do know why.

I had two different reactions when I saw her text—one as her ex-boyfriend and the other as a partner in my company.

The boyfriend reaction was immediate nausea, but the partner reaction was seeing dollar signs flashing before my eyes. I ignored the first and listened to the second—maybe I should have done the opposite, who knows? But here I am, pimping myself out because our firm could really use the attention and revenue that a big-time author like Maryanne could bring in. I hope this is all worth lying to Tori. This place used to be where we came to hang out with our mutual friends when we were together. I lost all of them—authors mostly—in our breakup.

Podcast or no podcast, I really can't wait to see Tori later. We had one of *the* most passionate nights ever, but then she was gone when I got out of the shower this morning. I had a full day of work, and now I'm walking into an old bar to see my ex. It's not exactly how I pictured the morning after such amazing sex with a great woman. But at least we can hang out later. And who knows—maybe she'll be up for another session!

But right now, all that's on the back burner.

I see Maryanne, already waiting for me at the end of the bar. She's looking good—I'll give her that—although I don't really care what she looks like much anymore. It's funny how thinking of her made me sad, but having seen her face to face twice in such a recent timeframe, I really don't miss her at all anymore.

She waves me over. She ordered me a vodka and Sprite. That used to be my drink when we were together. I haven't touched one since. She really is living in the past, it's kind of sad. "Hey."

"Hey!"

She gives me the biggest hug ever. She also yells hello a little too loud. The guy who's now staring at us at the end of a very crowded and loud bar should not have been able to hear her, but that's how screechy she is.

"Have you been waiting for me for a long time?"

"No, not long, like fifteen minutes. I had a meeting and I came here right after. That's why I look all fancy."

She really does. And I don't trust her as far as I can throw her, so I'm taking every word that's coming out of her mouth with a grain of salt. "How'd the meeting go?"

"Not so great," she says. "I left Mifflin."

Mifflin is our biggest competitor, and currently our most vicious competitor also. They pilfered three popular authors from us, including Maryanne, and another three more in the last year alone. I'm a little shocked to hear this, but I also don't completely believe her.

"Really?" I ask. "How come? I thought you were happy over there."

"The past tense being the key there. I *was* happy. I mean, I know you don't want to rehash our past."

"I'd rather not, no."

"But in terms of the deal they gave me, they don't get much better in this industry. They were great. They gave me money, distribution, a great royalty deal, all of it, but that was when I was on the rise. Now that my contract is up and I'm an established name in the industry, they want a much deeper cut of all of my profits, and I'm not having it. We've been going back and forth for a few months, trying to negotiate a new contract, but they just won't budge."

I smile. Part of me is doing the I-told-you-so dance in my head.

"They don't need to budge anymore," I tell her. "Not trying to be a dick, but after you jumped ship and took Terry and Jillian with you..."

"I know, I know. I empowered them."

That's an understatement. She made that company. And now they're acting like the predatory assholes I've always known them to be. Birds of a feather.

"That's right. And now they're realizing that they have the negotiating power. Are the others jumping ship with you? Or is it just you?"

"Right now, just me. But who knows? Maybe they'll follow me."

"So it's one hundred percent? You're leaving them for good?"

"I just did. Signed, sealed, delivered. Or maybe I should say 'unsigned.' I'm a free agent now."

"I promise you this isn't a disingenuous question, but why are you telling me all of this? We haven't exactly kept in touch since things ended—minus that weird coffee encounter."

"That wasn't weird—it was the universe trying to tell us something."

Holy crap. This is it. She's finally lost it. "How's that?"

"Think about it. I haven't seen you in forever, and then right as my contract is coming to an end with a publishing company I'm not happy with, we run into each other? What are the odds?"

"I don't know what the odds of that happening are, but there are a few things I do know. For one, we haven't spoken in forever—by your choice, not some accident of the universe keeping us from one another. If you remember, I tried to text you a few times after we broke up, and you ghosted me like I was yesterday's news."

"Do we really have to go over this old stuff?"

"Trust me, I don't want to talk about it any more than you do, but your whole theory of the universe bringing us together right now seems to be predicated on the idea that the universe was somehow keeping us apart—and that's not the case. You broke up with me, you didn't want to have anything to do with me after the fact, and us running into each other was just a random accident."

"So does that mean you don't want to resign me?"

And there she is—the real Maryanne—cutthroat, business like, and cold. I've been waiting for her to show her face, and she just did. Good to see you again.

"To tell you the truth, I haven't even thought about it. The tone of your text was a little strange and I wanted to see what was on your mind. I suspected we'd end up here, but I wanted to see for myself."

"And?" she asks.

"And what?"

"If—and that is a big if, by the way, you're not the only big firm in town—if I was interested in resigning, are you interested in having me back?"

"I'd have to speak to Elissa and Cynthia."

"I'm not asking about your partners," she says curtly. "I wasn't fucking them. I was fucking you, and I want to know if I come back how it's going to be between us. So? Are *you* interested in having me back?"

I was wrong before. This wasn't a mistake. This was exactly what I needed to say goodbye to the past. I was pining for the ghost of what Maryanne and I had—if we ever even had that at all—but reality is hitting me square in the jaw right now. Everything about how she's speaking to me—from the changes in her tone, to the strategic use of flattery, to her referring to a serious relationship as us 'fucking'—all of it gives me the clarity I lacked for such a long time.

I stand up, take the smallest sip of the drink she got for me, and get ready to walk right out the door and never speak to her again. It doesn't feel sad—it feels incredible.

"That's a hard pass for me, Maryanne."

"Excuse me?"

"You fucked me in more ways than one—and I'm all fucked out for a while. Go shop yourself around, I'm sure you won't have any trouble getting a contract that'll keep you happy for a long time to come, but we're done now. Goodbye. Thanks for the drink."

The look on her face is priceless. Maryanne's a cool customer, and it's rare that she lets herself get hit as hard as she can hit, but I can tell my rejection is stinging her a little—or at the least offending her. She's used to getting her way, and that ship has sailed when it comes to me and her.

I won't be mentioning this to my partners—they don't ever need to know. What I will be doing is getting out of this time machine of a bar and heading home to my present—to the girl I never thought I'd end up with. We have an interview to conduct.

RECORDING SESSION THREE

"**S**ORRY," I SAY AS I WALK THROUGH THE door. "I got home earlier than I thought."

"That's fine, we can do it now."

"Okay, perfect." I sit down on the couch, where she's already waiting with her recording equipment. "So what's on the menu for tonight?"

She hits record. "Kylo have you ever cheated on a woman you were seeing?"

Wow. That was kind of a jarring way to start. "Where did that one come from? I already told you my feelings on monogamy."

"I know, but some women consider cheating to extend past the traditional definition of sex."

"Extend how? Like what kind of things do you mean?"

"Well... things like private messages on social media, or even seeing them without telling your current partner."

"I see. Seeing them how?"

"Like going out with them behind your partner's back. Seeing them in private, without telling the person you're with that you're doing so. It could be anything. Going to the movies, hanging out at their house... going to dinner or getting a drink. Whatever."

"Wait, so you're telling me that women you interviewed thought that a DM or running into their ex was something they considered cheating?"

"Not running into—more like intentionally seeing them, but without telling their current partner the truth about where they were going, or who they were with, no matter what the activity was."

"So, what's the question? Have I ever done any of those things, or have I ever cheated— 'cause I don't have the same definition of infidelity that your female subjects apparently do."

"Fine. We can put that aside. Have you ever done any of the things that I—that *they* mentioned in their responses? Like meeting up with an ex behind your current partner's back. Yes or no."

"This is starting to sound more like an interrogation than an interview. What's with the tone shift?"

"I think you know."

"I really don't. Why are you shutting off the mic?"

CHAPTER 30

Tori

I HIT THE PAUSE BUTTON. It isn't all that I want to hit.

"Because I know, alright. I know about tonight."

I didn't want to do it this way. Really, I didn't want to be in this position at all, but he's put us here. I wanted to confront him gently—to ask him about his little meeting and have him look me dead in the eye and tell me the truth—that it was a meet up with his ex girlfriend. I wanted him to prove me wrong about men, to show me that all of my assumptions weren't fair—but here we go again—another liar.

The more I thought about it the rest of the day, the more steamed I got. Maybe bringing it up like this, under the guise of our last interview, wasn't the best idea, but something's come over me. I need to know if I'm being played.

"You know what?"

"Oh, come on, Cormac. I know you saw Maryanne."

"Jesus. How do you know about Maryanne at all?"

Here's the part where the conversation fully turns into the fight it's already becoming.

"Because I looked... I mean, I saw... you left your phone out in the kitchen this morning."

"And you read my texts?"

"Don't make it sound so shady. It popped right up on the screen in front of me while I was trying to make a cup of coffee. So, yeah, I looked down, but I wasn't going out of my way to snoop. It was just kind of there."

"Just kind of there. Right."

"Can you just answer me and stop repeating everything I'm saying?"

"Yes," he says right away. "I saw Maryanne tonight, but I didn't lie to you. Do you know who she is?"

"Your ex?"

"Yes, my ex, but I meant do you know who she is, professionally?"

"Can't say that I do, no."

"LM Branford."

"LM Branford? Isn't she the one who wrote..."

"The Cadence Chase Detective books? A New York Times #1 best selling author? Borderline famous? Yes, she's all of those things."

"I don't need her resume, I know the name." I can hear the pettiness in my voice, I just can't seem to stop it.

"I'm not giving you her resume," he says. He sounds frustrated. I don't blame him, I can be frustrating. "My point was, she's an author, and she used to be a client of ours."

"Oh, really. Do you always sleep with the authors you have as clients, or is it just me and her? Oh, excuse me, I'm not actually a client. So I guess I asked the wrong question—do you always sleep with authors and potential authors you offer contracts to? Is that part of the signing process?"

"Jesus, Tori, of course not. What do you think of me?"

"I'm not so sure anymore, Cormac."

"What the hell does that mean? Come on."

"Look, I think we can end this little... whatever it was we were trying to do here. I have the data I need. I'm sure you still think my work is total feminist man-hating shit, but hey, at least you got to fuck me before it was all over."

"Tori, listen. I don't know where all of this is coming from, but I promise that you're overreacting to everything right now. If you'd just let me explain."

"I'm overreacting? Just being a stereotypical woman, I guess."

I stand up. I have to leave. I can't be in this house anymore. He tries to stop me, but that's not going to happen right now.

"Tori!"

"Just let me go, alright? I can't be around you right now."

I go into the bedroom and grab my suitcase. I don't pack so much as throw my shit inside as fast as I can. I practically have to sit on it to get it to close, but I get it done. Now I need to drag it to my car and head back to my place in the city. When I get to the door he yells for me one more time.

"Tori! Wait. I can explain all of this."

"I don't need you to explain. I know all that I need to know. The experiment is over, I'll talk to you later."

I leave, holding back the tears and feeling like a fool. This isn't how I thought our experiment would end. I'm going to stop calling it that, because for me it was something much more, even though I never expected it to be.

I never wanted *us* to end this way.

PART THREE
THE THREE KISS
CLAUSE

CHAPTER
31

Cormac

Friday, July 21ˢᵗ

S O THAT WAS AN EPIC FAIL, HUH?

I shouldn't joke, it's not really funny, but what was supposed to be a month-long experiment turned into a week-long disaster.

I moved back to my place. I make the drive over to Cynthia's house every day so I can keep up with my 'house sitting' responsibilities, but I'm back at my apartment in the city full time now. I haven't heard from Tori except a few polite texts back and forth, and I have no idea where things stand between us, other than knowing that they can't possibly be good.

On top of that, there's the very real issue of her last book meeting. It's coming up in a couple weeks and I have no idea what I'm going to do. Right now, I'm sitting at my place, staring, once again, at a blank computer screen, fooling myself into believing that I could actually write something good at the moment. There's no way. I'm distracted from my intellectual stupor by a noise.

Someone's knocking at my door. I don't know who it could be.

I don't bother looking through the peephole. I don't bother with the cliché yell of 'who is it?', I just open up. Part of me lives out an entire fantasy in the two seconds it takes to go from doorknob grab to swing of the door—in it, I open the door to Tori, standing there looking all cute and vulnerable, apologetic for assuming the worst of me.

That image is replaced by the reality of her best friend, Shoshana, standing in my doorway looking anything but vulnerable and apologetic. She doesn't ask to come in, she just comes in.

"Shoshana?"

"We need to talk, sexy publisher man."

"What are you... how did you know where I..."

"Lived? I followed you. Don't be alarmed, I can be a stalker when I want to be, but I'm not, like, Glen Close in *Fatal Attraction* or anything—you don't mean that much to me. I'm not gonna boil your bunny."

She's like a cartoon character. "Are you always like this?" I ask as I close the door.

"Like what?"

"Nothing. Nothing at all. What's going on, Shoshana?"

I sit down on my couch. The growth on my face that I called a five o'clock shadow two days ago is now rapidly turning into that itchy ass, pre-beard mess that makes all guys look like scumbags. On top of that, I need a shower. I haven't done much since Tori stormed out on me. I should probably shower at the very least.

"You look like absolute hell. But you're still cute, even behind the funk and the lack of a razor you're clearly afflicted with. I see why Tori fell for you."

"Fell for me?" I ask. This is the last thing I need to hear. "She didn't fall for anything. We were a terrible social experiment, and that's all she ever thought of me. Otherwise…"

"Okay, Captain Dramatic, I'm gonna need you to stop whining for a second and listen to me."

What did this girl just say? "Whining? I'm not…"

"Oh, please," she says, putting her hand up. "You sound like me three days before my period. Actually no, no one is that bad, but you are legit whiny. Stop talking and listen for a minute."

"Shoshana, I don't feel good. And I think you can see that I don't look great, either. If you came over here to make me feel worse, I really think we can skip all that."

"That's not why I'm here, Cormac. I don't do that. That would be kind of a cool job, though, now that you mention it—kind of like the anti singing telegram." She looks up into the ceiling as she speaks, like some kind of demented fairy, and for a second, I think she might be insane. Then she kind of floats back to the actual conversation we were having. "But, anyway, that's an idea for the Shark Tanks of tomorrow—right now I'm here to talk about our girl."

Our girl. Yeah, right. "Your girl, maybe," I say. I hear the bitterness in my voice and I don't like it. That isn't me at all. "She's not mine. She stormed out."

"Listen, Cormac. Can I sit down?"

Without waiting for me to answer, she plops her butt down on my couch. And she goes from flighty to focused and serious, and as she does I start to wonder which one is the act—the sarcastic ditz or the serious friend. Like Tori said, maybe they're both the real her. "What is it, Shoshana? Why'd you stalk me to my own place if you're not going all Single White Female on me?"

"That reference doesn't work, first of all. Single White Female would mean that you were another girl and I was trying to take over your life. You're good looking and all, but I really don't want to be a grizzly, un-showered, bitter publishing exec. Sorry, just not my deal."

"And second of all?"

"Second of all, I need to ask you one question and one question only—I'll believe what you tell me because Tori can spot a liar a mile away and she never called you one. She called you some other stuff in the beginning, but that doesn't matter anymore. I'm sure she changed her mind if she slept with you."

"And that question would be?"

"Did you do anything with your ex? And do you have any romantic feelings for her, whatsoever?"

"Technically, that's two questions. And I'm not really sure what business that is of yours."

"Tori's my business, alright, and don't get cute, Cormac, this is serious."

I look her straight in the eye and tell her the truth. "No and no. I ran into Maryanne a few days ago when I stopped for coffee. I tried to blow her off, but she's a little south of sane at this point. She texted me to meet up because she wanted to do what she always did—use me to further her career. I stupidly agreed to meet her and as soon as she started talking I knew it was a mistake. I blew her off and walked out of the bar. That's the truth. That's the entire story. That's what Tori didn't give me thirty seconds to explain."

Shoshana listens closely, and she looks at me like she's examining my every word for authenticity, like some human bullshit detector. "Alright. Then I did the right thing coming here."

"How's that?" I ask.

"I'm the one who needs to do the explaining, I think—about Tori and her past. Did she ever tell you anything about her ex boyfriend?"

I think about it for a second. "Only that it was a bad experience. No real details."

Shoshana laughs. "Bad experience? That's our Tori, always keeping her cards close to the vest."

I lean in, wanting and not wanting to ask what I'm about to ask. I don't want to make Shoshana tell me anything that isn't her place to tell me, but for all I know I'll never see Tori again. I think I at least have the right to understand why she reacted the way she did to whatever text she saw.

"Can you?"

"Tell you the whole story? I don't see why not."

"You won't be betraying a confidence or anything?"

She laughs again, this time I can tell it's at me. "Cormac, dear Cormac. I'd never, ever, betray a confidence with Tori, even if you came to me begging and crying—which is actually kind of funny to imagine."

"Thanks."

"Oh, relax, you're not offended. A little hurt by what happened, but not offended. Am I warm?"

"Red hot. I did my crying already. Now I need to understand what happened. I know I lied, according to Tori, but we weren't really boyfriend and girlfriend so I don't get why she flipped out on me."

"Okay, I see the problem now."

"Thank God!"

"You're an idiot."

"Wait, what?" I ask. "Excuse me?"

"Oh, sorry, sometimes I speak too fast and people can't understand me. I said, you-are-an-idiot. Was that better?"

"No, it's not better. I heard you, that's not the issue. I don't know what you mean."

"Listen, there's a lot you have to learn. Not just about women, but about Tori, specifically. You may not have technically been a real couple, but I know you were acting like one. That's right, Cormac, I know about the animal sex!"

"Excuse me?"

"You gave the girl an orgasm for the ages, took her out to dinner, and have been her closest confidant for a while now. Face it, Cormac, this wasn't an experiment. You are her boyfriend, and when you lied to her, she took it like a girlfriend who was being lied to."

Fuck. I feel so stupid there isn't even a word for it. Shoshana's right, and it turns out that Tori felt the same way as me this whole time. And I went and fucked it all up. I bury my face in my hands and sigh. "So this guy, this ex, he cheated on her? And this reminded her of it?"

"Ha," she laughs. I'm starting to hate the sound of her laughing. "He did much worse than that, Cormac."

The protective male in me takes over. My mind goes to the worst place ever, and I look Shoshana in the eyes intensely. "You don't mean? He didn't...?"

"No. Not that. He didn't hurt her—well, not physically."

"What did he do?"

"Uhh." She takes a deep breath—the kind you would if someone asked you to tell them your life story. "I'll give you the short version—and the preface here is that he was Tori's first real boyfriend, and she was head-over-heels in love with him."

"Okay."

"They were dating for about eighteen months—long enough that she was making jokes about marrying him one day. It was the end of senior year when it happened."

"What happened?"

"Well, unbeknownst to our Tori, her ex was something of a player."

"So he did cheat on her?"

"Yes," she answers. "But, believe it or not that wasn't the worst part. The cheating was bad enough, but there were signs of that Tori chose to ignore, in my opinion. That wasn't it. It was the video that changed everything."

"What video?"

She sighs again. "Tori didn't realize this, but her ex used to set up a tripod for his cell phone whenever they had sex. He recorded her all the time. And not just when they did it—when she got changed, when she showered. Turns out the guy was a major perv. Even tried to sell a video of the two of them to an amateur porn website. She had to take him to court and everything to get a judge to take the video down. Everyone on campus saw. It was going around that if you wanted to see 'that girl in Dorm G' fucking her boyfriend, all you had to do was pull out your phone and log onto PornHub."

Holy shit. No wonder she didn't trust guys. No wonder she didn't want to give the details. "I can't believe that happened."

"Oh, it happened alright. I went with her to court on more

than one occasion. Eventually the video got taken down by court order, but it wasn't fast, and by then the cat was out of the bag. Everyone knew. She was devastated. Depressed. Worse than depressed—whatever that is. But it took a long time for her to come back. It took a lot."

"And you were there for all of it?"

"Every step of the way. But don't worry, she's no victim. She's just damaged. We all are. She just turned her damage into a podcast with a million loyal fans. I wish we could all do that."

"Have you... talked to her?"

"Of course," she says. "Every day."

"Do you think..."

"She doesn't want to talk to you right now."

"Jesus, would you let me finish a sentence? How do you always know what I'm going to say?"

"It's a gift and a curse. And time is money, Cormac. I'm cutting off valuable seconds that don't need to happen. That, and I have to get my nails done in about fifteen minutes and I don't have the time for you to process as slowly as you do. But look, I tried, okay? I really did. I'm on your side because, even though this was all some experiment, our girl is complicated. It takes her longer than a week to show everything she has inside of her. Hell, I haven't even seen it all. But like I was saying, I tried to tell her she was overreacting, to get her to call you, but when it comes to this stuff she's hyper sensitive. I think she'll come around, she just needs some time."

Time.

Shoshana using that word reminds me that Tori has her final pitch meeting with us in a little over two weeks. Cynthia will be back from Europe by then. Elissa will be there. And, of course,

I'll be there, looking across a table at the girl I just fake broke up with—even though it feels like a pretty real break up to me.

"Well, thanks anyway, Shoshana. You're a strange bird, but I like you."

"Awww," she says, clutching her heart. "See, if it wasn't for Tori, you could have been one of my ex boyfriends. Oh well. Twists of fate and all that."

I smile at the cartoon character that is Shoshana. It's the only thing I've smiled at since Tori walked out on me. "Go get your nails done. Hopefully Tori will change her mind."

"Stranger things have happened. Goodbye for now, Cormac."

"Bye."

She walks out and my head starts spinning. I don't know how I'm going to handle this whole situation, but I do know that I'm dreading that meeting.

CHAPTER 32

Cormac

FUCK THIS COMPUTER.

It's not the computer's fault, I know this, but fuck it anyway!

Fuck these blank pages, fuck this empty screen that's practically calling me a pussy.

I smile thinking about that conversation with Tori. I smile thinking about Tori in general, but I'm guessing that I won't be seeing her again in person until that meeting, and whatever I thought we might have had is definitely over. It is what it is. If I told Tori I just had that thought she'd probably tell me I was being a typical man—unable to express my feelings and going all sour grapes on something meaningful. Maybe she'd be right. But what else can I do? Mope around the house? Take a vacation from hygiene again? I've got to move on. Clearly, she has.

Looking back there is one thing Tori did to change my mind—not about her book, but about the woman herself—she helped inspire me to finish this damn book. I've always hated that word—inspire. It always rang of artistic pretension to me, but I can't think of anything better at the moment for what Tori did for me. She believed in me even though I had ripped her book to shreds right in front of her—almost literally—and she had every right to laugh mine down that crowded city street when I told her what I was writing.

But she didn't. Not even a little bit.

Instead she propped me up, told me I could do it, took me someplace I'd never been before to kickstart my brain, and gave me some techniques of how to get out of my own way. Whatever we had, and whatever we lost, I still have that. And I'm not going to waste it.

I get up, make a cup of coffee, tell myself to stop being such a... to stop being such a pair of *balls*, and sit down, ready to fuck this laptop up in the fight we're about to have with one another.

But for the first time in months I think I have the advantage, because all of a sudden, I have an idea of the story I want to tell.

CHAPTER 33

Cormac

Two Weeks Later

I SHOULD NOT GO OUT with my brothers.

Strike that, I should not go out with Conor.

Aidan can be a wild man like the rest of us, but he's also got the maturity to know when to turn it off and slow down the crazy. Conor is missing that gene. He wanted to celebrate me finishing my book, so he took me and Aidan to a bar that was truly a hole in the wall. Calling it a 'dive' doesn't do it justice. Think of a meth lab, only they serve drinks. I don't know how Conor found that place and I don't think I want to know.

Now we're sharing an Uber. I live closest to the bar, so I'm the first drop off. It's only six blocks away, but in Manhattan-traffic-time, that's a good half hour of driving, accompanied by horns and middle fingers and possibly an accident if our driver is as bad as he looks. Next time, I'll let Aidan plan any celebrations.

"I can't believe my older bro is going to be a published author! That's sick!"

Conor's wild, but he's a good guy, and genuinely happy for me. "Thanks, dude. I don't know what came over me in the last couple weeks, but once I started hitting those keys I was busting out a chapter or two a night."

"I know what came over you," Aidan says. "You finally got away from all the crazy women in your life—Maryanne, and that Tori chick. Freed your mind to do its work."

I smile even though he's dead wrong. I don't have the time or energy to explain that it was Tori who kicked me in the ass to finish the book in the first place. "Yeah, I guess. I don't even care what it was, I have a book now."

"Oh, shit," Conor says. "I just realized I didn't even ask you, what's it called?"

"I'm not sure yet." Lie number one. "I'm playing around with some different titles." Lie number two. "But I'll let you know when I settle on one." Finally, the truth.

"Cool, bro. Or maybe I'll just see it at the bookstore."

Aidan bursts out laughing. "Bookstore? Who are you lying to right now? Your ass hasn't read a book since high school, and even then, you always got some girl to read it for you and tell you what it was about."

"Yeah, true. That trick worked in college, too. But I'll read this one for sure." Aidan and I both shoot him the side eye. "Alright, I'll read that little paragraph on the back at least. Maybe even a chapter or two."

I reach over and put my hands on his shoulder. "Coming from my half illiterate brother that means a hell of a lot."

"Thanks. Hey, wait a second..."

"God, you're slow," Aidan jokes.

"Not as slow as this traffic. My place is literally a block away, I think I'm gonna jump out and walk, I'll get there faster."

"You sure? I read *SuperFreakonomics*. They said in there that you're more likely to die drunk walking than drunk driving."

Aidan always worries about me. Sometimes I wonder who's really the older brother. "I'll be fine, I promise. I'm not drunk, and my place is literally right there. You guys get home safe. Text me, alright."

"We will. And congrats, man!"

"Congrats, bro!"

I leave them behind and weave in between the barely moving cars. About thirty strong steps later I'm at the front door of my apartment building. When I get to my door there's a package waiting for me. I wonder what it is because the only thing I ordered recently was a copy of my book that I'd had bound, but it's too soon to be that.

Inside, I grab a cold water from my fridge and use the edge of my keys to slit the tape open. Inside is a fresh copy of Tori's book, and a hand-written note.

"Cormac,

I haven't been ignoring you. I mean, I have been ignoring you, but not because I don't want to talk to you, but because I just needed time to let things settle. I know that I probably over reacted to what happened. You don't seem like the type to do what I thought you did, and if I made assumptions about you, I'm so sorry.

I need some time to myself. This whole experiment was for me to get to know men better, but I think maybe I learned more about myself than I did about men. I learned that I have some thoughts that need examining, and some viewpoints that need questioning. You helped to show me that, and because of that I'll withdraw my application to have my book published, just like we agreed to. Maybe the book shouldn't be published.

I know that you're probably really busy with your job and your book and, well, life, but if you want you can read the revised chapters I've sent. It's the same book, but I took out some of the gross generalizations that were wrong from the start. Our experiment is over, and you were right.

On the personal side of things, I'm not sure where we go from here. We started out as an experiment—as a fake couple—and along the way we became... something. I don't have a name for it, but I know that what I felt when I was in your arms is as real as anything I've ever felt. I don't know where you were emotionally through the whole thing, but I'm sure you'll move on from me to other girls who won't give you such a hard time along the way.

Thank you for showing me that I can be wrong—sometimes, anyway.
XoXo—Tori"

So many thoughts are running through my mind when I read that. First, I'm super happy to hear from Tori, even if it is in a weird package instead of her returning my numerous (really numerous—like, embarrassingly numerous) calls and texts. Even so, I'm not mad, I'm... something. Happy at first, then a little melancholy that she thinks I didn't feel the same way as her about everything.

If she doesn't want to be with me because I'm not the guy for her, then I understand. But I don't want it to be because of a misunderstanding. That's not okay with me. But besides us, there's something else in that letter that doesn't sit right with me. I take out my phone to send yet another text that I know she's not going to respond to—but it doesn't matter. I just need her to read it.

Me: Got your package, and I'm going to read your entire book this time. I read your letter also, and, no matter what else happens, I refuse your withdrawal. I want you to come to that last meeting. It's why we did all this. It's the least I owe you. I'll see you back in my office. I hope you're well.

I hope you're well! I sound like some sap in a bad movie. I don't know what I was thinking writing that, but the rest I meant. There's no way she's pulling out of this last meeting. I'm going to make myself a cup of coffee, and then I've got some reading to do.

As the smell of sweet, sweet caffeine fills the room, I start to think of Tori.

Despite what happened, I can't wait to see her.

I have a few things to say to her also.

But even more than that, I have something really important that I need to give her.

CHAPTER 34

Tori

Four Days Later

I MIGHT VOMIT. I HAVEN'T DECIDED yet.

That would be a bad look, right? Blowing chunks all over the publisher's floor while you're here practically begging one of the partners to give your book a shot.

I actually have enough natural adrenaline right now to last a while. I think this is the first time in years that I haven't started the day with a few cups of coffee. I'm not sure what I'm so nervous about, I know how this is going to go. They're going to go through the motions, just to be polite, but I know that Cormac is going to vote no.

I hurt his feelings. I probably hurt his pride. Now this is his chance to get back at me.

I think that for about two seconds, and then I hear Shoshana's voice—which, trust me, is an alarming thing to hear in your head first thing in the morning! She's nuts, but she's also really wise, and she has way more experience than me when it comes to guys and relationships. She's told me this whole time—no, actually, she's told me as long as I've known her—that all guys aren't bad, and she seemed to really like Cormac.

I mean, what's there not to like about him? He's great. He's sexy. And after all, he chased away the spiders in my vagina.

Here goes nothing.

I have that awkward moment where I have to walk inside the room last. They're all sitting there—Cynthia, Elissa, and of course, my fake ex boyfriend. It's the first time that I've seen him since that night a few weeks ago, and there's no escaping the situation any longer.

I walk in and he makes eye contact with me right away. If it's even possible, I forgot how deep and how blue his eyes are, and for a second, I forget books and contracts and meetings, and I'm just stuck in place.

He stands up and fidgets a little, like a kid trying on new clothes. I guess that's what he does when he's nervous. "Hi Tori. Thank you for coming."

"Hi."

I sit down, and so does he, and for a second, I forget that there are two other people in the room.

"Tori, it's so good to see you again. And I trust that we won't have any shenanigans like last time?" I'm always team Elissa. I love her.

Cynthia is right next to her—a woman I've never met before, but who I feel a tremendous amount of guilt towards for not screaming out that I had crazy sex in her bed. It was crazy, God! His tongue was like... Shit, focus!

"Shenanigans?" she asks.

"Nothing," Cormac says, jumping in to defend himself. "Tori and I just had a little... spirited back and forth, you could say."

"Ah. Well, I'm only back from Europe a day and I still feel pretty jet lagged, so I don't have any time for shenanigans. Let's do this. Elissa, you want to lead off?"

"Certainly. Tori, first of all, how are you doing?"

"I'm nervous," I tell them. "Very nervous, if I'm being honest. But I'm happy to be here."

"I understand. This is important to you. I'd be worried if you weren't at least a little bit nervous, but you're among friends."

More than friends, Elissa. If you only knew what he did with BOB, you'd turn bright red just like I did.

"Thanks, Elissa."

"How this works is kind of like a reality show—we each say a little piece about how we interpret your work, followed by our vote of yes or no. As you already know, the vote has to be unanimous."

I know, Elissa. I concocted a whole experiment because of it.

"Yes, I'm aware, thank you. So which one of you is the Simon Cowell of the group?"

I secretly die inside when they both look at Cormac. We all know he's Simon Cowell on steroids. Luckily for me, Elissa goes first.

"I'll begin. As I said last time, Tori, I think that your work is progressive and highly appropriate in the era of the #metoo movement. While it's not without its issues, I believe that they can be worked out in editing. That said, you have the same vote of 'yes' that you had from me at the initial meeting. I'd be happy to count this among our books."

Deep breath. "Thank you so much, Elissa. I really appreciate it."

Cynthia goes next. "Tori, first off it's great to finally meet in you in person. I have to admit that I was on vacation when I received the initial copy of your book."

"I know, I really appreciate you reading it when you were off trying to relax."

"It was my pleasure," she says. "And anyone who knows me knows that I'm never truly off of work, even when I'm walking the streets of Hamburg and Dublin. I had a copy of your material in my backpack at all times."

"Really?"

"Well, my husband did. He carried the backpack, but I'm taking full credit."

I laugh. It's a little strained because I'm still too nervous to really laugh at anything, but this woman has my fate in her hands, so I'll smile like the Joker if I have to. "You really didn't have to read it, so thank you."

"No, thank you, Tori. Not only do I love your social media presence and message, I loved every bit of this book. I loved seeing a written version of your podcast, plus your own thoughts on these issues. I loved it, and it's a solid 'yes' for me. Which leaves our last partner, the sole 'no' in our last vote. Cormac, it's your turn."

Here we go.

"My turn, huh?" He stands up. It kind of freaks me out. It looks like he's about to accept his party's nomination for the presidency of the United States. But damn, does he look good in that suit! He walks around to the other side of the conference table and sits next to me. I can smell him from that chair—that musk that comes off of him. I lose my concentration for a second as I wait for him to speak.

"Tori, as you know, I was... pretty harsh on you last time. You didn't deserve that, but I did have some questions that needed answering. One, in particular. Do you remember what it was?"

What the hell is he doing? "I remember. You asked me how I could speak about a subject that I didn't have a lot of personal experience with, if I remember correctly."

He turns back to Elissa and Cynthia. "I don't think you two have this." In his hands he has the new edition of my book that I sent to him, with my little post it notes still attached to the revised sections. He passes it to Elissa and she starts paging through it. "It's a revised version of her book, one that she sent to me."

"Revised?" Elissa asks. "Revised how?"

"I... made some changes, based on the feedback that I got from Cormac. We spent some time over the past couple of weeks discussing the pros and cons of the book—what he found convincing and what was putting up a barrier to him saying yes. It's pretty much the same book, only now I added a new foreword where I'm a little less general about *all* guys being such pigs."

I still have no idea what he's thinking, and I'm still expecting a hard no. After putting him through all the experiment stuff, where he still played along even though he didn't have to. And then I walked out on him He's got to be pissed.

"Alright," Elissa says. "Well we'll definitely need time to see the changes in the book as well, but right now it's time for you to tell her what you've decided, Cormac."

He looks right at me, and I swear that I can see that look he gave me back at the house—he doesn't look angry, he looks like he wants me still. Maybe that's just wishful thinking, I still have to wait and see what he's about to say.

"I started this process a month ago, not knowing who you were or what your message was about. I thought a lot of things about you, Tori. That you were a man hating feminist, that you had an agenda, that you were just doing this to get more followers on your social media pages. I'm really happy to say that after spending some time with you... *talking* like we did over coffee a few times, that I couldn't have been more wrong about you. You're not a man hater, and you don't have any agenda other than trying to give women a voice to talk about very real issues. This book— like your podcast, like your vlog, and like you, are there to help other women out, and I think that's beautiful. So, Tori, I guess what I'm trying to say is that my vote has changed from a no to a yes, and I'm thrilled to publish this under our banner."

I'm not a cryer. Not at all. Not even a little bit. But I can't help the tears that are forming in my eyes when I hear those words. I never expected them. I try to keep my composure, but it's almost impossible. But then I realize that holding my breath, squeezing my face and trying not to cry makes you look ten times crazier than if you just cried in the first place—so I cry. It's my normal cry face, not the ugly one.

"Oh, Tori, it's so nice to see the emotion. We're happy to have you in our little family."

"Thank you, Cynthia." *But that's not the only reason I'm crying, but you can't know that. And, also, what the hell is with that coffee maker at your place? Oh, right, can't tell you about that, either, can I?*

We celebrate—and, by that, I mean everyone comes over and hugs me. I try not to get tears on their fancy suits. After Elissa and Cynthia excuse themselves, and it's just me and the fake ex standing around in the room.

"You know you didn't have to vote yes if you really hated the book. I was thinking, and ..."

"Do you like coffee?"

"Huh"

"Coffee," he says slowly. "Do. You. Drink. It?"

I smile. He doesn't need to say the last part, but I kind of want him to.

"Uh-Huh. I'm actually a little tired. This getting a book deal after a social experiment goes terribly wrong thing is tiring."

"Great! You're in luck, there's actually a Starbucks down the street. I'm sure you knew that already. I'll buy you a cup. I always like to treat my new authors to an overpriced cup of coffee. Let's go."

Oh, Cormac Delaney, what am I going to do with you?

CHAPTER 35

Cormac

"Another Americano?" I ask.

"You know me too well."

I smile. I wish that were the case. I want to know her more than I do. I'm just not sure that I'm ever going to get that chance with the way things have gone between us. "We know some things about each other, but there's probably much more that we don't know."

"Yeah," she says. "I guess you're right. It was only a little over a week that we were living together."

A week. It was, wasn't it? Wow, it does not seem like such a short time that we were with one another. "That's so crazy. I think for that short amount of time we got to know a lot about one another."

"That's true. I learned that you pack lightly and that you can be a slob sometimes."

"Hey."

"Stop, you know it's true. If I hadn't stepped in to play a 1950's housewife you wouldn't be sitting here with me, you'd be explaining to Cynthia why she has an infestation of mice and roaches. Just thank me. But back to what I was saying, I also learned that you're thoughtful, sweet, and have some talent with BOB."

I have no idea what that part means. "Who the hell is BOB?" I ask.

She giggles. "I'll explain later."

"So there's going to be a later? I thought you were done with me."

"That's only because I thought you were done with me. Can I ask you?"

I know what she's going to ask—the same thing Shoshana asked me, the thing I finally need to explain to her in person. "Before you do, let me answer."

"Huh?"

"Sorry, that sounded confusing. I meant, if you're going to ask about Maryanne, the answer is no, nothing is going on between us."

"She's your ex?"

"She's my crazy, driven, borderline sociopathic ex, yes. It's a long story, but right now just understand that I ran into her randomly a few weeks ago. Seeing her was like Chinese water torture, and I tried to get away but she went on about wanting to see me for drinks, so I said yes just to blow her off, but she ended up texting me. I met with her to let her know that nothing was ever going to happen, once and for all."

"Because of me?"

"Two reasons—one, because I hate her and she's nuts, but also, yes, because of you. I swear, I'm not a cheater, and I'm not a guy who'd ever have what we had that night, and then meet my ex the next day."

"Now I feel really stupid," she says. "I guess it's apology time."

"You don't have to apologize. Shoshana came and saw me."

"Wait, what?"

"She told me the whole story about your ex in college. And side note—if I ever ran into that douche I'd beat his ass. Don't be pissed at her, she was trying to give me some insight on what had happened. And then I listened to that early podcast where you discussed it all."

She takes a big deep breath, like she wasn't expecting me to say that, of all things. But then she has a different look on her face—it looks like relief.

"I'm glad that you know. It was a horror show for a while."

"I can't even imagine what that must have been like," I tell her. "But I can't even begin to tell you how much I respect what you did with that situation. You could have folded—dropped out of school, sat at home and cried all day, but instead you made something positive out of it. That takes strength I can't even imagine."

"Thank you," she says. "And trust me, there was plenty of crying and feeling sorry for myself also."

"Nothing wrong with that. But when you were done feeling sorry for yourself, you got up and made something incredible out a horrible circumstance. That's amazing."

"And that's also why I wrote this book—that's what I was trying to explain to you all along."

"I know that now," I tell her. "And I appreciate the little

changes you made. I'm so happy you're going to be a published author now."

"Me too." For the first time in a while she has a real smile on her face—a happy face that you can't fake.

"I'm sorry," she says. "About misunderstanding what happened between us. With storming out. With thinking the worst of you. I guess the damage from that experience wasn't totally gone yet. You helped me see that. I needed some time to reflect, to work on my book, to just think about everything that had happened. I wasn't trying to ghost you. And you know I didn't change the book just to get your approval. I changed it because you changed me."

I smile. "I know you didn't do it just for me—that's why I voted yes. And you're not the only one who was changed by the experiment, you know?"

"Should we start singing For Good from Wicked to each other right here? That would be epic."

"Only if I get to be Elphaba," I joke.

"No," she says. "I'm so Elpahaba. You can be Glinda. You're the happy go lucky—and sometimes obnoxious one. I'm the dark one."

"So you're calling the Wicked Witch part, then?"

"Always. And we can start singing at any point. I may not need to sell books, we can just get YouTube famous when someone takes out their phone and records us."

"You're crazy, you know that?"

I drink my coffee fast, because I need the energy for what I'm about to ask her. All this is great. It feels amazing sitting here with her, but I don't know where everything goes from here. "So?"

"So?"

"What now?"

"I figure you finish your drink, and then I go tell Shoshana and my parents about the publishing deal and we celebrate. What are you up to this afternoon?"

"Stop it, you know what I mean."

"Maybe," she jokes. "But I want to hear you say it."

"Still with that? You're still gonna torture me?"

"Always, Cormac. I'm always gonna torture you."

"Fine. You win. What I'm asking, is where do you and I go from here?"

"Cormac Delaney, are you asking me to bump your status up from fake boyfriend to actual boyfriend?"

"I think I am.

"In that case," she says, smiling. "Hell yeah I want you to be my real boyfriend!"

I'm not going to sing broadway show tunes to her, but I am going to kiss her. I stand up, walk to her side of the table, and lift her to her feet. I put my hands on her hips and pull her into me, and I don't give a damn who's watching.

We kiss.

Like, we really kiss.

We might be making other people uncomfortable at this point.

Phones might be out recording us.

The manager might be on her way to our table to politely ask us to leave and never come back.

It's that kind of kiss.

"Wow!" she says when we finally separate. "That was amazing."

"I only have one more question for you," I say, looking intensely in her eyes.

"What is it, Cormac?"

"Who the hell is BOB?"

She starts cracking up and buries her head in my chest. I still don't get it.

"I promise I'll tell you later."

"How about dinner at my place?" I ask her.

"You cook also?"

"I'm a man of many talents."

"You certainly are. How's eight sound?"

"Sounds perfect. Wanna go?"

"Sure."

Once we're outside, I pull a special package out of my bag. "Oh, and I wanted to give you this. It's not packaged all nice like yours—it's basically brown paper bags poorly cut and even more poorly taped, but I didn't have a whole lot of time this morning."

"What is it?"

"Open it."

She rips away the paper like a kid on Christmas morning. "Oh my God, you finished!"

"I did. I wanted you to see."

"That's amazing, I'm so proud of you!" She gives me the biggest hug ever. "I redid the whole thing, almost from scratch. It's still a rom-com, and still about two opposites who get together even though it seems like they never would. All I needed was a catchy title. What do you think?"

"*The Three Kiss Clause*," she reads. "I love it. Although I have heard that somewhere before, are you sure it's original?"

"Pretty sure."

"Okay, just checking. Last thing I'd want is for my boyfriend to get sued for copyright infringement—might be a bad look for a partner in a publishing company. Just looking out for you."

"I appreciate that."

"There's just one more thing."

"What?"

"We only kissed twice."

"No, it was three times."

"I was thinking, though. If I don't remember it, it really shouldn't count. 'Cause then it would be two kisses I remember and three that you remember. Doesn't seem fair."

"So what do we do?"

"I have an idea." She steps forward and grabs me by the tie. Before I know it, her lips are pressed into mine. It feels like the rightest thing that's ever happened to me. "What was that for?"

"See. Now the title makes sense."

It sure does.

Now a lot of things make sense.

EPILOGUE

One Year Later

So I made it to Barnes & Noble for my signing after all. Did you ever doubt your girl?

I'm just kidding around and being cocky—the truth is I doubted myself along the way several times, but here I am.

The time for insecurity is over. Take this as a reminder, TorMenTors—never let anything—or anyone—in this world tell you what you can't accomplish. A few years ago I was just a college kid with a broken heart and a shitty ex boyfriend—nothing original at all. And now, I'm one of the most successful people I know, and saying that doesn't make me arrogant, it makes me what I've always claimed to be—a self assured, badass woman.

I always knew that part.

The parts I didn't know are the things I learned during my experiment with Cormac.

I learned that it's not just women who can be self assured

badasses—there are some great men out there who balance out all the shit heads like my ex, and all the exes out there. I learned that some of the qualities in men that I used to roll my eyes at aren't always bad. In fact, some of them are downright amazing, as long as they belong to the right guy.

And then I learned the most important lesson of all—that Cormac Delaney is the perfect guy for me. It's been a year since his company agreed to publish my book, and we've spent most of those days around one another. And guess what? Now we're living together for real!

Cynthia never did find out about the naughty things that happened in her bed while she was touring Europe. Maybe one day that'll make for a funny story for Cormac to tell her, cause I'm never saying a word about what he did with good old BOB! But speaking of which—we've had some amazing experiences that are never going to make my podcast. Let's just say that trying to remember a time before incredible orgasms is like trying to remember a distant memory.

Things are amazing.

Cormac is everything I didn't know I was looking for. I thought I hated him. I thought he was everything wrong with the male sex. I've never been so happy to be wrong in my entire life. Not only did I end up not hating him, I kinda sorta love him like no one I've ever loved before, and I know that he feels the same way about me, because he tells me that every single day.

I'm the luckiest woman there ever was.

Speaking of lucky, I can't believe that I'm about to do my first legit signing. I speak to millions of people every week between my podcast and my YouTube channel, but seeing them line up around the corner is something different. I'm inside, sitting at a little table with Shoshana and the manager of the store. Looking through the window I can see the crowd. They're all wearing my merch. TorMenTor shirts are everywhere.

"I've never seen the #slavestotheirdicks shirts before. They came out good."

"Of course they did, silly," Shosh tells me. "I had them made. Did you think they'd come out anything but awesome? Silly rabbit."

"You're right. How dare I question you?"

"Oh, Tori." She jokes, taking my hand. "I've been waiting to hear those words for forever. This is a great day. For you also cause of the whole book thing. But especially for me."

"You're crazy, you know that?"

"Well, if I was crazy, I probably wouldn't know it, right?"

"You do have a point there, Shosh."

"I'm just me. That's all I know how to be."

The manager of the store comes forward. "Are you ready to meet your adoring fans?"

I am. I really, really am.

She opens the front doors and the line starts to form in front of my table. Each one of them has a copy of Fu*&$Boys in their hands, and each has a TorMenTor shirt of some kind on their body. This is so amazing I can barely believe it's happening.

Now, you remember those hashtags, right? Probably not, it's been a hell of a journey to get here, so let me remind you just in case you're one of the fifty people on line to take that epic selfie with me. #slavestotheirdicks (of course), #torikleinisawesome #shessoapproachable #myfavoriteauthor #fuckboys. You get the idea—just remember to tag me on IG and I might add you to my story!

I can't even tell how much time has passed—maybe twenty or thirty minutes. I've been signing my ass off, and taking crazy amounts of pictures, and line looks like it's getting longer, not shorter. I haven't even had time to look up yet. The whole time Shosh is standing behind me, keeping things moving.

"Have you seen Cormac in the crowd?" I ask her. "He said he was taking the day off so he could be here but I haven't heard from him."

"He's your boyfriend experiment, shouldn't you be keeping track of the man?"

"That's not quite how it works, Shosh. And I think we can drop the experiment part—he's just my regular boyfriend now, remember."

"My mistake. Let me go see if I can find him. Maybe he's caught up in the wave of TorMenTors outside. Hold on. Can you handle things while I'm gone?"

"I think I've got this." I joke. "But if anything gets dicey I'll just use our secret word so you can come choke some fools out."

"Is it strange that I hope that happens? Wait, don't answer that, it is strange. Let me run before I say something silly."

"Too late." She disappears into the distance and I sign a few more books. It's great seeing my fans. They came out in droves—young girls, older women, and even a few guys. After a while Shosh comes back and sits next to me.

"I texted him for you. He'll be here soon, I'm sure."

"Thanks."

I lean down underneath the table because the points on my sharpies are running down to flat little nubs. As I'm bending over I hear a copy of my book slam down on the table above me. I'm still bent over, and all I can see underneath is..."Hey. I know those shoes."

Then I hear his deep voice. "Excuse me, would you mind signing this for me? I'm a huge fan." I lift my head up so fast that I almost bang it on the edge of the table.

"You're here!"

"You'd think I'd miss this for anything in the world?"

He's the best. He's really the absolute best.

"I should have known better than to doubt you."

"You got that right. Now would you please sign this for me?"

I look up into his deep blue eyes and get lost for a second. "Wait, you really want me to sign this? I have a million copies at your place. I can sign any of them for you."

"I realize. I had to climb a small book mountain just to get to my closet this morning."

"Sorry about that."

"It's alright. You can make it up to me by signing this one. This is a special copy, and I'm going to make a special place on my bookshelf just for it."

"Why is this one so special?" I ask, a little confused.

"Open it up."

I do. I pull the front cover to the left and stare down. It looks like there's a little carved circle in the middle of all the pages. "What the?"

"Look inside." I can't believe my eyes. I put the book on its side, and out from that hole falls the shiniest, most beautiful ring I've ever seen in my life. The shine of it hits me in the eye. Or maybe those are just the tears forming that I seem to have no control over. I look back up at him, and he's smiling ear to ear.

"Cormac? What?"

He steps around the side of my signing table and as he does I see that Shosh has her phone out and is pointing it in our direction. "Smile, Tori, you're live on your social media."

"What? You knew?"

"I know everything, girl. Now stop looking at me and look over at that gorgeous man in front of you."

I turn and Cormac is down on one knee. I can't control the tears that are streaming down my face. A year ago I hated this man—I thought he was representative of everything wrong with men. Now he's down on one knee, looking up into my tear soaked eyes.

"Tori Klein, we started out as an experiment and we became something very real. I love you with all of my heart and soul. Would you make me the luckiest man in the world by becoming my wife?"

The whole room is silent. I forget where we are for a moment, and then I look up. Everyone's phone is on me, and the smiles in the room are too many to count. I have the biggest one of all.

"Of course I will. I love you so much."

I pull him up off of his knees, and we kiss the best kiss I've ever had.

"You know we'll have this moment forever now."

"I don't need the cameras for that, Cormac. I'll always have this moment forever."

The End

Where can you keep up with my new releases, deals, discounts, and other cool news? Just make sure you click 'follow' on all these links below!

My Newsletter Sign up
http://eepurl.com/cg0vav
BookBub
https://www.bookbub.com/authors/christopher-harlan
Goodreads
https://www.goodreads.com/author/show/15894914.
Christopher_Harlan
Amazon
https://www.amazon.com/-/e/B01M1KU74Y
Instagram
www.instagram.com/authorchristopherharlan

ALSO BY CHRISTOPHER HARLAN

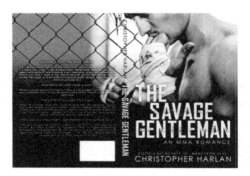

The Savage Gentleman

My name is Lucas "The Ghost" Esparza.

I'm the best MMA fighter in the world that you've never heard of, but if I have my way, I'll be a household name soon enough. My life's been nothing but hard training, crazy partying, and fast women, and that's just how I liked it. No man had ever gotten the better of me inside the cage, and no woman had ever been able to slow down my lifestyle outside of it.

And then it all came crashing down.

When I tasted defeat for the first time in the biggest fight of my life, I was a broken man—my pride destroyed and my dreams of greatness deferred.

That's when Mila walked into my gym.

When my trainer told me I had to give her self defense lessons because she was a 'special case', I had no idea what he meant. All I knew was that she had a body to die for, and a face that made me forget my own name. I'd been with my share of women, but she was easily the sexiest I'd ever laid eyes on.

There was only one problem—we hated each other with a passion!

I thought she was whiny with a bad attitude. She thought I was full of myself. But then something happened that changed everything between us. She gave me the confidence to pursue my dreams once again—to be a champion, to make it into the UFC, and to be the savage gentleman that I was born to be.

Amazon
http://Amzn.com/B07WLN711T

FREE SAMPLE CHAPTERS
https://dl.bookfunnel.com/am39zd94rn

Goodreads
https://www.goodreads.com/book/show/47515165-the-savage-gentleman

Away From Here: a young adult novel

Synopsis:

When I was seventeen years old there were only three things that I knew for certain: I was a mixed up mixed kid, with weird hair and an unhealthy love of comics; I wanted to forget I'd ever heard the words depression and anxiety; and I was hopelessly in love with a girl named Annalise who was, in every way that you can be, a goddess. What can I say about Anna? She wasn't the prom queen or the perfect girl from the movies, she was my weird, funny, messed up goddess. The girl of my dreams. The reason I'm writing these words.

I'd loved Anna from a distance my junior year, afraid to actually talk to her, but then one day during lunch my best friend threw a french fry at my face and changed everything. The rest, as they say, is history. Our History. Our Story. Annalise helped make me the man I am today, and loving her saved my teenaged soul from drowning in the depths of a terrible Bleh, the worst kind of sadness that there is, a concept Anna taught me about a long time ago, when we were younger than young. So flip the book over, open up the cover and let me tell you Our Story, which is like Annalise, herself - complicated, beautiful, funny, and guaranteed to teach you something by the time you're through. Maybe it'll teach you the complexity of the word potato, something I never understood until the very last page.

Our Story: an Away From Here Prequel
(Amazon FREE download)
http://a.co/fYScly5

#1 bestseller—Away From Here: A Young Adult Novel
Amazon
http://a.co/di866wQ

Goodreads (4.61/5 stars)
https://www.goodreads.com/book/show/38212508-away-from-here

The Impressions Duet (HEA Contemporary Romance)

This duet follows the interrelated stories of two best friends, Mia and Dacia, as they encounter the Marsden brothers—two mysterious, handsome, and intriguing men whose family has a sordid history that they must discover together:

Impressions of You (book 1)
http://a.co/786mkFA

Impression of Me (book 2)
http://a.co/4MI4gw3

The New York City's Finest

HEA contemporary romance—My 5 book series, a blend of contemporary romance, action, suspense, and adventure—each book features a different sexy NYPD detective and takes place in a different borough of New York. Follow these NYPD detectives as they meet the women of their dreams while trying to solve the crimes of their careers!

Calem (book 1) **http://a.co/hEyPn3Q**
Jesse (book 2) **http://a.co/eyTkL7I**
Quinn (book 3) **http://a.co/gO9YJ7m**
Noah (book 4) **http://a.co/2xvrb7p**
Riley (book 5) **http://a.co/5YRvjxv**
Or, you can get all of the books bundled:
The New York City's Finest Boxed Set (all 5 books) **http://a. co/1D3kw4i**

The Wordsmith Chronicles

HEA contemporary romance—A group of aspiring romance writers struggle with trying to make it big in the indie publishing world while navigating their love lives.

Knight (book 1) http://a.co/iBcVaK5
Colton (book 2) http://a.co/dy2Ojmq
Grayson (book 3) http://a.co/d/43MNyLS

True North: A Wordsmith Chronicles Standalone MC—>
http://a.co/d/iSlpvVo
North: A Wordsmith Chronicles Standalone
https://www.amazon.com/dp/B07QZHV28D

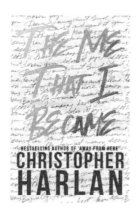

Standalone HEA Contemporary Romance:
The Me That I Became

Synopsis:

We were destined to never end up together. You an empath, and me the woman who can't feel anything. It never should have worked. Then, our hands brushed together. It was serendipity—a happy accident that made me experience the world like I never had before. You said all the right words, and for a time I remembered what it felt like to be alive. But, my shadows have returned, threatening to extinguish the light you brought into my life, and I'm terrified that our future together is slipping away. I need you now, Brandon. I need you to chase away the demons, to make me whole, and to teach me once again what it means to love. Now only one question remains. . . Will you?

Amazon

http://a.co/d/0rjzTBu

Goodreads

https://www.goodreads.com/book/show/42551351-the-me-that-i-became

The Sick Parents Club: A Novel

Synopsis

"*The bullet let loose on July 22nd, 1939, destroyed a house full of children who went to sleep normal, but awoke forever deformed. The bullet ricocheted, lodging itself so deep inside each of them that none realized they'd been hit until years later. There were no survivors that day, even though there were many.*"

So begins the latest work from bestselling novelist Nathan Dunbar, as he chronicles the dark secret that forever altered the trajectory of his family. As he struggles to complete that book, he realizes that another story begs to be written—the story of his own teenaged years, a time he spent asking questions about the origin of his parent's mental illnesses, and forging a bond with the best friends he's ever know.

As he writes memories flood back—of summer days spent playing basketball, of surviving his household with his twin sister, Clover, and the way he felt when Serafina moved in to the neighborhood. That summer he experienced something he only told her, something he's never allowed himself to express until now, and when he does it will force a confrontation between the future he wants and the past he struggles to reconcile with.

Welcome to the Sick Parents Club.

Amazon
https://www.amazon.com/dp/B07Q2HKXX8

Goodreads
https://www.goodreads.com/book/show/44076471-the-sick-parents-club

Made in the USA
Coppell, TX
05 December 2022

87924452R00168